Comes the Warrior

Portals of Light – Doors of Despair
Book 1

Evelyn Rainey

ISBN: 0997051248
ISBN-13: 978-0-9970512-4-7

BLISS Books Online
An imprint of Denouement Literary Agency, LLC
PO Box 973, Eagle Lake, FL 33839

BLISSBooksOnline.com
DenouementLit.com

DEDICATION

To those who are no strangers to despair…
Neither are you strangers to joy, so choose joy.

CONTENTS

ACKNOWLEDGMENTS

I would like to acknowledge my great appreciation and respect for Daniel LeBoeuf – my editor and my friend. He is one of those rare writers who actually understands and is gifted with the Art of Writing.

I would also like to express my appreciation for Susan Krupp, whose cover designs and enthusiasm has made being a publisher so enjoyable.

Chapter 1
The Warrior

"D'ya hear about the jewelry heists up in Tacoma?" The trucker kept his eyes on the road. His Stetson danced on his head in tandem with the bouncing cab on this rough road, tempting Gwen to reach up and steady it.

Gwen had been traveling for two and a half weeks, going from one safe-house to another, fed by strangers, hitching rides with men and women who knew not to ask personal questions. She hadn't realized how vast the safe-house network was, nor had she realized just how many battered women depended on it.

"No, I haven't heard much in the way of news." She tried to imitate his Alabama twang.

"Middle of the day about a week ago, bold as brass, a dozen men in robes carrying swords marches into the mall, killing anybody got in their way –men, women, children – didn't matter none. They get to the jewelry shops and takes nothing but rings. You know them malls got six or seven jewelry shops and kiosks and the like. These weirdoes just went from one to the other, taking only the rings. And slicing and dicing the folks as they went."

"Did the police catch them?"

"Naw. And see here's the really weird part. They all troops into a girly bar next to the mall and up and disappears."

"You're joshing!" She hoped she sounded convincing.

"Scout's honor!" He gestured with his right hand. "Heard it on the radio late last night. Ain't been a word of it on CNN or Fox, 'cause you know the government is covering it up."

"Tacoma? Up in Washington?"

"Or Oregon, can't never remember."

"Now, if you'd said N'Orleans that would make sense. All those devil worshippers there. But Tacoma. Well, that's just unnatural." Gwen's response tickled the trucker and they laughed together. She prayed that the Dark soldiers still believed she was near Tacoma.

She left him at the next stop and decided to walk for a while. Before she left the rest stop, she unscrewed the head from a broom and secured the stick beneath her coat. She slept under the stars for two weeks, wandering south.

There were plenty of things to eat, Gwen knew where to forage and didn't mind too much what it looked like.

She was crossing a bridge over a rocky stream in Georgia when an old blue Ford pick-up rattled up behind her. She pressed against the railings to let it pass. It didn't. The driver stopped and rolled down the passenger-side window. "Need a lift?"

Peeking into the cab, she saw a man in his late thirties, short blonde hair, brown eyes, a wide nose and full lips on his handsome face, and a winning grin. "Nope. Thank you. Just out for a stroll." She continued walking.

"You're a might far off the beaten path." The truck slowly kept up with her.

"Never cared much for beaten paths," she increased her step.

The truck kept pace. "I'm not trying to pick you up, Sister."

She hunched her shoulders and strode forward.

"It's just, I know you're not from around here and – and – you look half-starved and a might wind-swept."

She was nearing the end of the bridge.

"I just can't stand the idea of one of God's servants being cold and hungry. And it's going to snow."

Gwen stopped and looked at the man. "It's the first of May."

"Well, it's gonna snow sometime." He grinned. "My name's Atticus. I'm pastor at Morning Creek; it's just up the road."

Gwen grinned and began walking again.

The truck crept forward. "We're a huge church. We had nigh on twenty-five people last Sunday. And dinner on the grounds. So the fridge in the fellowship hall is stocked with fried chicken and apple pie."

Gwen didn't stop, but she peered at Pastor Atticus again as her stomach growled.

"Well look, our insurance agent says we have to keep the church and hall locked when not in use, but if someone were to look behind the stone angel by the double doors, they'd find a key. And if that person were to take what they need and return the key later, wouldn't nobody mind."

Gwen stopped and stared open-mouthed at this total stranger.

He smiled. "I gotta go serve communion to the shut-ins. God bless you, Sister."

He drove away. She numbly raised her hand and saw him smiling at her through the side mirror.

She ate cold chicken standing at the counter and surveyed the room Pastor Atticus had called a fellowship hall. The setting sun sparkled through the jalousie windows, illuminating the dust specks she'd stirred up as she walked across the linoleum floor. She refilled the water bottles and stored them in a raggedy backpack she'd been given in Utah. She wiped the counter and looked back at the full fridge longingly.

A door led from the hall to the sanctuary. The church had a dozen nine-foot wide pews on each side of a central aisle. It smelled of cedar planks and bees wax. The altar shone with lemon oil. The evening light fell gently through the nine stained glass windows: Matthew, Mark, Luke and John on the left; Grace, Joy, Hope, and Charity on the right; and Jesus on the cross behind the pulpit. An upright piano guarded the presbytery and a drum set flanked the pastor's pulpit. A massive carved mahogany table served as the altar. It held a Protestant cross, a chalice and a paten resting on its charger, and an ancient Bible opened to Luke. There was a brass strip underlining Luke 24:49. *And behold, I am sending forth the promise of My Father upon you; but you are to stay in the city until you are clothed with power from on high.* The two brass candlesticks held half-burnt white candles.

Gwen's vision blurred with unshed tears, her chest expanded, trying to gather in the essence of the air. The happiest times of her life had been in churches. Singing in the choir, praying, teaching Sunday school. Her feet led her forward and she sank onto the front pew. A tiny puff of dust escaped the thin cushion. She bent her head and began to sob.

She woke with the surely that someone was watching her. A man was kneeling next to her, his right hand stretching toward her. Before he could register that she was awake, she grabbed his wrist with her left hand and his throat with her right. Pushing him backwards, she landed on top of him.

"Whom do you serve?" her voice echoed in the tiny church.

"God the Father Almighty," the man spoke calmly. "And Jesus Christ his only Son our Lord."

It took her a second to realize where she was and another second to relax her grip. It took a third second to roll off the pastor's chest. He sat up and asked in a humorous tone, "Whom do you serve?"

She put her right hand over her heart, "I serve the Light, the Bringers of Light, and the Light Eternal."

Atticus got to his feet and held out his hand, "Sounds like we're on the same team."

She took his hand and stood up. "I'm sorry. I fell asleep praying. You just startled me."

"You got a strong grip," he gently rocked her hand in his.

She eyed the side door that led back into the fellowship hall.

"Do you have a name?"

She gently but firmly pulled out of his grasp. "Thank you for the chicken." She took a step away.

"There's plenty more." Light from the full moon through the stained glass of Jesus cast a hallo around the pastor's head and shoulders.

"I tucked three pieces in my pack. For the road." She took another step and bent down to catch the pack's straps, keeping her eyes on his face.

"You running away?" He stepped toward her.

"I'm just traveling." She hoisted the pack over her shoulder.

"Well, maybe you've traveled as far as you need to." He kept his voice soft. The colored halo seemed to follow him as he stepped closer.

"That would be nice," she heard herself whisper.

"So stay."

She looked up into his face and tried not to cry again. "No. No, I have to keep – I'm just traveling." She spun and marched quickly into the fellowship hall.

"He told me you were coming," his voice echoed from the sanctuary and she froze.

"Who?"

The moonlight barely illuminated the dusty jalousies. The pastor moved into the hall and around until he faced her. This close, she noticed he smelled of cedar and lemon oil and brass polish. His golf shirt was frayed at the collar and his jeans were worn to paleness around the knees. Slowly, he reached out and moved a strand of her hair out of her eyes. "When I was five years old, the Angel of the Lord appeared to me in a dream. He told me to hide under the bed. I had no sooner crawled under my bed than a car screeched down the street, spraying every house in the block with gunfire. My bed was riddled with bullets."

Gwen shivered.

"When I was eight, the Angel told me not to let my mother marry a certain man. She beat the living tar out of me, but she listened. Three months later, he was arrested when a plumber discovered the remains of twelve little boys under his house."

Atticus' hand touched the bag's strap and he gently slid it to the floor. "All my life, the Angel of the Lord has spoken to me. And I listen. He told me about the war that's coming. Five years ago, he sent me to this church because he said this place was going to be vital to the war. He told me not to despair; that he would send a warrior to hold back the Darkness. Those were his words, 'to hold back the Darkness'!"

He cupped her cheeks. "And here you are. But the Angel of the Lord didn't tell me your name."

Gwen hesitated and then took a step backward. "I'm gonna guess that I'm not the first person to tell you this sounds a little crazy."

He stuck his hands in his pockets. "No, you're not the first."

He walked into the kitchen and flipped on the lights but didn't raise his voice. "I brought you some things. Shampoo, soap, deodorant. And I brought you a dress." He picked up a paper sack. "It was my wife's."

Gwen meant to head out the door, but found herself in the kitchen instead, reaching for the offered bag.

"I don't reckon you'd accept an invitation to my home."

She glared at him in silence.

"But you're welcome to use the baptistery. I turned on the water heater this afternoon."

"I'm not a warrior."

His nostrils flared and his voice hardened. "I can't abide a lie."

She held his gaze. "I don't want to fight anymore."

"You're not here to fight. You're here to train us."

"Us? Us, who?"

Pastor looked at her lips. "The ones that are coming. Refugees. He'll send them, too."

She said nothing.

"Have you been baptized, Sister Warrior?"

She nodded.

"Good, then it won't be blasphemy if you bathe in the pool. Because, quite honestly Sister Warrior, the Angel of the Lord said you might need it, and again, he was right." Pastor pointed back toward the sanctuary and grinned. "I'll make us a pot of coffee, 'cause we have a lot to discuss."

He followed her into the sanctuary and then took the lead up the steps. Under the stained glass was an eight by four foot empty pool. Pastor knelt down and reached below the rim. Water steamed from a huge faucet above three steps leading into the pool. When he stood up, his eyes traveled over her body with immodest longing.

She crossed her arms and glared.

Fixing his eyes on her arms, he spoke hoarsely, "The Angel of the Lord told me a lot about you. What you liked, what you don't." He raised his eyes to her face. "I'll never betray you. I'll never force myself on you." He seemed to be having trouble breathing. He took a deep breath and looked at the filling pool. "Well, listen to me yammering on. I've got coffee to make. I'll leave you to your privacy."

As she watched him all but flee into the kitchen, she wondered how far she could run before he caught her, and what he might do if he did catch her. She looked up at the stained-glass Jesus. "Guard and guide. Protect and preserve. Defend and direct."

"Just so I understand," she walked into the kitchen. He spun around from the sink at the sound of her voice. "Am I a prisoner here?"

"A prisoner?" He gaped at the transformed creature before him. She was holding her walking staff with her pack slung over her shoulder. The cotton floral dress was too small at her breasts, too large at her waist. Her auburn curls had wet the shoulders. A memory of Martha in that dress, wide-eyed and innocent and laughing tore into his guts. He bit the inside of his cheek. "No, you're not a prisoner. There's the door."

"Thank you for the dress. I'll mail it back to your wife when I can." She walked toward the door.

"Don't bother. You can't mail packages to hell."

She stopped and then kept walking.

"No matter where you go, Sister Warrior, you'll wind up back here. I guess it just depends on how much walking you want to do."

"Bye!" She waved over her shoulder and snatched open the door.

Its stench reached her first, and then its fist. The ragged claws missed her by mere centimeters; the stench enveloped her like gaseous oil, filling her nostrils more surely than water would have. The ukera snarled from its throat as it advanced.

Gwen dropped her pack and grabbed up her staff. The once-common broom handle arched gracefully through the air, pheasant takes flight, but the ukera bowed out of range.

"Sweet Jesus! What is that thing?" Pastor picked up a knife.

Gwen backed up; juggling the end of the staff between her hands causing the free end to spiral in a sideways 8, infinity blossoms. The ukera growled again.

"Don't move. It can't sense you very well if you are still."

The pastor stopped. "What is it?"

Gwen rapidly tapped the butt of her rod twice on her right, chicken on the worm. The ukera's head wobbled. It turned toward the sound.

Gwen tapped again, manipulating the ukera around until its back was to Atticus.

"This is a ukera. It's like a reptilian bloodhound, but it's got a soul." She swirled the staff an inch above the floor, waves on sand. The ukera lithely hopped over it.

"A soul?"

Completing the circle, she raised the staff shoulder high and sliced it at the creature's left shoulder, panther strikes. The ukera leaned backwards avoiding the strike. Letting the weight rock the end, she pulled it back at her left waist, sheathing the claw and immediately projected the staff into the ukera's chest, clanging the gong.

It staggered backward.

"Tell me what to do!" Atticus yelled.

The creature spun toward his voice, striking with claws extended. Atticus ducked and swung out with the knife.

"Not in here!" Gwen shouted too late. The smell of rancid cat litter filled the room as the ukera's blood oozed out of a shallow wound on its arm.

"God Almighty!" Atticus backed up, covering his nose and mouth. His eyes were streaming with tears.

Gwen poked between the ukera's shoulder blades three times rapidly, woodpecker on the oak. Then she swung the rod down, connecting with the back of its knee, hoeing the garden.

The ukera toppled sideways and rolled against the wall, leaving blotches of dark blood along the linoleum.

"Run into the sanctuary and stay there!" she commanded.

"I'm not leaving you," Pastor insisted.

Chopping wood, the staff cracked the exposed ribs. The ukera snarled and slithered along the wall out of reach.

Gwen examined the ceiling as she repeated chicken on the worm. "Turn on the ceiling fans, Pastor."

She heard a click and the blades began to turn. She tapped again and again, stepping backward toward the outside door. The ukera slithered toward the sound.

She enticed it across the room and stood in front of the door.

The ukera crawled to its feet, clutching at its side. Its head wobbled and it began to hum.

"Pastor," Gwen spoke softly. "Go into the sanctuary and wait there. Walk lightly. The ukera can't sense you over the motion of the fans."

"I'm not."

"You will do as I command, Pastor."

Atticus blinked and then began to tiptoe past the ukera's back.

Chicken on the worm became rain on the roof. The ukera was mesmerized by the fans, taunted by Gwen's tapping. The pastor exited the fellowship hall. Gwen rushed the ukera, bear on the mountain, reigning blows on each shoulder, both arms, both thighs. Enraged, the ukera lunged. Gwen leapt backward, spun and ran out the door. It followed her, unaware that she'd sidestepped just outside. As it ran across the doorway, Gwen stabbed the staff onto its ocular scales. She ducked, covering her head as the ukera's skull exploded, spewing vile-smelling brain matter out the opposite ocular scales.

Soundlessly, the ukera took three more steps, slumped forward and was still. Gwen turned her head and became ill. She clamped her hand over her nose and mouth and stepped over the ukera's leg back into the hall. She slammed the door behind her and made her way to the sink. She turned the water on full and put her head under the gooseneck faucet, gagging.

When the stench was washed away, she turned off the water but remained slumped over the sink. She was dizzy and nauseous and bone-weary. She heard Atticus walk up behind her, but didn't move.

He touched the small of her back, his palm cool against her sweat. He put his other hand on her shoulder and gently pulled her around to face him. He cupped her wet face and spoke firmly, "Never send me away again. I'm supposed to fight at your side, not cower in hiding."

She straightened. "Take your hands off me. Don't touch me. You don't know me. You have no right to be so familiar."

His face hardened in anger, but he dropped his hands. He towered over her for moments, then stepped away, "Forgive me."

She glanced down. The tight buttons had burst

during the fight. She pulled the bodice halves together, embarrassed. "I didn't send you into hiding. What did you learn about ukeras?"

"Ukera – it looked like an upright snake with four legs."

"What did you learn about it?" she repeated.

"They stink."

"That's one thing. Their skin smells, their blood stinks, but their viscera is strong enough to sicken you. So what is the lesson you have learned?"

"Never slice one open inside a building."

She nodded gravely. "What else have you learned?"

"The fans and your tapping. They can't differentiate between constant vibrations."

"It blinds them. Good. What else?"

He shook his head, looking around for answers. "I don't know."

"Why did I send you to the sanctuary?"

"For safety."

"With the fans going and my staff tapping, you were safe enough where you were. Why did I send you to the sanctuary?"

"I don't know."

"What did you do there?"

"I prayed."

She nodded, "I expected you would."

He cocked his head in confusion.

"Do you have any idea what kind of war I fight?"

"The angel said it was a war against the Darkness."

She nodded again. "Why did I send you to the sanctuary?"

"To pray?" His eyebrows furrowed. "Because you were fighting against the Darkness. A creature of the dark. And the sanctuary is a place of light."

She nodded. "Ukeras and others who have fallen to darkness cannot stay in a holy place for long. It becomes physically painful for them. I'm surprised the ukera could enter this fellowship hall, it glows with Light."

"It seemed very determined."

"It was. So even though a holy place can keep you safe, don't depend on it. Given the right incentive, ukeras can go anywhere."

Gwen walked over and picked up a mop and bucket. "Knowing this truth, what does the opposite teach you?"

"The opposite?"

She plopped the bucket into the sink and began to fill it. "There are holy places which ukeras avoid. Holy places weaken them."

He took a bottle of cleanser from under the sink and poured a stream into the bucket. "So, there are also places of evil. And these places strengthen a ukera."

"That ukera was weakened by being in this holy place. He was also suffering from having his sternum split by me a month ago, and killing ten Marines and only God knows how many others, and traveling by foot all the way across the country to find me."

"You fought that thing once already? Where? How'd the Marines get involved?"

"It's a long story, and not important right now. Imagine

what that fight would have been like if he had found me in a dark place full of despair and sorrow?"

Atticus shook his head sadly. "We have so much to learn."

"Do you have a shovel?"

"In the shed. Why?"

"I need to bury the ukera and then we'll need to clean up the yard."

"We can toss it in my truck. There's a gully down the road by the river, a place called Black Creek. I'll get rid of the body there."

"It had a soul. You can't dispose of it like some worthless road kill. We'll bury it in the cemetery and pray over the grave."

He thought this over and then nodded. "You mop up in here. I'll go dig a grave."

She took the mop and bucket from the sink. "Cover your nose and hold your breath until you're clear of the body."

They buried the ukera at dawn with full Christian burial rites. A steady rain began to fall, alleviating them from the need to hose off the church yard.

"I'm going to ask you something, but I don't want you to get mad. I'm asking you honorably." He held the door as she entered the hall. "I want you to come home with me. I live on the other side of the cemetery. I have a spare room, and a shower. I hope this blood washes off."

"It will, but it helps to soak in tomato juice."

"I had a dog got sprayed by a skunk once. My

mother poured tomato juice over him. You going for the same thing?" He grinned.

She smiled and bent down to retrieve her pack.

He ogled her breasts. "I also have some clothes that might fit better. T shirts and some of my jeans. We'll go to town tomorrow and buy you some things."

She straightened and shouldered her pack. "You are so out of your league, Pastor, it's frightening. You have no idea what you're asking."

"Yes, I do. The angel told me."

"You're a nice man, Pastor. I will not be the reason you're slaughtered in your sleep." She walked to the door.

"It wasn't your fault."

She glared at him over her shoulder.
"Your family. The angel told me. It wasn't your fault they were slaughtered in their sleep."

She yanked open the door. Rain flooded in.

"I know it sounds crazy that I listen to the angel. But he tells me the truth. The Darkness will destroy us all if you don't stay here. You have to train us. You have to teach us how to hold back the Darkness. You know it's true! You don't have to believe in angels, just stay."

She turned, squinting at him. "I do believe in angels."

He caught his breath. "Then stay."

Chapter 2
The Preacher

Gwen drenched herself in tomato juice and then showered quickly. She locked the guest room door and slept for twelve hours. When she awoke, the house was quiet. She found her few belongings laundered and folded outside the bedroom door, along with a ball of white socks, an extra pair of jeans and a white dress shirt. She took the pile of clothes back to the bed, locked the door again, and got dressed in the jeans and T she'd taken from the women's shelter she'd taken refuge in, after Sanchor and his band of Dark soldiers and the ukera had first found her in Tacoma. There was a note on the refrigerator: "Ms. Pearl has taken ill. I've gone to the hospital. Fix whatever you want to eat, I'll be late. Atticus."

The thought of food made her feel queasy, so she wandered around the cottage. It was clean but worn. A hand-crocheted granny square afghan covered a small sofa. The maple coffee table was dented and stained; one of its legs had been broken and re-glued. Prints were scattered on the walls, each depicting pastoral scenes of lambs, trees and wagons. The curtains were muslin tie-backs. She moved into the hallway. The pastor's bedroom was on the other side of the bathroom from the guest room. The double bed was covered in another afghan – a ripple design in maroon, hunter green and navy blue. Green cotton curtains covered the large window looking out on the backyard. There was a dresser covered with river stones, feathers and leathery dried leaves. A golden wedding ring hung on a tarnished sterling chain from the corner of the dresser's mirror.

The room had a pleasant odor, like the smell of warm flesh and sunscreen lotion. Gwen felt safe in that room.

A small TV rested on a book shelf, but it only crackled with snow when she turned it on. Next to the TV was a calendar. Today was the first Tuesday in May. The date niggled at her memory. It had been the last Thursday in March when she'd been driven from her home. She lost herself in memories of the ukera in the moonlight, the lightener masks on the soldiers, the sound of Sanchor's voice.

The feel of him touching her, inside her.

He pressed his lips against her ear and whispered, "Do you still love me, Gwen?"

He slowly lowered her to the ground, relaxing his grip on her staff.

"Whom do you serve?" She asked him the same first words he had ever spoken to her.

His hands moved from her staff to her shoulders. She maintained her grip. "Do you still love me?" He bent down to press his lips first against her ear and then against her neck. His left hand cupped her breast and pulled her against him. "Do you, Gwen?"

"Yes," she moaned.

"Then does it really matter whom I serve?"

"Yes," she sobbed and tried to pull away.

"Gwen, don't fight me." His left arm imprisoned her against his chest while his sword snapped her staff in two.

She brought both halves around and down, planning to sink them into his thighs. They clunked on armor instead.

She spun in his grasp and pushed his chest with open palms.

He chortled, sheathing his sword, as she fell backward from the impact against his breast plate. She blinked up at him from her seat on the ground. The moonlight caressed his face as her fingers had once longed to do. A seven-pointed star embroidered in gold thread decorated the left breast of his cloak. It was the mark of a *Strategia Oscuro*. Gwen shuddered; Sanchor was a general of the Dark Forces.

He reached down and took her hand. Pulling her to her feet, he whispered, "I need your help."

She met his request with numb silence.

"There is only one thing standing between my master and victory. A ring. The Ring of Gothiaren."

"A ring? Don't be stupid. A ring is just a thing. Dark and Light don't—"

He grabbed her forearms and shook her, "Listen to me. We don't have much time. The Ring of Gothiaren, remember it? We found it, you and I, in the crypt of Martolia. Gold with emeralds and diamonds, and a cabochon ruby in the center."

He'd kept the ring. He taunted her with it, promising to give it to the one he loved as a betrothal gift. She'd kept the pearl necklaces and the silver dagger, but he had kept the ring. He saw her memory reflecting in her expression, but she refused to speak.

"It is the only thing that stands between my master and the total annihilation of the Light on my world." He bent down as if to kiss her. "Do you understand?"

She pushed against his chest. "There was a ukera in my house. I tried to kill it. And three Dark soldiers. They think I have this ring?"

Sanchor's grip tightened. "He knew that only the two of us were in the crypt. He believes I could never defy him, so he assumes you have the ring. He sent me to retrieve it from you."

"Son of a gelding!" She threw her weight forward. Her knee connected painfully with the metal of his thigh guard but she punched his jaw and he staggered backward.

He wrestled her down from the top of the fence and threw her against the oak, pinning her with his arms, thighs and torso. She drew a huge breath to scream and he covered her mouth with his own.

She fought him, but she fought her own body more. When she was on his world Gothaira, fighting at his side against the Darkness, she had longed for him, thrown herself at him, and he had turned away. But now. She turned her face, breaking away from his possessive

tongue. *"I love you,"* she admitted, *despite her fears.*
"There has got to be some part of you that doesn't
serve the Darkness."

Gwen pushed away her memories. She felt warm
and dizzy. Then a coldness swept up from her stomach
and flamed in her throat: she hadn't had a period
since that first week of March.

Her hands pressed against her belly in panic. She
was pregnant. She knew it with a certainty that
bordered faith. She was carrying Sanchor's child.
Terror vied with joy. She counted the months on her
fingers; the baby would be born in December.

Her feet led her to the church across the yard from
the parsonage. She unlocked the doors and knelt at
the altar.

She prayed for strength. She prayed for this child
whom she'd been given. She prayed for Sanchor. She
prayed that he would somehow find out he was this
child's father and the joy of that news would turn him
away from the Darkness. Then she became ashamed
of such wistfulness, and prayed that God's will be done.
Her prayers dwindled away as she knelt, listening for the
voice of God. It wasn't a corporeal voice, not like the
pastor's angel. It was a stillness, a peace which filled
her, strengthened her, calmed her.

The church doors burst open and Atticus strode in.
His face was masked in fury. She jumped to her feet in
alarm. He saw her and stopped. Anger fought surprise,
then his face reddened in embarrassment. "I thought
you'd gone," he explained.

She blinked. Pastor looked so sweet now, when seconds earlier he'd looked like a Strategia Oscuro in battle.

"How's the woman in the hospital?" Gwen balanced her weight, wary.

"She'll be fine. She let her sugar get out of control. But she'll be just fine." He stopped at the first pew. "Thank you for asking. Were you praying for her?"

"No." Gwen pressed her hands on her abdomen, possessively.

He sported a cocky grin, "Were you praying about me?"

Gwen pursed her lips and scowled. "My prayers are private."

The grin slid off his face and he reddened again. "Forgive me. I didn't mean to pry."

"I didn't mean to snap." She nodded. "I'm sorry. It's just – you act like you know me. Like I'm supposed to know you."

"You don't like it when someone tries to get close to you."

She couldn't deny it, but she didn't want to admit it.

He held out his hand, "Would you pray with me?"

She meant to turn and walk away, but found she had taken his outstretched hand. He reached for and took her other hand, too, and bowed his head.

The peace she'd sought earlier flooded through her, spreading like living warmth from her hands, through her arms to her stomach and from there up to her head and down to her toes. She gasped and opened her eyes. He was looking at her. His lips were open but gently smiling. She felt herself drawn into his eyes, drowning in his soul.

"Amen," he whispered.

"Amen," she replied, reluctant to release his hands. That cocky grin returned, "So what's for dinner?"

She laughed. "I didn't look."

"Well, I'm hungry, and you haven't eaten since last night. What do you feel like eating?"

"Something simple, but very filling."

"Eggs, bacon, grits, and biscuits?" He kept hold of one hand and walked with her down the aisle to the church yard.

"Cheese grits?"

"I can make that happen." He released her hand to lock the doors.

"How are you going to explain me to your parishioners?"

"I don't have to. They all knew you were coming. The Elders do, at any rate. That's all that matters."

"Does your angel talk to them, too?"

"No, just to me. But I've been preaching about you for a year now. About the war and the warrior."

When Atticus took Gwen's hand at the kitchen table, she tingled. "Father, bless this food to our bodies and bless us in your service. Keep us faithful and prepared for the coming days. Amen." He popped open a biscuit and picked up a mason jar. "This honey comes from just down the road. Brother Easton rents hives to the farmers and his wife jars the honey."

Gwen spooned it onto a buttered biscuit. "Pastor, what is it you think you know about me?"

He took his time studying her features as if she were a masterpiece at a museum. Then he shook his head, "I thought I knew everything there was to know about you, except your name. But," his eyes lingered on her lips. "I don't know you at all."

He shifted his focus lazily upward to her eyes. "I want to know everything. But I want you to do the telling. I don't want to know your secrets, until you trust me enough to tell them to me."

"I don't have any secrets."

He pointed at her, warningly, "I told you, I can't abide a lie. You don't have to utter another word to me, but each and every word we share has got to be the truth. Understand?"

She frowned. "There is a difference between keeping a secret and being discrete. I don't have any secrets. There are parts of my life that are none of your damn business. And I have the right to keep quiet about them."

His nostrils flared, but he nodded. "Fair enough."

They finished the meal in silence. The silence lingered while she washed the dishes and he put them away.

"Good night," she dried her hands.

"Just tell me one thing, please."

She sighed.

"What is your name?"

Gwen shook her head. "I'm Guinevere Hampt."

He put out his hand and took hers. "Nice to meet

you, Guinevere Hampt."

She felt the strange tingling again where his flesh met hers. It seemed to connect them at a spiritual level. She took a deep breath and laughed. "You know how crazy this is?"

He laughed too. "Yes, ma'am. I reckon I do."

But still, she locked her door that night.

Chapter 3
The Beginnings

Morning Creek was a very small town nestled in the curve of the river's bend. It had two grocery stores, a hardware store, and one bank. It also had a dozen churches and a half-dozen bars. The children were bussed to Blakely Elementary in Pineview, twelve miles away. Pineview was three times the size of Morning Creek and boasted a Sears and a Salvation Army store.

Wednesday morning, Atticus drove Gwen to the Sears, where she bought a week's worth of underwear, bras and three nightgowns. She insisted he drive her to the Salvation Army. When she proudly brought him her findings, he seemed angry.

"Four church dresses at seven dollars each, a pair of high heels and three skirts at four dollars each, eight shirts at three dollars each, and three pairs of pants."

Atticus looked at the tag, "Four dollars each."

"Look at these dresses: Lesley Fay, Coldwater Creek, George. I'd pay ten times this much in a department store."

"They're real pretty." He handed the clerk the correct amount of cash.

"Is it too much?" she worried.

He glared at her. "No. No, it's too little. You didn't have to buy used clothes. I can afford better for you."

"Atticus," she slammed the truck door and turned to face him. "I have always bought my clothes at the Salvation Army and thrift shops. They're clean, they're good as new, one-tenth the price, and the money spent goes to charities I believe in. The money you spent at the Salvation Army here will be used for 'soup, soap, and salvation.' Those are important things in this world that's teetering between the darkness and the light. It had nothing to do with what you can afford. It had to do with me being who I am. This is me."

He started the truck.

"Is there a drug store here?"

The pastor nodded.

"May we go there?"

Atticus sighed and turned the corner.

"Are you mad at me again?" She couldn't keep the tinge of irritation from her voice.

He shrugged.

"There is nothing in those bags that would shame you. You wait; I'll have the men in your church drooling when I wear that Leslie Fay."

"Old Brother Rutger drools already. He's eighty-five years old," Atticus scowled.

"Well!" Gwen grinned. "There you go!"

He returned her smile as he pulled into the parking lot.

"I need twenty dollars, and you can stay in the truck." She held her palm up confidently.

He blushed furiously and handed her two tens.

Chapter 4
The Church

"Prayer meeting starts at seven," he called to her from the outside of the bathroom door.

"What time is it now?" she called into the hall.

"Six o'clock. You've been in there since five-thirty."

"OK."

"I always get there by six-thirty."

"OK."

"You gonna be ready?"

"By the time I finish shaving my legs, my mask'll be dry. And there's some more things I haven't done in over a month that I plan to do. Do you want me to tell you about them?"

"Well," Atticus touched the door. "Yeah. You can tell me."

She thumped the door. "Go away."

"You gonna be ready?"

The shower came on. "Yes, Preacher. I'll be ready."

He walked away, turned back to the bathroom door, then left again.

She dressed in a floral skirt, pale blue blouse, and stepped into leather sandals she'd bought at the drug store. She threw away the grimy pink cotton braid she'd worn around her neck and transferred Sanchor's ring to the chain she'd bought at the store. The chain was just cheap metal, but it was thick and the clasp was strong.

"It's six-fifteen," he shouted from the hall.

She opened the bedroom door and nearly stepped into his arms. "Yes, I reckon it is, Pastor."

He drank in her metamorphosis. "Oh Gwen, you are breath-taking."

She opened her mouth for a snappy reply, but nothing came to mind. It surprised her how pleased she was with his compliment.

He licked his lips.

"See, drooling already, and this is just the Wednesday-go-to-meeting outfit," she smirked.

"Lord have mercy," he laughed.

They walked across the cemetery.

"You all don't dance down the aisles, do you?

He shook his head, "Hadn't planned to."

"No," she shivered, "Snakes or anything like that?"

"You know," he scowled at her. "You got a mean mouth sometimes. What makes you think I'd pastor a church like that?"

"Sorry," she snapped. "I don't have an angel who's been filling me in about you for the last five years."

"Well, you got a sarcastic side he never revealed."

"This is me." She stopped and held her hands out from her hips. "I get mouthy when I'm scared. Deal with it. You want me to walk in that church like some kind of trophy. I don't know what to expect."

He bowed his head. "You've got nothing to be scared of. 'For I will not leave you nor forsake you until I have done that which I promised you.'" He held out his hand. "Don't be scared, Gwen."

"That's my favorite verse."

He stepped closer and took her hand. "Believe it," he whispered.

Gwen sat in the third row on the right and watched the pastor's back as he knelt to pray. The evening light filtered through the stained glass Matthew, bathing Atticus in patches of sky blue, red, and green. A peace fell heavy in the sanctuary as Atticus prayed.

A tall black woman in her fifties sat down at the piano and began to play *Sweet Hour of Prayer*.

Atticus rose, glanced back at Gwen, and sat beside the pulpit. A man in Wranglers and an oxford shirt ushered a teen-age girl in black Goth into the pew opposite Gwen. The girl peered around the man and looked unsmiling at Gwen.

A couple walked in, followed by five children all under twelve. They genuflected in the aisle and sat two rows behind Gwen.

The pianist shifted to *Shall We Gather at the River* while the biggest man Gwen had ever seen scooted into the pew behind the man and teen. He glanced at her and looked knowingly at the family across from him. The huge man raised both hands palms up and closed his eyes.

An ancient couple walked in with three women in their sixties. The women looked so similar; Gwen wondered if they were identical triplets. The old man, he must be Rutger, touched his wife's arm and pointed at Gwen. The woman squinted and sat down, but the man smiled warmly and nodded his head in greeting.

The pianist shifted to *The Old Rugged Cross* while others came in until the church was half-filled.

Atticus glanced at his watch and was about to stand when all eyes seemed to latch onto a big-boned woman who was ambling up the aisle. She was in her early thirties, dressed in a white cotton lace sun-back dress. Her bottle-blond hair was permed and held away from her broad cheeks with scarlet combs. The scent of Chantilly was so strong Gwen could almost see it trail behind her. The woman's eyes were locked on Atticus's bowed head, as if daring him not to see her. When she sat at the end of Gwen's pew, the wooden planks squeaked.

The church, which had been murmuring softly, stilled with anticipation. The girl peered around her father again and looked first at Gwen, then at the newcomer, and back to Gwen. She smirked as if she were about to witness something hilarious.
The woman in white glared at the teen, and then realized there was someone else on the pew. She snatched her head sideways. The look she gave Gwen was pure venom.

Atticus stood at the pulpit but stared nervously at the third row. Gwen smiled her sweetest, opened her eyes in friendly innocence, and spoke quietly, "What a beautiful dress. I love eyelet lace."

The woman cut her eyes at Atticus and returned a fake smile. "Thank you. I always enjoy wearing something special to church."

Gwen blinked. She heard someone behind her hiss, "I was afraid of this."

Gwen glanced up at Atticus, who stood like a deer in headlights. She grinned and spoke in a normal voice which she knew would carry, "Well, I sure hope the pastor appreciates how your efforts enhance the worship service. He would be an absolute fool not to notice how beautiful you are."

One of the children behind them giggled.

"I welcome you in the name of Jesus. May we stand and declare our belief one to another." Atticus raised his arms.

The congregation quoted the Apostle's Creed.

"Hymn 579, *Come Ye that Love the Lord*." The pianist shouted and immediately began playing. The congregation seemed to fumble finding the right page, but the woman beside Gwen never looked at her hymnbook. She belted out the verses in an incredibly clear soprano.

They sank to the pews and looked expectantly up at Atticus at the hymn's end.

Atticus caught and held Gwen's eye, smiled wistfully and then winked. He turned his attention to the congregation. "I've been here for five years this coming August. I've been a widower now five years this coming January. Some of you here knew Martha." He took a deep breath and nodded, "And you knew our child Andrew."

Atticus shook his head and sighed again. "Andrew was the sweetest creature in all of creation."

The woman beside Gwen rubbed under her heavily mascaraed eyes as if wiping away a tear.

"Those of you who joined us in the succeeding years didn't know Martha or Andrew. But there's not a doubt in my mind you have been told the story. Horror stories. Tales of tragedy. Wicked women and innocence lost. Don't these make the best gossip of all?" Atticus looked at Gwen for a moment while the congregation shifted guiltily.

"I've never used that story as the topic of a sermon. And I never will. I only bring it up to say, I am not a stranger to death.

"I am not a stranger to death," he repeated. "And neither are you."

He walked around the pulpit and stood behind the altar table. He pointed at the man and teen. "Brother Tyler, are you a stranger to death?"

"No Pastor. I know it well."

"Taralyn, are you a stranger to death?"

The girl next to Tyler shook her head.

"You both lost someone you loved. Tyler lost his helpmate. Taralyn lost her mother."

He craned his neck as if to see the back of the church. "Sister Beatrice, how long's it been since your son died?"

Gwen heard the woman catch her breath, "Twenty years, Pastor."

Atticus nodded, seemingly unaware of his cruelty.

"And you, Brother Rutger. Why, you must have outlived most of your kin. Even those beautiful daughters sitting beside you have outlived some of their own families and friends."

"Naught but me left out of eight siblings," Rutger assured the congregation.

"Definitely not a stranger to death." The pastor took his time looking at each person, who nodded in agreement, glared in defiance, or dropped their faces in despair. He looked at Gwen. She felt panic rising. He was going to tell these strangers all about her family.

"None of us here is a stranger to death," he told her.

He took a deep breath and moved back behind the pulpit. "When death came, long awaited after years of pain," he pointed to someone at the right of the church. "Or like a thief in the night," he pointed at Beatrice. "It caused the Darkness to fall. We, each and every one of us, crept into that darkness, seeking refuge, seeking solace, wallowing in despair. Some of us are still wallowing in the darkness.

"Mitchell, you're about to graduate from third grade. What's the opposite of dark?"

One of the children behind Gwen answered, "Light, pastor."

"Good job. Light is the opposite of dark. Just as death is the opposite of life. Joy and sorrow; hope and despair.

"You can wallow in darkness or dance in the light. You can lose everything to death, or gain everything in life. You can drown in sorrow or soar in joy. You can rot away with despair, or you can heal with hope."

"The choice is yours. The choice has always been yours. It always will be yours.

"Hope or despair. Joy or sorrow. Life or death. Lightness or darkness. What is it you are going to choose? It's your choice. Both of them happen to you, each and every day! You are handed joy or smacked with sorrow. You stumble over death or rise above in life. Which do you choose? Which do you cling to? Which do you allow to sink into your heart and ooze out of your pores?

"Mitchell, which do you choose?"

The little boy jumped to his feet, "Light!"

"Brother Tyler, which do you choose?"

He stood, "Joy!"

Atticus pointed at the teen. Tyler asked, "Daughter, which do you choose?"

"Hope," she grinned and stood. "Sister Elke, which do you choose?"

One of the triplets stood, "I'm going to dance in the light!"

They continued calling out names, asking for choices, and declaring for the light. They adlibbed when Atticus nodded in permission: faith chosen over disbelief, love over hate, trust over suspicion, promise over betrayal.

Patsy, the soprano in the white dress chose love and turned to Gwen, "I don't know your name, honey. Which do you choose?"

Gwen stood up and swallowed. "I choose the light." She put her hand over her heart and swore,

"I serve the Light, the Bringers of Light, and the Light Eternal."

"Amen!" Atticus shouted.

Gwen looked up at Atticus and then couldn't seem to look away. He glowed, as if there were a spot light aimed at the back of his shoulders. His face was radiant. She couldn't seem to breathe. She didn't hear him over the congregation, but she watched his lips, "Don't be afraid."
She took a steady breath and grinned. He grinned in return. She smiled. He laughed. "Sister Eduviges, we need to sing!"

"Angels We Have Heard on High!" she shouted.
After six verses, they sat back down.

"There will be a meeting of the Elders at my house Saturday afternoon. Bring food. Sister Sara, I would be delighted if you'd bring a jar of your green tomato relish."

"Gladly," Mitchell's mother beamed.

"Keep Le'Vander's mother Sister Pearl in your prayers. She's still in the hospital with her diabetes. Tom, we're praying that your loan goes through. Young Airman Doug, stationed in the oilfields, praying for peace and safety for him. Others?" Atticus searched each face and rested at last on Gwen. "The peace of God which passes all understanding keep your hearts and your minds on Jesus Christ our Lord. Amen."

He stepped down from the pulpit and touched the woman in white's elbow. Patsy beamed up at him. He bent and whispered in her ear. She turned beet-red

and stepped out into the aisle. Atticus held out his
hand to Gwen. "Don't be afraid."
She slipped sideways to him, her fingers wrapped
around his, eager for his touch. She was suffused with
confidence. He held her firmly as they walked down
the aisle to the narthex.
"This is Gwen," He introduced her to each member of
the congregation as they exited the service.

They were all kind and polite as they shook her
hand. The bear of a man, Matthew Kellerman hugged
her gently. The teen, Taralyn Fogel nodded at her and
walked away. Her father, Tyler hugged Atticus and
kissed Gwen's cheek.

"You're prettier than I thought you'd be." Rutger
Perkins patted her arm. "Not all manly like Xena the
Princess warrior. You're not. Right pretty young lady."
"Thank you." Gwen blushed.
Rutger continued, "This is my beautiful bride, Kaela.
And my beautiful daughters Milia, Elke, and Hetta.
Don't ask me which one is which. Sixty years and I still
can't tell them apart."

"Oh, Papa," Elka kissed his cheek and shook
Gwen's hand.

Atticus stuck out his hand and took Patsy's hand in
his. She sank toward him, as if to hug his neck, but he
locked his elbow, keeping her at a stiff distance. "Sister
Patsy, what a pretty dress. Gwen, may I introduce
Patsy Welden, one of the best singers in the area."

The two women shook hands. Gwen felt as if she
was shaking a frozen brick. "I run my own beauty shop,
Peggy's Parlour. Why don't you come down this week

39

and let me touch up that gray? Have Atticus drive you.
He knows exactly where I live."

Gwen blinked as Atticus tensed beside her. "Why
thank you Patsy, but I've earned every single one of
these gray hairs. I don't mind them; I'm rather proud of
them."

"I got some gray hairs you could touch up for me,
Patsy." A tall thin man dressed in stained over-alls
grinned at her.

"You don't have a gray hair on your head
Le'Vander McAfee."

"I didn't say it was on my head." He shook hands
with Atticus and kissed Gwen's cheek. "And I also know
exactly where you live."

Her face scrunched in frustration. They walked
away together, bickering.

The last one out of the church was the pianist
whom Atticus introduced as Eduviges McGuinna. She
kissed Atticus on the cheek and wrapped Gwen in a
warm embrace without uttering a word.

He closed and locked the doors. Taking her elbow
he led her into the cemetery toward his home.

"There is nothing between Patsy and me," he stated.

"It's none of my business if there were."

"I'm making it your business."

"In that case," Gwen leaned against a headstone
and shook the sand from her left sandal. "You preach
a phenomenal sermon, Atticus. It was the most moving
sermon I've ever heard. But maybe you didn't listen to
the words yourself."

Atticus shook his head. Moonlight fell in splotches

across the graves.

"Your sermon was about choices. She has chosen you. Every single person in that church knows it."

"I have never--"

"But she has."

"No. Love doesn't work that way."

"Honey, she doesn't know that."

Atticus stumbled at her endearment, but she continued without a pause, "You represent everything that's good in the world to her. Nothing else would compare to the qualities you possess. You're God in the flesh to her. It doesn't matter that you're unattainable. It's not going to matter if I escort you to every church function. She's made a choice. And until she chooses something else you're going to have to deal with her."

Atticus frowned.

"Not me. You."

He hung his head and crossed his arms.

"However," a smile played across her lips. "You might consider strolling her by the ukera's grave, and telling her how good I am with my battle staff. You might want to explain to her exactly how I got each and every gray hair on my head and that I am not afraid to get more of them."

Atticus snorted.

She took his hand and led him toward the cottage.

"You really liked my sermon?"

"Absolutely."

Chapter 5
The Morning Meadow

At dawn Thursday, Gwen started a pot of coffee and gazed absently out into the backyard. The yard was deep and - other than a large oak tree near the house – was clear of trees for about one half of an acre. Deep green grass covered the ground. A huge picnic table and trestle benches which could seat two dozen people bordered the left side of the yard. There was a brick and cement barbecue pit. From the light pungent odor on the breeze, she guessed the fenced field beyond was probably cattle pasture. Woods, beginning with the oaks and maples, surrounded the right edge and a pecan grove stood sentry at the bottom of the yard. It was too beautiful to stay inside. She retrieved her well-worn broomstick from her room and went quietly out the kitchen door.

Gwen stood in the center of the yard and drew a deep cleansing breath. She hadn't done the Morning Meadow ceremony in over six months. Morning Meadow was a ritual that taught spiritual lessons and physical skills. Everyone who served the light learned it.

42

Children begin the practice as soon as they are old enough to hold a wooden dowel. Morning Meadow was a beginning. The basic steps for all the complicated steps to come. With mastery, the lessons learned in Morning Meadow were sufficient to protect oneself in simple battle.

Simple battle, she snorted at her thoughts. She thought she was done with battles. The Light had other plans for her. She cleared her mind and held the stick horizontally to the ground at shoulder height: Dawn.

She sank to her knees, keeping the staff steady: Awareness.

She lowered the stick to the ground, pressing her forehead to the cool dewy grass: Awe. She held that position while her muscles stretched and her joints popped. Curling upwards from the small of her back she stretched the staff as far as she could reach: Surrender.

She returned to the Dawn position and drew in another breath.

She dropped the rod end, allowing the tip to dip level to her waist and repeated it with the left end. She did this six times. Then the rod dipped to her hip on the right and the left six times. She dropped the staff to her knees on the sides and eventually allowed the staff to touch the grass. The Spider's Web wasn't complete until she'd walked the staff ends back up to Dawn position again. Her wrists ached from disuse.

She transitioned to Frog in the Pond, alternately swinging the staff outward from chest to side with the right hand snapping the free end into her left hand and then arching the staff with her left hand out to the side and back to snap into her right palm. She repeated Frog in the Pond a dozen times.

She brought her hands together in the center of the rod and stretched it up as far she could lift it and then bent at her waist touching her knuckles to the ground: Rainbow. Holding the staff parallel to the ground and keeping her feet flat, she began to twist it around to the back of her ankles to the left and then to the right. Rising slightly, she twirled it around behind her left calf and then her right. A little farther up with each pendulum she worked the staff to her waist and then all the way inch by inch until she stopped twisting her torso and began twirling the staff. It had taken her two weeks to learn how to perform the Journey without falling over with dizziness. Smiling with joy, she repositioned her hands and returned to Dawn.

She began the exercises again. Dawn, Awareness, Awe, Surrender, Dawn. She added steps to Morning Meadow working her way across the yard. A box step for Spider's Web, grapevine steps for Frog in Pond, but nothing for Journey because balance was the key to that exercise.

As she arched to the ground with the Rainbow she followed through with a somersault. She arched and rolled across the yard. Then she turned around and worked her way back to the center of the yard in box steps. Sweat was pouring down her arms, torso and legs and her mouth was fuzzy with thirst. Dawn. Awareness. Awe. Surrender. Dawn.

She laughed and lowered the staff. She smelled

coffee and turned at the sound of pastor's voice, "That was beautiful, Gwen. Thanks for brewing the coffee. Didn't know what you wanted in it so I brought the works."

He stood behind her carrying a tray laden with a steaming pot, mugs, a jug of milk and a sugar bowl.

Still breathing hard, she smiled and followed him to the picnic table.

"It is so beautiful here," she sighed over the mug she had to hold in both hands due to her aching wrists.

"You're beautiful here," he replied.

"Atticus, please don't. You don't know me."

"I agree. I don't know you yet. But I do know beauty when I see it. And you are beautiful."

She put down her mug and frowned.

"Do you do that exercise every morning?"

"I stopped for a while but I plan to get back into the habit of the *Morning Meadow*. That's its name. It's a spiritual ceremony as well as a physical rendition. Every individual step has a name too, but they are all things from a meadow."

"Tomorrow morning, will you let me try it with you?"

She nodded. "It's not as easy as it looks. Don't get discouraged."

He snorted, "That didn't look easy at all!"

"What are your plans for today?"

"It's Thursday. I work on my sermons for Sunday and Wednesday, prepare the agenda for the Elders' meeting, and go fishing in the afternoon."

"Is there anything I can do to help you?"

"Are you any good at cooking?"

"With the right ingredients," she replied softly. "There's only so much I can do with peanut butter."

"I happen to like peanut butter."

"You have four jars of it, and very little else."

"Peanut butter on a spoon, easiest meal there is."

"You know, there's this terrific way of fixing peanut butter --you spread it on bread and sometimes you put jam on a piece of bread and stick them together."

"See! I knew you'd be a good cook!"

They laughed together then he sobered, "I never got the grocery store, menu, recipe thing right."

"I can do the grocery stores and recipes but I'd rather us do the menus together." She drained her cup. He picked up the pot to pour her some more but she shook her head, thinking of the effect caffeine might have on her baby.

"What do you like to eat?" He refreshed in his own cup. "I have to say my favorites are barbeque chicken and any kind of fish. Hush puppies are okay but I love cornbread. And black-eyed peas with green tomato relish."

"Southern. I can cook southern."

"Really?"

"Well, we'll see, but I think I can."

"Do you know how to make peanut butter pie?"

She grimaced. "I've never heard of peanut butter pie!"

"I've got a recipe."

She shook her head.

"What do you like to eat, Gwen?"

"Hot and spicy Thai. Doritos and tamales.

Szechuan chicken. And," she thought for a moment. "My favorite dessert is Moose Tracks ice cream."

"We got a serious breach of compatible recipes here."

"I reckon so, pastor." She shrugged.

"It's alright. I reckon we'll make do." He stretched out his hand. "Will you pray with me to begin the day?" She took his hand and was pulled to her feet. He took her other hand too, and bowed his head so close that she felt his breath on her forehead.

She waited and stillness filled her with a warmth bordering passion. She squeezed her eyes shut knowing he was staring at her.

"In the beginning was the Word. And the Word was God. We thank you for this day. We thank you for this life. We ask you fill us with your word and your purpose. Bless us to your use Father. Amen."

Gwen held his hands and spoke, "Lord of Light, guard and guide. Lord of Light, protect and preserve. Lord of Light, direct and defend. Amen."

She opened her eyes and she was right; Atticus was barely inches from her. In a voice filled with intimacy he said, "Good morning, Gwen."

Her skin tingled and she caught her breath. Taking a step backwards she smiled sheepishly and pulled her hands out of his grasp. "Good morning, Atticus."

After a thorough inventory of the kitchen, Gwen bought one hundred dollars' worth of groceries, for which Atticus paid in cash.

A hardware store next door to the grocery caught

Gwen's eye as they loaded the truck bed. "I could really use a new battle staff. And if you're going to train with me, you'll need one, too."

"You can get battle staffs in a hardware store?"

"It wouldn't be my first choice for one, but I could probably find something that'll do for training rods."

Atticus tied a tarp over the bags and nodded.

She found the dowels an inch in diameter. She glanced around and spoke softly. "Training rods are as thick as a thumb. Battle staffs are about the same diameter as your closed fist. They should be as tall as the bearer. I like yew."

"I like you, too." He grinned. "But this is pine."

"A fruit wood works well for battle staffs but they're hard to find."

She held a six foot dowel in front of Atticus and nodded. She selected a five foot dowel for herself.

"Take them all: four, five and six foot lengths." Atticus commanded.

"Won't that look a little suspicious?"

"We'll need them." He reached around her and began pulling them out of the cylindrical holders. "Eighteen. There won't be enough."

"Enough for what?"

"The army. You're going to train an entire army." He tucked the dowels under his arm.

"With eighteen dowels?"

"They'll order more of them when the computer shows they are out of stock." He led her to the checkout. "This will be enough to begin training the Elders."

"Good morning, Reverend Jordan!" A young woman named Christy Gwen recalled meeting Wednesday night was at the register. "What you doing with all these dowels?"

Gwen raised her eyebrows in an *I told you so* expression.

"I'm planning to use them for the church."

Christie waited for more of an explanation.

"A project for the church," Gwen supplied.

Christie began ringing them up. "They'd make a good show and tell for your children's sermon. You know, something like spare, the rod spoil the child. Too many children today don't know the benefits of a pop on the butt."

Atticus frowned. "I've never thought of it that way. You mean you think the Scriptures mean you shouldn't spare the rod?" He handed her a wad of bills. "I always thought it meant one *should* spare the rod so that you *can* spoil children. Jesus admonished his followers that hurting a child is one of the worst things that the man could do."

It was Christie's turn to frown as she handed him his change and receipt.

Chapter 6
The Choice

"Hold the rod as if it were made of cloth. Not tight, it's not going to go anywhere unless you want it to." The sun was just rising above the trees as Gwen and Atticus stood in the backyard Friday morning. "Hold it out at shoulder height, feet below each hip, well-balanced. Comfortable?"

"Not especially," Atticus mumbled.

"Good."

He glanced at her.

She explained, "This first position is called Dawn. It's a beginning where you have to make sure your body is ready to begin. You never go beyond Dawn until you are sure of yourself. Now, look at your rod. Shut out everything around you except for the rod. Feel your blood pumping and your lungs breathing -- breathe through the nose. Feel your shoulders tighten and consciously relax them. The sun is rising and the earth hushes for a moment. Let your body hush for a moment. Absorb the Dawn."

She paused, "How do you feel?"

"Glorious."

"You are aware of the Dawn. You are ready for the next step. Keep the rod even at your shoulders, stay relaxed but kneel."

Atticus wobbled.

"Slowly. I've seen you do this. Kneel at the Altar of Light with reverence. Keep your eyes on the rod." Atticus bent one leg, then the other. He grimaced as an acorn cut into his knee.

"From Awareness you move to Awe. Awe of the light. Awe of its glory and your part in its glory. Let your hips roll down to your feet and stretch your rod to the ground. Keep your chin in the same position so your forehead touches the earth." Gwen observed him. "Good. Now listen."

The birds chirped around them.

"Relax your toes and your ankles, unclench your calves. Allow your thighs to sink down all the way. Feel the pressure in the small of your back? Cast it upward, up your spine through your shoulders, down your arms onto the rod and away into the ground. Do not move until your jaw is slack and you are at peace."

She waited until he drew a deep breath. She placed her hand on the small of his back. "Pretend I fasten a rope right here and I'm pulling it up into the sky. The rope is going to slip forward only when you've used the right muscles."

She pulled him to his feet spine first. "Keep the rod at arm's length parallel to the ground. Now raise it slowly above your head, stretching each vertebra until you grow another three inches."

She walked around him twice and stopped in front of him. "This is Surrender. Don't move, but be aware of yourself. If you ever are in this position in battle you will die. Your neck is exposed; your ribs, spine, abdomen, groin, thighs, hamstrings, arteries. A nick here," she touched his hairy armpit. "Or here," she touched where his thigh met his torso. "And you will bleed out in seconds."

He looked at her with a worried expression.

"Never forget how this feels. Never forget that you must surrender yourself to God in all you do. You must accept death as a possibility, with eternal life beyond this mortality, as the reward for absolute surrender. Concentrate on the rod but feel your body. Remember the feelings Awareness and Awe and Surrender." She circled him. "Do you understand? Then return to the Dawn to begin again."

He held Surrender for a full minute. When he lowered his arms his face was peaceful.

"Now go sit over there and watch me go through the Morning Meadow. Just observe. We take each portion one day at a time. You did well."

Chapter 7
The Elders

The Elders' meeting was Saturday at four o'clock. Gwen dressed in a wraparound skirt, T-shirt and sandals and peered nervously at her very first peanut butter pie. There was no baking involved but it had been rather complicated. Atticus was pleased.

The first to arrive was Tyler Fogel and his daughter Taralyn. Tyler took Gwen's hand and kissed her cheek. Gwen offered her hand to Taralyn but the teen stepped backward. "I don't touch people."
Gwen nodded awkwardly.

"Come out to the backyard. Gwen can greet the Elders and send them back to us."

Gwen caught her breath. Atticus took her elbow. "You've already met them, Gwen. There's nothing to be afraid of."

"Goten Auben!" a voice called from the front porch.

"Brother Rutger, come on in. You remember Gwen."

Rutger snorted. "Couldn't forget her." He touched her cheek with his cold fingertips.

The tall pianist stood at the screen door. Rutger opened it for her. She bent and kissed his forehead and stopped in front of Gwen.

"Hello. It's Eduviges, right?"

The pianist lifted her chin and nodded. She held out her hand, which felt like sandpaper over chicken bones when Gwen shook it. Rutger took Eduviges' arm and led her into the backyard.

An SUV pulled up and five children swarmed out. Four of them hugged Gwen around the waist and raced back out front to the cemetery. The fifth child, Mitchell, stared up at Gwen. His parents, Sara and Larry Sveete, shifted uneasily while Mitchell continued to stare silently.

"Pastor's out back," Gwen offered.

Sara smiled weakly. Larry took her arm and led her into the kitchen. The boy remained.

"How's third grade?"

"It's okay. Algebra's easier than it looks."

"Algebra? In third grade?"

"My mom home-schools me."

"Hey fart face," Taralyn came into the living room. "Leave the warrior alone. She'll eat you for breakfast."

"Na-uh."

"Pastor's ready to start. You know how rigid he is when it comes to the clock."

The bear came next; Matthew gave Gwen a kiss on the forehead.

Bea Horne walked across the cemetery, returning the children's greetings. She stopped at a grave and straightened the silk flowers resting on the die stone before walking the rest of the way to the parsonage.

"Hi Bea. They're all out in the back yard."

Bea was drab and weary looking. She sighed and headed into the kitchen.

A car pulled into the dirt drive and beeped its horn twice. A hand waved out the passenger window as the car rolled to a dusty stop. Two people Gwen didn't recognize walked onto the porch.

"I'm sorry we're late!" A pretty woman with jet black hair and chocolate skin flung open the screen door. She stopped in her tracks when she saw Gwen, her companion bumped into her.

"Hello. I'm Gwen. Everyone's out back. I think they have already started, but you're not too late."

"You are her." The regal black man in his early forties gently pushed his wife aside. "You are really her."

"I'm Gwen." She crossed her arms.

The woman wrapped her arms around her swollen abdomen protectively and backed away.

"I am Chi Abubakar. And this is my wife Visolela." He had a firm grip.

"How do you do?" Gwen kept her eyes on the frightened pregnant woman.

Chi looked back at his wife. "She will not bite, Visolela. Tell the warrior hello."

Visolela's eyes widened and she licked her lips. "Hello."

Gwen nodded.

Chi retrieved his wife, gently pulling her around Gwen and out the back door.

Gwen wandered into the kitchen and looked at the

table laden with casseroles and desserts. Her peanut butter pie sat there - a testament to her insecurities. Footsteps pounded toward the house and Mitchell slung open the kitchen door. "Pastor says you can come out now. We're all here except Sister Rawan. Her sister's grandson is dying of cancer up in New York and she's gone to heal him. But the rest of us Elders are here. So come on." He took her hand and pulled.

They were all seated around the picnic table except Atticus who paced at the head of the table.

"You can sit next to me. I don't bite either."

Gwen slid in between Taralyn and Mitchell and glanced at Atticus.

"Let's begin. Treasurer's report?"

Larry put on reading glasses and peered into a Blackberry. "Tithes and offerings are minimal. They're enough to cover utilities and insurance. So everything looks right on paper. The legacy from the Widow Prunella's estate is covering Atticus's salary, so again everything is right with the IRS."

Gwen frowned and looked around. Everyone else looked attentive.

"The market dipped somewhat this week so I pulled $100,000 out of the Steel fund and put it into Xenographics. Corn dropped three points but it will go back up again I'm sure, so I took $50,000 from the month's profit on K.L. Amit and pumped up corn. Net gain this year to date: $2,521,903 and some change."

"What?" Gwen gasped. "How?"

"We're a 501 (C)-nonprofit organization," Larry stated calmly replacing his Blackberry and removing his glasses.

"I know this is new to you Gwen, but there'll be plenty of time for in-depth explanations later. Matthew, how is the compound proceeding?"

"Well." The huge young man grunted. "Blue prints were approved. Permits are all in except one. We should be breaking ground in three weeks."

"Which permit is still out?" Atticus asked.

Matt answered, 'The agricultural one. We've asked to build a water filtration system and the state requires a lot less in the way of environmental safety then we have planned for. They are curious why we want to spend so much when we don't have to, so they're dragging their feet."

"Ideas?" Atticus leaned on the table.

"University of Graz Chechnya is trying to develop something similar, but is having funding problems. Maybe we could offer a few of their students a grant to come study our methods. The state would have to acknowledge the necessity of our plans." Tyler spoke up.

"You'd have to handpick the students," Rutger warned.

"I need to see a list of names," Atticus stated.

"I can get you the complete enrollment roster for the University of Graz Chechnya and their majors," Taralyn offered.

Atticus turned to Mitchell. "Mitchell, I'll need the schematics translated into Chechnya."

"They don't speak Chechnya, they speak Ingushetia," he giggled.

"Oh." Atticus blushed. "Can you do it?"

"I have to practice for my piano recital Monday but I can do it Tuesday night if Matt can bring me the documents."

Matt nodded.

"Medical supplies? Chi."

"I am just waiting for a place to store them."

"Rutger, what's the status on the power station?"

"Stalemate. Foreman wants a little more grease on his palms."

Atticus looked at Larry.

"The money's there ..."

"No," Rutger argued. "I've got another avenue. I think I'll pursue a housing developer I know. He can open the door easier -and cheaper- than my first mark, without setting us up as known bribers."

Atticus nodded. He glanced around the table. "Weapons? Gwen, you already told me yesterday about the battle staffs. What exactly will you need along the lines of full weaponry for one thousand soldiers?"

"A ticket out of town?" She smirked.

The Elders laughed.

"Thirteen hundred staffs made of hardened wood, five inches in diameter varying lengths between five and six feet. The ends need to be blunt cut. No varnish, just sanded wood. And training rods the same lengths, two thousand in number, diameters ranging between one and five inches."

Atticus spoke up, "We can get those at Lowe's."

"Really?" Mitchell perked up.

Eduviges answered, "Really. What else do you need?"

"I don't know. I don't know what you are facing. The only weapon I have is the staff. I can train someone to use a sword without cutting off his leg. But the weapons of each world are so different. And so is the armor. Where will you be fighting? Against whom?"

"Black & Decker has these really cool handheld nail drivers," Mitchell suggested.

Atticus grinned at the boy, but his voice deepened. "We'll be fighting against the Darkness. I thought I made that understood. They're coming across the barrier to this world. They've been coming here for centuries, a little at a time. But something is allowing them greater and greater access to this world. A mighty battle is coming. That's why the angel sent you to us." Atticus leaned towards her. "In a year or two, refugees will start pouring into our little world. They will be fleeing the destruction of their worlds by the Darkness. We'll gather those refugees to give them shelter and began training them."

He pushed off the table and began to pace. "More of them will be drawn here. They'll be like us - who have been made to face the Darkness and chose the Light. Prayer will be our greatest weapon, and the warrior's training will lay the groundwork for discipline and service. Eduviges, what else can you get us in the way of weapons?"

"Uncle Morris has offered me a small nuke."

"We can't use nuclear weapons!" Gwen pounded

the table.

"She was kidding," Taralyn stated with an unspoken *duh* quality.

The pianist raised one eyebrow before continuing, "Uncle Morris can get me two gross of handguns - nothing traceable and twice as much ammo as we need. Plus he'll sell us a trainer."

'The trainer will have to come to us willingly. We can't risk the possibility that he'll be turned to the Darkness," Sara insisted.

"He'll come willingly. We're paying him a healthy salary, if the budget is approved." Eduviges looked at the treasurer and tilted up to peer at Atticus. "It's up to you to make sure he is strong enough to stand in the Light."

"It's the Lord's will, sister. But I'll put him on my prayer list."

Everyone chuckled.

"Well, let's see - finances, building, electric, medical, weapons. That leaves food and education."

"We've ordered two hundred PCs, twenty printers and the blue prints take into account the necessary electric and LAN lines needed," Sara spoke shyly. "Wireless is a possibility, if we can make accommodations for security. With the satellites we'll be set to piggyback into Harvard, Duke and University of North Dakota e-classes."

"Wait," Atticus put his hand up. "I can understand Harvard and Duke, but – North Dakota?"

Sara grinned proudly, "Best Veterinarian College in the continent. I assume we'll have animals as well as humans coming across the great divide."

Atticus nodded pensively.

"We've hired our communications expert," she pointed at Taralyn who rolled her eyes. "We'll need teachers. There are two in the congregation. We'll need a minimum of thirty teachers."

Bea spoke up, "I can help with that. I'm the president of the retired teachers league."

"Wonderful! Food?"

All eyes turned to Visolela. She looked sick with nerves. "There," she began pushing a small notebook down the table. "It's all there in my report."

"I'm sure it is an excellent report. But I'd like you to tell us about it."

Visolela blushed and bit her lip. Her husband reached his arm around her shoulder and gave her a little hug.

"It is all taken care of. The minute the refugees begin to arrive, I will notify various warehouses around the world. Private planes will pick up the supplies -- I wish you could have worked in an airfield in the compound. They will rendezvous with the helicopters and begin delivering the food and supplies. Three days from notification to delivery. Then a continuous supply every week thereafter until-" she blinked and grew pale.

"Until the Darkness has been defeated." Chi squeezed her shoulders again.

Visolela's eyes brimmed with fear as she looked at Gwen.

"Any other business?" Atticus looked around the

table. "Good! Let's have a prayer then and bring the food out here and eat."

They stood and circled around the table. Atticus stepped in next to Mitchell. "You don't mind if I hold the Warrior's hand do you, boy?"

"No Pastor, that's all right." He dashed around and stood between Taralyn and Tyler.

"The hand of fellowship," Atticus took Gwen's and Eduviges' hands. Everyone else held hands around the circle. Power surged from Atticus' hand into Gwen, but also from Taralyn. Gwen glanced around. Each face glowed; a golden halo seemed to encircle the group. "The fellowship of faith. The faith of destiny. The destiny of good versus evil. The assurance of victory. These things we lift to you, O Lord. We have sworn ourselves to you. We have pledged our lives, promised our hearts, consecrated our bodies and our children. We are yours. We are your vessels, we are your weapons, we are your word. Let your will be done. Amen."

Fire swept through Gwen's body. It ricocheted between the Elders. They all stood with ecstasy etched on each face. Sara moaned; Matthew panted. Gwen's body arched as she gasped.

"It's too sweet to let go, pastor," Eduviges laughed.

"It's only going to grow stronger," Tyler said with difficulty.

"Praise God!" Atticus shouted. He released Gwen's hand and she slumped forward. He caught her around the waist. "It can be a little overwhelming at first."

"It's always overwhelming, Pastor," Bea laughed. "I wouldn't know I was praying if I didn't get weak in the knees."

Chi was patting his wife's hand from where she sat at the table.

"Here, come sit next to Visolela while we go get the food." Bea steered Gwen away from Atticus' arms and around to the pregnant woman's side. Visolela glanced up; her eyes glazing with fear again.

"Don't be afraid," Gwen whispered.

"How can you say that?" Visolela whispered back. "I was scared when my husband started having dreams of this place. I was scared when we left Nairobi and traveled to this place. I was scared when the pastor told us of the coming war. And then you came. The warrior who would help us hold back the Darkness. I was scared before. But you are here now. You are proof that everything I've been told is going to come true. You don't scare me, Warrior. You terrify me."

Gwen stood up. Visolela took her arm and pulled her back down. "I'm sorry. This is not your fault. It is not you that terrifies me; it is the war. For my baby. I am scared for my baby."

"I understand that." Gwen placed one hand on the woman's womb and one on her own. "When are you due?"

"Three more months. The end of August. It will be a boy. A fine healthy boy who will not die at birth."

"Do you have a good doctor?"

"The best! My husband."

"Oh that's good to know. In case I ever need one." Gwen glanced at the forests beyond the yard.

"I have never carried to child to full term. I have

tried many times but--" her eyes filled with tears.

"I can't imagine how hard it must be to lose a child."
She rubbed her abdomen protectively.

"It is a clay jar filled with despair. A huge clay jar big
enough to stand inside and drown in."

Gwen swallowed hard, "I've been inside that clay
jar."

"So you are not just a warrior; you are one of us,
too?"

"I don't know." Gwen got up as people began
reaching around her to set platters of food on the
table. "I don't know who you are."

"Well, what do you think?" Atticus grinned at her as
she tentatively placed a forkful of peanut butter pie in
her mouth.

She swirled her tongue around and nodded.

Chapter 8
The Singer

She lay awake the next morning listening and thinking. She liked the feel of the cotton sheets and light faux-quilt as she stretched. The walls of this tiny room were a soft white, somewhere between moonlight and ivory. The curtains had once been sheets; the rods supported the fabric through what had once been the head of the sheet. It ruffled limply along the top of the window and stopped about an inch above the floor. The patterns on the re-purposed sheets were tiny dinosaurs in primary red, blue and green and matched the thin quilt. She knew the closet had two shelves at the bottom with a sturdy wooden rod at the top, and another shelf above that; empty except for her purchases. The mismatched chest of drawers and bureau were also empty, devoid of the child's toys and clothes which had once filled both this room and this home with love.

"Gwen?" There was a light tap on her door. "You up?"

"Yes."

"Is it too early to practice the Morning Meadow? Sunday's pretty full for me. I'd hoped to get an early start."

"I'm awake. I'll be out in a minute." She pushed aside thoughts of the room's previous inhabitant and dressed in jeans and her thread-bare T.

Heading out into the hall, she picked up her dowel. He was waiting in the back yard, dressed only in jogging shorts.

She caught her breath. With the sun coming up and illuminating his body like a torch, he was gorgeous. "Dawn," she spoke sternly.

She led him through Dawn, Awareness, Awe, Surrender, and Dawn and then commanded him to practice the same three times while she completed the Morning Meadow.

As she finished with the final Dawn, he stepped behind her pressing his chest against her back and cupping her shoulders gently in his hands. Fire filled her as he whispered in her ear. "Strength for today. Fortitude for tomorrow. Faith for eternity. These things we ask in your name oh Lord."

She couldn't move; she could barely breathe. She arched her back against his body; he hardened against her touch. His lips brushed her shoulder, she moaned. His hands caressed their way down her arms across her waist, pulling her further into his embrace. She turned her head to meet his lips with her starving mouth.

A perfectly pitched voice sing-songed from the front yard. "Hello! Anybody home?"

Gwen shuddered and forced herself away from him.

The front doorbell rang and the scent of Chantilly Lace wafted toward them. "Atticus! I hope I'm not calling too early."

Atticus grumbled softly, "Patsy Welden. What the hell does she want?"

"I'm just guessing, but I bet she wants you." Gwen gave him a sassy grin.

He grabbed her, pulling her against him so there was no doubt as to how he felt. "She's out of luck." He moved to kiss her and she dodged his mouth, grinning wickedly.

"We're back here, Patsy!" Softly Gwen whispered, "You better get some clothes on or Sister Welden is going to think you're mighty happy to see her."

He dashed into the kitchen, slamming the door.

"Hello?" Patsy opened the gate. "I thought--I was looking for Atticus."

"The pastor is taking a shower. He just got up." Gwen smiled at her own pun.

"Oh." Her nostrils flared. "I see we both came too early. I guess one of us should've called first."

"If you called any earlier I'd have had to tell you Atticus was still asleep."

She crossed her arms. "Really?"

"Yes, really. Atticus takes about ten minutes to shower and shave. I was just going to have some coffee. Would you like a cup while you wait?"

"I-" she could barely speak. "Gwen? Isn't that your name? I didn't catch how you are related to Atticus."

Gwen began twirling the dowel in one hand then the other. "I'm not."

"Are you a friend of his mother's?" She snarled the last noun.

"I've never met his mother. Have you?"

"No." She tilted her chin defiantly. "Not yet."

Gwen nodded and began arcing the dowel in Sails against the Winds stance.

Patsy snorted and began tapping her foot.

"Are you sure you don't want some coffee?"

"I see I came at an inopportune time."

Gwen nodded, "It is sort of early."

"Kindly tell Atticus that I won't be able to sing a solo next week after all. As a matter of fact, First Baptist has asked me to join their choir."

"Patsy, don't do that. You're the best singer this church has. Why, the pastor was telling me last night that he'd like you to start a choir here."

Patsy tsked in disgust and stomped to the gate. She hesitated as the latch opened. "Does he really want me to start a choir?"

"I think that's a wonderful idea," Atticus walked out of the kitchen in a white dress shirt and black slacks, toweling his hair. "We are a small church, but we are growing. I couldn't offer you much in the way of salary. I think First Baptist has more in their choir than we have in the congregation. I'd understand if you thought you could better serve the Lord elsewhere."

"Well!" Her head wobbled just like a ukera's. "I'll have to give that some thought."

"When school starts up again, I was thinking of

starting a children's choir," Atticus stopped an arm's length from Gwen's side. She ground her rod in *Pine Tree at Rest*.

Patsy licked her lips, looking from Gwen to Atticus. "That might be fun."

Chapter 9
The Children

"Come sit with us." Chi took Gwen's arm outside the church and escorted her inside.

Patsy walked in, preceded by the scent of her perfume. Gwen smiled sweetly and waved. Patsy waved back. She glanced around and sat next to a surprised Le'Vander. Chi leaned around Visolela toward Gwen and whispered, "I didn't know you could work miracles."

Gwen blushed. "You just have to know what a woman wants and be able to give it to her."

"I thought everyone knew exactly what Patsy wants--Atticus."

Gwen shook her head, "What she wanted was to please Atticus. To be important to him."

Visolela cocked her head. "Igala - not English- is my first language. What is it you have given to Patsy?"

Gwen hunched her shoulders and leaned forward conspiratorially. "She's our new choir director."

The pew shook with Visolela's silent laughter.

"That was brilliant!" Taralyn spun around from the

pew in front of them. "Totally brilliant!"

"Thanks!"

Her father turned, too. "She could have become a real liability. She is too nosy and too egocentric. She would eventually have found us out."

A wrinkled hand fell on the doctor's shoulder as Rutger leaned down, "I was hoping you'd have to kill her."

"What would've been the fun of that?" Gwen whispered, pleased with the success of her idea.

After the benediction, Gwen turned to the doctor. "Have lunch with us today, please?"

They agreed.

The four friends feasted on baked chicken, kidney bean salad, black-eyed peas, corn bread and iced tea around the picnic table.

"Ladies, that was wonderful. Chi, how do you feel about a little fishing this afternoon?" Atticus stretched.

"Visolela," Gwen spoke firmly. "Since we cooked, why don't we go sit on the rocking chairs on the porch while they clean up?"

Visolela hobbled sideways and escaped from the bench. She kissed her husband's cheek, "Soak the chicken pan in soapy water. You and Atticus can go fishing this evening before service."

A breeze cooled the porch as the women rocked.

"Can I ask you something, Visolela?"

"Yes."

"Do women frequently have miscarriages?"

She rocked for a moment before answering. "My

husband says that a great number of fetuses are aborted naturally at the sixth week, when the umbilical cord is supposed to attach the fetus to the womb. Something happens and this attachment does not take place. He says most women do not even know they were with child that early in the pregnancy."

"But you knew."

She nodded gravely. "Each and every time.

"I heard once that a child is given a soul at the sixth week."

"I have heard that, too." Visolela nodded. "After the last miscarriage, we stopped trying. For six years, we made sure we could not conceive. But then we came to America. And Atticus prayed over us. And I knew."

"His prayers," Gwen hesitated, blushing.

Visolela smiled knowingly. "When we pray in a circle, the power is strong. But the first time Atticus took me aside and prayed with me alone, I thought I would have an orgasm. Orgasm? That is the correct word?"

Gwen nodded.

"It is the same for you?"

"Oh yes. Lord yes!"

"When he taught Chi how to pray the same way, and then Chi taught me to pray, we stayed in bed for three days. We were so filled with power. That is when I got pregnant. That is why I know this baby will be born alive."

"So, Atticus prays this way with everyone? It's not just--me?"

"Atticus prays with everyone. For everyone."

Visolela rocked again. "But you are special to him. Set apart. There will be no shame when your child comes. Atticus has seen this."

Gwen's feet slapped onto the porch. "Atticus knows I'm pregnant?"

"He must. He has spoken about the children you will bear him. Especially the first child. She will be as great a warrior as you are, and will also hold back the Darkness."

They rocked in silence as the wind spun dirt devils down the drive.

"Gwen, Atticus has spoken of his first child as if it were his. You have been here less than a week. Has he already fathered a child within you?"

"No!"

"But you're already with child?"

"Yes, I think so."

"Atticus is a good man, a great priest, but a proud man with a terrible anger. You should tell him now."

"I will. There is no reason not to tell him. But Visolela, let me tell him first. Promise me you will not tell anyone."

"I will tell my husband if he asks. It is a wife's duty." Visolela frowned. "But no one else."

Chi and Atticus burst onto the porch with fly rods in their hands. "The fish are calling us!" Atticus declared.

"Don't keep them waiting," Gwen commanded.

Chi knelt beside Visolela, stroking her abdomen and kissing her deeply. He bent his head, "I will take you fishing as soon you can hold a pole, son."

Gwen looked away, pleasantly embarrassed by their intimacy. She glanced up at Atticus; his face had darkened. He looked like someone had stabbed him. A twinge in her abdomen caused her to gasp, drawing Atticus's attention to her.

He strode in front of her and placed his hands on the arms of her rocker. As slowly as Awareness sinks to Awe, he leaned forward and kissed her lips.

"Atticus," Chi spoke. "Atticus, the fish are calling."

He broke off gently and smiled into Gwen's glazed eyes. "The fish are calling."

Gwen nodded breathlessly.

The men laughed as they climbed into the old blue truck and drove away.

"I may not be." Gwen's voice trembled. "Pregnant. I haven't had a period since March. I've been under a great deal of stress. That can cause a skipped period."

"Perhaps."

"Maybe after another week of good food and safety, I'll start."

"Maybe."

They rocked in silence for a while, with Visolela sneaking glances at Gwen's face. "Would you like to know for sure?"

"Yes."

"I will speak with my husband."

"Thank you."

"How far along are you?"

"Just six weeks."

"You are sure?"

She nodded, grimacing.

"He knows? The man who is the father of this child?"

Gwen shrugged, "No, but it doesn't matter."

"I see."

They rocked while a helicopter traced across the sky.

"I love him."

"Atticus?" Visolela asked.

"Sanchor. I love him."

"And where is this Sanchor? Where is he while you seek refuge away from all you knew?"

"Not here."

"Is he dead?"

"No." Gwen got to her feet. "He was a great warrior. He served the Light with all his heart. I loved him so dearly, and then, something terrible happened and he was lost. I couldn't bear it. So I left him and came home--back to Earth. You understand that this war is being fought on other worlds?"

"I understand."

Gwen leaned on the porch railings, looking beyond the cemetery. "He came to see me the last week in March. He told me he loved me, but that I couldn't save him."

"Did you believe him?"

Gwen didn't answer.

Chapter 10
The Promise

They moved together as one: Dawn, Awareness, Awe, Surrender, Dawn.

"Open your right hand. Now close your right hand and open your left. Do you feel the muscles in your hands and wrists respond?"

"Yes."

"Good. Use only those muscles, not your shoulders or your arms. Release your right hand and allow the rod to drop as low as your waist."

The rod wobbled.

"Take a slow breath and concentrate on the rod. Good." Gwen circled Atticus. "Now bring the rod back up and repeat it with your other hand. Better. Do this six times each until you no longer control the rod; you are the rod."

A mockingbird deposited a grasshopper onto the picnic table and began disemboweling it.

"Open your right hand and allow the rod to drop to your thighs. Now the other side. Five more times." Atticus puffed at a drop of sweat on his nose.

"Knee level," she commanded and he responded well.

"Ankle level."

He groaned as the rod slipped from his hands.

"Return to the Dawn and began again. Six times each level - waist, thighs, knees, ankles." While he moved, practicing the forms, she spoke gently. "Long ago, darkness covered the face of the world and the animals were afraid that the light would never return. Grandmother Spider fashioned a web around a clay pot, climbed across the sky, scooped up the sun in her pot, and dragged it back to the world. She landed on the Sequoia tree and climbed down its trunk to tie her web at its roots, anchoring the sun in the sky. Then she climbed back up the Sequoia to admire her work."

Atticus successfully lowered the rod to ankle height six times.

"As you allow the rod to touch the ground at your feel, think of the rod as Grandmother Spider's web, and you are the Sequoia. It is to you the Light is anchored."

Atticus closed his eyes. Sweat dripped from his chin and ears.

"Now Grandmother Spider climbs back up the Sequoia: ankles, knees, thighs, waist, shoulders."

Atticus groaned.

"Where are you?"

"On the Sequoia tree."

"What do you see?"

"The Dawn?"

"Again; we have returned to a place of beginnings."

"Does that mean I can rest?"

"You can hold the Dawn and watch me." She began at the beginning and worked her way through the Morning Meadow. They sank onto the picnic bench and drank their coffee.

"I visit the shut-ins and the hospital on Monday."

"I remember."

'That's right! You've been here a week now. We need to celebrate." He squeezed her arm; her skin tingled with his touch.

She moved away. "Before we do any celebrating, or anymore praying--I need to tell you something."

He wrapped his hands around his mug. "You can tell me anything, as long as it's the truth. Don't be afraid."

"I don't know you. And you don't know me."

'The angel--"

"I don't know the angel! Who is he to tell you certain things about me and leave other things out? Who is he to tell you anything about me at all?"

His face clouded and his voice deepened. "He is the Angel of the Lord."

She pressed her hands on the bench between them. "Who is he to me?"

Atticus peered into her eyes. He brushed the hair from her cheek, leaving a trail of arousal through his fingertips. "He is the Angel of the Lord."

"Don't." She moaned as his fingertips painted her lips.

"Don't tell me no." He cupped the back of her head and pulled her to him.

"Atticus, I have to tell you something."

He engulfed her, his lips consumed hers, his tongue possessed her mouth. She soared in his arms.

He broke away. "Gwen, we can't, not yet. I want you so much, but we're not married, not yet."

His words pulled her down out of the skies. She blinked dazedly up at his face and shuddered. She took a ragged breath and pushed away from him. "Married? I don't even know you! You don't know me!" She sprinted into the house and locked the guest room door.

Atticus kept his distance reluctantly for the rest of the week. Gwen never found the courage to tell him she might be pregnant. Thursday morning, she taught him Frog on the Pond, relating it to the concepts of metamorphosis and rebirth.

Occasionally he took her hand or brushed his lips across her cheeks, but he controlled his passion. She put off telling him about the baby, hoping that her mense would return soon.

Saturday, Gwen taught Atticus *the* Rainbow. "The frog signifies new life. For the first time, you will use the rod as a tool. A frog uses its extended limbs to move across the pond; you use the rod as an extension of your arms, striking farther but with much more force." "The frog brought new life, a new way to use the rod, and now you will learn a new way to hold the rod. At Dawn, don't release the rod, but pull your hands together to the center. Caress the rod as you slide your hands together. Tell me what you feel."

Atticus focused on his fists. "I don't have as much control over the rod. It feels wobbly."

"Learn this lesson, Atticus. From this point onward, you have no control over the rod. You are the rod. It is an extension of you. Once tadpoles become frogs, they can never turn back. Once we face the darkness and choose the light, we will not turn back. Once you've become the rod, you -- not the rod -- are a weapon." She waited for this to sink in. "Tell me God's promise."

"I will never leave you nor forsake you until I have done that which I promised you."

"What did God used to represent his promise?"

"The rainbow."

"The next step is called the rainbow; it marks the promise you as a weapon against the darkness have made to God. Keep your feet flat, stretch as high as you can. Lean forward."

He stumbled.

"Begin again," she admonished gently. "Follow the rainbow up, over, to the ground. Bowing before the light. Promising yourself to the light."

"Oh!" He lost his balance and tumbled against her, knocking her feet from under her. She fell with a grunt and shoved at him, laughing.

He grabbed her legs and rolled against her. "My legs are broken!"

"I told you it was harder than it looks."

"I can't walk." He grabbed her arms.

"Quit your whining!" She sat on her knees and tried to pull him up.

He shifted his weight, pulling her on top of him. "I'm in pain," he laughed.

She wound up straddling his hips, her palms pressed against his chest. He reached up, pulling the hair back from her face.

Time stopped.

"You were going to tell me something."

She couldn't speak.

He tucked her hair behind her ears and slowly let his hand slip to her breasts. His thumbs flicked her nipples. She closed her eyes. His hands grabbed her waist and shifted her. He arched upward, his tongue repeating what his thumbs had done.

She nestled his head against her breast, gasping. His hand slipped under her shirt, exploring the firm flesh beneath. His mouth replaced his hand. Her hands traveled down his back, kneading their way to his bare skin.

Shirts were flung aside as he toppled her onto her back. She was lost. She found his mouth and surrendered to her desires.

"No." He moaned. "Not yet." His hand continued against the advice of his words.

"Atticus," she murmured.

"We have to be married first." His hand stopped just inside her waistband.

"We what?" She unbuttoned his shorts.

He pushed his chest away grinding against her pelvis. "We have to get married. Then we can become one."

She rubbed her face, as if awakening. "I can't

marry you."

His fingers dug into her shoulders as he gave them a shake. "You will be my wife."

She sobered, swallowing down her desire and looked at him. He frightened her. Passion mottled his cheeks. "Or what?" she calmly asked.

He trembled.

"Get off me," she commanded.

His fingers dug deeper.

A shift of her weight and she flung him over her head onto his back. She jumped into a crouch and retrieved her shirt.

"I'm sorry, Gwen. I lost control. It'll be different once were married."

"Reverend Jordan," she shook her head and arms into her shirt. "I can't marry you."

"Why?"

"For one thing, you didn't ask. You just assumed that what your angel told you would happen."

"It--"

She rode right over him. "And for another thing, there is someone else. Someone I loved. Someone I wanted to marry. I still love him." She lowered her voice. "I'm not going to marry you."

She ran out of the yard into the cemetery. She watched as he left the house dressed in his white shirt and black slacks. She watched as the parishioners arrived and entered the fellowship hall for Sunday school. She knew what she had to do. She packed quickly, leaving behind her church dresses and high heel shoes. She took off the ring and tucked it deep under the mattress. She filled a plastic bag with fruit, cheese, and water; grabbed up her staff and hopped over the back fence into the forest. She hiked for ten minutes and then collapsed against an oak and began to sob.

Chapter 11
The Seeker

"Found her!" Taralyn looked up from her laptop. The Elders filled the fellowship hall around her. "She was arrested for vagrancy in Greensboro."

A haggard Atticus stopped pacing and exhaled. "Can you access her VITA?" Her father asked. She rolled her eyes. Visolela stepped behind her, silently reading the screen.

"She was arrested in connection with the jewelry store robbery. She was fighting the robbers. The police arrested all of them. Oh, red flag!"

Her father peered at the screen. "FBI was notified about the other men who were arrested with her. The robbery suspects matched identity with a string of gang-related crimes from Washington, Oregon, Nebraska and Illinois."

"Hey, she's--"

Visolela smacked Taralyn so hard on the back of her head her teeth clacked together, silencing her. Visolela reached down and closed the health document on the laptop. She gave the teen a serious look. Taralyn nodded.

"I can get a helicopter here in an hour. We'll go get her." Rutger declared.

"What, just drop into the detention center yard and grab her? Nothing like being conspicuous." Sara remarked.

"We could bail her out," Larry suggested.

"Twenty-five thousand dollars," Taralyn read off the screen. "Court date is in July."

"Did the FBI flag her, too?" Eduviges asked.

"No, they have her listed as Jean Louis Finch. They don't know who she is."

"How did you figure that's her?" Bea asked.
"I didn't. Mitchell did."

The third grader explained as if it were simple. "Your name's Atticus. Atticus Finch was the lawyer in *To Kill a Mockingbird*. The little girl's name was Jean Louis but everyone called her Scout."

"Huh?" His mother grunted. The boy sighed.

"What's the plan?" Rutger rubbed his hands together.

"I'll drive over tomorrow and bail her out." Atticus rubbed his face.

"And then what?" The doctor asked, glancing at his wife.

"I'll bring her home."

"Atticus," Chi took a deep breath. "What if she does not want to come back?"

Taralyn glanced up at the doctor and then aside at Visolela. "Oh."

"What?" Tyler asked.

"Oh," Taralyn repeated, thinking quickly. "We could go get her. And she could stay with us. Just for a while."

"That is a good idea," Visolela agreed.

"I'll bring her home to my house." Atticus' face turned red.

No one met his eyes.

"They are planning to begin clearing the field next week for the compound. Maybe Gwen would feel more comfortable in a quieter environment," Chi suggested.

"She's going to be my wife. She belongs home with me."

"Mitchell, why don't you and Taralyn come help me fix snacks in the kitchen?" Sara stood.

"It's not like I don't know what's going on," Taralyn snarled.

"You may, but Mitchell doesn't. And he doesn't listen to me when you're around."

Taralyn turned to Visolela, pointed at her and put a finger phone to her ear. "Come on, Mitch. I'll let you lick the oatmeal cookies before we put them on the plates."

When the children closed the door behind them, Atticus exploded, "Who do you think you are, telling me I can't go get my wife!"

"She is not your wife!" Visolela snapped.

"There's been talk in the town. A minister shacking up with a single woman," Eduviges warned.

"I'm not shacking up with her. She's my wife!" He held his hand up to block the protests. "She's going to be my wife."

"Well, when she is your wife, you can live under the same roof, like decent people," Bea snipped.

"Then I'll grab a preacher on the way home. We'll be married before we return."

"Just like that?" Tyler asked quietly.

"In Africa, it is still acceptable for the man to kidnap the woman and force her into marriage." Chi spoke calmly. "However, we are in America."

"Kidnap!" Atticus roared. "I didn't force myself on her. I'm no monster. What, you think I'd rape a woman?"

"Calm down." Rutger snapped. "Atticus, calm down."

"No one's saying you raped Gwen," Larry growled.

"We just don't understand," Tyler paused.

"Why did she leave?" Bea asked.

Atticus trembled, trying to calm.

"Did she tell you something, and you lost your temper?" Visolela took her husband's arm.

His face turned red again.

Chi and Visolela exchanged looks.

Tears streamed down Atticus' face.

Rutger clamped a hand on Atticus's shoulder and pulled the younger man against him. "You have such a great faith, Atticus. Your belief is as strong as iron. You see how things should be."

The elders gathered around, forming a close circle. "But sometimes you don't see how things are. You see that Gwen will be your wife. But you don't see that Gwen is a stranger to you now. She doesn't know you."

"She doesn't love me." Atticus wrapped his arms around the people near him. "She's in love with someone else."

"She will love you. But it takes time." Bea assured him.

"If you rush into this, you'll scare her away. We can't afford to lose her." Eduviges stated.

Atticus nodded.

"Taralyn and I will go bail her out tomorrow. We'll use fake IDs and pay the fine in cash."

"Swing by my house on the way. I'll have unmarked bills ready for you." Larry instructed.

"And we'll bring her home. We'll get this sorted out. It will take time."

"But we believe in you." Chi reminded him.

"You can show us by example how to be patient and understanding," Visolela smiled.

"Atticus, we're going to pray for you now. Fill you with the power of prayer, just as you taught us how to do." Rutger kissed the side of his face and began to pray.

Chapter 12
The Colonel

"Mom!" Taralyn rushed into Gwen's arms in the release room. "Mama!"

Gwen hugged the teen, blinking in surprise. Tyler wrapped the both of them in his arms and declared, "Thank God we found you Jean Louise! I brought your medicine. You'll be right as rain soon. We've come to bring you home."

"Play along," Taralyn whispered.

"I'm not going back." Gwen stood her ground.

"Now honey," Tyler cajoled. "You're going to stay with us."

"At our home." Taralyn whispered.

"No one's going to harm you. There was just a big misunderstanding. We know things got to moving fast for you. We understand that."

"I'm not who you think I am!"

"Hush now," Tyler took her arm, appeasing her. "The doctor explained your condition to me. I won't say I wasn't surprised. But, we understand how you feel now. Won't nobody make you rush into anything."

"You know?"

"It was in your detention health records," Taralyn whispered.

"Atticus knows?"

"This isn't the place to discuss things," Tyler whispered. Louder, he continued, "I already claimed your belongings, they're in the car. Come on, Jean Louise. We're going home."

"I've read the file; your men did good work, Sheriff." The man in the brown Armani perched on the chair in the sheriff's office.

"Your papers for extradition were impressive, too, Colonel. And real prompt."

"Well, no reason to mess around with paperwork. That's for desk jocks, not soldiers like you and me."

Sheriff Johnson glared in contentious silence.

"The woman that was arrested along with these terrorists--is this a complete inventory of her belongings?" Colonel Morgan Forest handed Johnson a folded sheet of paper.

"Yep. Just clothes and food. No ID."

"No jewelry?"

Johnson shook his head. "Maybe it got left off the list accidentally."

The man in the brown suit squinted in irritation. "We'd like to ask her a few questions."

"Well, that's a damn shame." The sheriff smirked. "Her family came and got her."

"When?"

"About two days ago."

Colonel Morgan Forest spoke into his cell phone. "Get me the records on Jean Louise Finch, Malcomb, Alabama, and everything you can find on her."

"Wasting your time, Colonel."

"How's that?"

The sheriff opened a drawer and pulled out a folder. "A man and teen girl came in with proper IDs and twenty-five thousand in cash. Professed to be Jean Louise Finch's husband and daughter: Jim and Scout Finch. According to a signed document from one Alonzo Sanchez, M.D., Mrs. Finch had been prescribed a drug for depression, and had had an unusual reaction to it, triggering temporary dementia and amnesia. Me? I thought the husband had knocked her around a bit and she'd run off." Johnson yawned, "The only charge we had against her was vagrancy, and she was instrumental in capturing your terrorists. The woman went willingly with the man and the teen-ager. We saw no reason to keep her."

"But?"

"This morning, her fingerprints came back, with big red arrow next to her real name." He handed the agent the folder. "Guinevere Hampt. Tacoma, Washington. Wanted in connection –

"Shit!" Morgan pulled out the cell again. "Immediate pickup order--"

"Wait, won't do no good. You much of a reader, Colonel Forest?" The sheriff plopped a paperback on his desk. Morgan flipped through *To Kill a Mockingbird* while Johnson continued. "Alonzo Sanchez isn't a doctor at all, it's is a coffee shop."

"Description of the man and teen," The colonel tucked the book beside the folder.

"Average. Average. Forty-five and seventeen."

"Where did they go?" Veins bulged at the agent's temples and throat.

Johnson leaned back and rested his hands behind his head. "I'm not rightly sure. Tracking them down sounds like a job for a soldier, not a desk jockey like me."

"I want the surveillance camera films of the couple." Morgan stood.

The sheriff opened another drawer and pulled out a disk. "Oh, one more thing, might interest you. The woman Guinevere Hampt, a.k.a. a Jean Louise Finch, is pregnant."

Chapter 13
The Family

"It's not as clean as it could be," Taralyn walked her through the living room. She whispered, "Dad's a slob,"

"It's fine. Really." Gwen glanced around at the piles of newspapers and books. Empty water bottles circled the center.

Taralyn led her down the hall and into a small bedroom. "You'll sleep in here. The couch makes out to a bed."

The room was filled wall to ceiling with computer equipment. The only bare space was a frayed couch.

"You can put your clothes in this closet. I'll go get the rest of your things from Atticus tomorrow." Taralyn hovered nervously.

"Taralyn, why don't you let Gwen get some sleep?" Tyler came into the room and had to walk sideways to get to the couch. He flung the cushions off and grabbed the mattress handle, struggling to unfold the bed. He scolded, "I don't want you folding or unfolding this bed. We'll just leave it open while you're here."

"I put fresh sheets on it last night. I didn't know if you needed a blanket or not. Dad keeps it cold as the tundra in here!"

"Your mother--" Tyler began.

Taralyn froze. Gwen looked between the two.

"My wife Beth had a very high metabolism. It was like sleeping next to oven baked bricks."

Gwen smiled sympathetically.

"Well, goodnight Gwen. It's nice to have you back." Tyler nodded and sidled out of the room.

Taralyn perched on the mattress while Gwen put her bag on the floor. "I'll need to wash these clothes before I hang them up."

"The washer and dryer are in the garage." Gwen sat next to Taralyn and sighed. "Was he really mad?"

Taralyn nodded. "But we calmed him down. Sort of made him see reason. He still doesn't know you're pregnant. I mean – we're not morons with a death wish or anything."

Gwen dropped her head into her hands. "This is all so crazy."

Taralyn began to pat her back, but withdrew her hand. Gwen saw it.

"After my mother died, I didn't let anyone touch me either."

"Your mother died?"

Gwen sat up. "And my father, my two bratty sisters, and my little brother." She glanced sideways at Taralyn. "I was about your age."

"Visolela said you were one of us. Not just a warrior, but one of us."

Gwen blinked. "Visolela said that; not the Angel of

the Lord?"

"Yeah, well, you know."

"No, I really don't."

"We don't either. Know about you, that is. I mean, we know what Atticus tells us, but it has suddenly become obvious he doesn't know everything, either. And that sort of makes me a little nervous. I mean, I'm not even old enough to drive a car, and I'm hacking into the educational systems of the University of Chechnya." Taralyn bumped her shoulder gently against Gwen's.

"As long as you don't try to speak Chechnyan to them." Gwen bumped her back.

"My mom was killed by terrorists, but it wasn't in the papers or anything. What about yours?"

Gwen sighed. "My family was assassinated seventeen years ago. It was covered up, too. I guess it's alright to report that terrorists bomb foreign countries, but Americans must be too delicate to be entrusted with the truth. My father had been an ambassador to a friendly country with unfriendly revolutionists at large. On vacation back stateside, I slipped out one night to meet some friends, intent on underage bar hopping. While I was dancing in some skank dive, my parents, sisters, and little brother had their throats cut. I returned to the hotel, snockered, and remember throwing up on the FBI agent's shoes. It's weird what you remember. His name was Morgan Forest."

"It sure sounds like you're one of us."

"One of us?" Gwen turned so she was facing

Taralyn.

"The elders." Taralyn yawned.

"The elders. I got that. But who are you? What are the elders?"

Taralyn got up yawning. "Why don't you ask Atticus that question? As a matter of fact, I think Eduviges is right; maybe you and Atticus should do a lot more talking and a little less praying."

Gwen blushed.

"You need to tell him he's not your child's father."

"Why is that anyone's business?" Gwen snapped.

"Because the Angel of the Lord told Atticus a lot of stuff about you."

"So how come this angel left out that I'm pregnant?"

"He didn't leave it out. Atticus knows your first child will be a daughter."

"And he assumed it's going to be his."

Taralyn held up her hands. "None of my business. Why don't you talk to Atticus? Good night."

"Goodnight."

Chapter 14
The Pride

"Atticus, she's still asleep!" Tyler's voice flowed through the house. Gwen got up and tiptoed down the hall, peering around the corner into the living room.

"Is she all right?"

"Yes, she's fine. But she needs her sleep."

"Do you mind if I wait here? Until she awakens?"

"Yes, I do mind." Tyler's voice was stiff. "I have to take Taralyn with me to this site this morning. The schematics for the security system aren't fleshing with the electric system."

"What's up?" Taralyn walked in wearing shorts and a T.

"Morning, Taralyn."

"Atticus, what are you – stalking Gwen? Let the woman come to you!" Taralyn perched one foot on the couch's arm to tie her shoe.

Atticus blanched.

"Out of the mouths of babes," Tyler raised his eyebrows.

Atticus blew out a long breath. "You're right. I'll be at the parsonage. Will you give her this?" He handed

Tyler a practice dowel.

By the evening, when Taralyn and Tyler returned, Gwen had laundered her clothes and cleaned the living room, and made a dent in the kitchen.

"Wow! Someone stole all our dirt!" Taralyn exclaimed.

The next morning, Tyler read the paper while CNN droned on the TV. Taralyn watched Gwen go through the Morning Meadow.

"Are you going to church tonight?" Taralyn asked. "It's Wednesday."

"I don't see why not." Gwen handed her the rod. "Here, want to learn?"

Gwen dressed in jeans and a T -- all her skirts and dresses were still at the parsonage. She headed to the car with her pack and rod. Tyler raised an eyebrow but didn't say anything.

She sat beside Taralyn on the third row and listened attentively to the service. Atticus's sermon was based on trials and tribulations. Patsy sang *God Leads His Dear Children Along*. There were a half-dozen new men in the congregation. Tyler said they were construction workers from the compound's building site. After Atticus gave the benediction, he paused at the third row and held out his hand.

"Forgive me my pride and arrogance." His voice spanned across the sanctuary.

Gwen's eyes welled with tears.

"Don't be afraid," Taralyn whispered, giving her shoulder a slight shove.

Gwen reached out and took his hand. The elders collectively shouted "Hallelujah!"

They walked hand-in-hand down the aisle.

As the last of the congregation drove away, the elders returned to the sanctuary. They stood in a tight circle, arms around each other's waists and shoulders, heads bowed. The prayer filled them all until they were glowing so brightly that the stained glass windows cast colored lights on the grass outside. No words were spoken. None needed to be.

Finally, Atticus spoke, "Amen."

"Glory!" Eduviges shouted.

"Elders meeting at the parsonage this Saturday, four o'clock. Bring food." Gwen announced.

They looked startled and then pleased. Rutger chortled and threw his arms around her. "You gave us quite a scare, little Xena."

"Nice to have you back." Both of the Sveete's hugged her at the same time.

"Did you really fight off robbers?" Mitchell peered up at her.

"No." Gwen replied. Glancing around, she raised her voice. "I fought with seven soldiers of the dark. I don't know how they got to South Carolina but I do know why they were robbing the jewelry store. There's something I need to tell all of you. But not until Saturday. Atticus and I have things to discuss first."

She stood by his side, waving as the last car pulled away. He shouldered her pack and took her hand. "Don't ask me any questions. Not yet."

"Okay." Atticus agreed.

Chapter 15
The Darkness

Dawn.
Awareness.
Awe.
Surrender.
Grandmother Spider.
Frog.
Rainbow.

Gwen and Atticus moved as one.

"You've been practicing," she complimented him.

"Every morning for two and a half weeks."

"The next step is the hardest."

He met her gaze. "Yes ma'am. I reckon it is."

She waited three heartbeats before continuing. "The journey begins where the light is anchored."

"The roots of the sequoia."

"Yes."

He bent over.

"Your journey through this life is full of twists and turns. Gently move your rod as far left around your ankles as you can. Slowly. Let your muscles stretch without injuring them. Now, twist to the right."

Atticus groaned. His spine popped noisily.

"That's good. Now, like the transition from Awe to Surrender, straighten from here." She put her hand on the small of his back. "Raise up to the calf level and twist to the left. Not so fast. Now right." She kept her palm on his back.

"Knee high. Continue the journey. The Journey represents the spiral of Life. We retrace our steps but work our way higher and higher on the path to enlightenment."

He raised the rod and twisted left and right.

"Thighs."

"I'm getting dizzy."

"You're doing great! The first time I did this, I fell over twice."

"I have a good teacher."

"Concentrate on the Journey." She watched as he journeyed at waist level and then stopped at Dawn. "Keep going. Journey beyond your beginning until the rod is at Surrender."

"Easier now," he panted.

"Now, spin the rod over your head, using only the muscles you used for spider. One hand, then the other."

The rod spun three times, and then flew across the yard clattering against the picnic table.

"Oops."

"Again. Start from the beginning. When you get to journey's end, keep the rod spinning while I finish the morning meadow."

"Yes, ma'am."

The sun rose in rays of magenta and Lapis with swirls of ocher and ecru.

"Return the journey to Dawn."

He did so.

She faced him at Dawn position and bowed. He copied her. "Lord of Light, guard and guide. Lord of Light, preserve and protect. Lord of Light, direct and defend. Amen."

Atticus repeated the prayer. They straightened.

"I'm pregnant."

He sank to his knees, gasping for breath.

"That's why I can't marry you. It wouldn't be fair."

"Fair?" He growled.

"It wouldn't be."

"She should be mine!" He roared.

She took a step back.

"Mine! My child!" He clawed at the dirt, flinging clumps of grass into the air.

"She's not."

"Who? Who did it?" He snarled up at her from a crouch.

"His name is Sanchor."

"Where is he?"

She stared down at him, so he shouted, "Where is the bastard?"

"He's lost," she whispered.

He watched as tears began to slide down her cheeks. He wanted to rage at her. Condemn her. Kill Sanchor. Power surged from within him, erupting like vile puke from his mind.

Gwen cried out, "No! Don't open it!"

In the space between them, a darkness expanded. It began as a dull shimmer, expanding up and out while the space within darkened to jet black. When it was a circle four foot in diameter, a gauntlet punched through it, followed by an armored chest, legs, and head. The glass lightning mask sparkled in the morning light. The dark soldier stumbled and fell through the Door of Despair toward them as Atticus stared in shock. The black hole blinked and disappeared.

The soldier leapt to his feet, unsheathing a sword.

"Whom do you serve?" He bellowed.

"Atticus, *frog on the pond!*"

Without thinking, Atticus extended his rod in an arch, smacking the soldier on his thigh.

Woodpecker followed by hoeing the garden, followed by chopping wood; Gwen became the weapon of light as she declared, "I serve the Light, the bringers of the Light, and the Light eternal."

The soldier lay crumpled at her feet.

"The broken ribs punctured his lungs. His spine is snapped. He was probably dead before you called me." Chi washed his hands at the kitchen sink.

Atticus stared out at the yard at the body concealed by a blue tarp. He'd helped Gwen remove his mask and was sickened by the sight of the face of such a young man. Trying not to vomit, Atticus remembered again Gwen's explanation for what she called a lightener mask. Lighteners were made from the skins of some luminescent sea creature on a far distant world and allowed the wearer to see in the darkness. The easiest way to blind someone wearing such a mask was to shine a light into it.

The doctor continued, "Who was he?"

Gwen looked at the silent pastor and replied in his stead, "A dark soldier."

Chi's nostrils flared. "What are you going to do with the body?"

"We'll give him a proper burial. He was lost, but he had a soul."

Atticus's head jerked up at Gwen's words.

"I will call the elders. We can bury him at noon."

"Don't worry about it, Chi. We'll do it." Gwen sighed.

The doctor took Gwen's elbow. "How are you feeling?"

She opened her mouth, but Atticus interrupted.

"She's pregnant, Chi. Did you know that? The Warrior the Angel of the Lord sent me is already pregnant."

Chi took a calming breath. "Congratulations. I will bring you some vitamins. And I would like to examine you, make sure everything is all right."

"Thank you, doctor." She escorted him to the door. Gwen showered and changed into a broomstick skirt while Atticus continued his vigil at the kitchen window. She put a mug of coffee beside him and waited.

"You said he was lost." Atticus turned slowly.

She nodded.

"A dark soldier? You said he was lost but he had a soul?"

"Yes. A dark soldier is lost to the light."

"He was so young."

"Despair doesn't wait for maturity."

"Where did he come from? What was that black hole?" Atticus turned back to the window.

She took his arm. "Atticus, look at me."

His eyes were glazed.

"You opened a door of despair. You opened the door between his world and ours."

He snorted. "How?"

"Don't you remember?"

"I remember what you said."

Gwen pursed her lips. "It's not what I said, or what you said. It's how you felt."

He shrugged off her hand. "I was angry."

"You were more than angry. You lost yourself to the fury within you. You opened a door to the darkness."

"No."

"It's true. It happens that way. Someone surrenders to the darkness and opens a dark door, or someone surrenders to the light and opens the light portal. That's how I crossed over to Sanchor's world. I was praying and the halo appeared right in front of me. It grew and grew and I stepped inside."

"I do not serve the darkness."

"You don't have to be lost to open a door of grief. Even a Strategia Oscuro can open a portal of light." Gwen took his arm again. "It's rare, but it does happen. They can't go through one, but they can open one. Just like you, a true servant of light, despaired and opened a dark door. It happened because you are so powerful."

"Can it happen again?" There was fear in his eyes.

"If you let it."

He reached down and covered her hand with his. "I didn't mean to."

"You have a terrible temper."

"You killed him, just so quickly."

"I am a warrior. I have killed before. If I am to be your warrior, I will kill again. Many times. That's what warriors do."

He held his breath.

"The first time I killed someone, I became violently ill. Sanchor told me, *You can't go into battle wishing to only maim and wound. He said, You should never relish in the death, but there are some things which need killing.*"

"Did you kill Sanchor?"

Gwen frowned. "No. Why would you think that?"

He shrugged. "You said he was lost."

"Sanchor was lost a year and a half ago. But before that, he was a soldier of the light. He was as strong in the light as you are. He trained me and commanded me in many skirmishes. He was glorious in battle!"

"You loved him."

"Yes," she replied fervently. "Yes, but he didn't love me."

"You slept with him anyway," his words were tinged with bitterness.

She straightened and walked away. "I didn't sleep with him at all."

"Then how did you get pregnant?"

"He threw me up against a tree while his soldiers ransacked my house."

"He raped you?"

"He told me he loved me," she swiped angrily at her tears. "And I believed him!" She flung her words at Atticus. "I believed him and he threw me against a tree and now I'm pregnant!"

He took three steps toward her but didn't touch her.

"You tell me I've been preordained to marry you and bear your children and fight your war. Like I'm some breeder-slave? Like I have no say in my own life?" She turned away from him.

He followed her as she walked to the church shed and grabbed a shovel. He did likewise. They buried the young dark soldier next to the grave that held the ukera, working in silence.

Chapter 16
The Good Guys

"Tyler? Hey, Tyler!" A young man in a hardhat jumped down from the girding and ran toward Tyler.

"Doug?" Tyler squinted. "Doug Tompkins?"
The two men embraced, thumping each other on the back.

"What are you doing here?" The young man grinned.

"I'm designing the security system for this complex. What about you?"

"Heard they were hiring construction workers. I was sort of," the young man shrugged. "Broke. I was flat broke and thought, what the hell, I've never been to Georgia. So here I am!"

"Dad, talk to Matthew. The satellites are going to be in the wrong places!" Taralyn walked up behind her father and stopped, staring at the newcomer in tight jeans and a wife beater tee.

"Taralyn, do you remember Doug Tompkins?"

"Taralyn?" Doug took off his hardhat. "This is Taralittle?" He swooped down and lifted her off the ground.

"What are you doing here?" Taralyn blushed when she regained her balance.

He jerked his thumb behind him. "Mostly being a lazy bum, but occasionally I move a stack of cement blocks from place to place."

"But -- Quantico!" Taralyn stuttered. "You were mom's favorite student. Every weekend you told me how you couldn't wait for your first tour of duty!"

Doug's foot scuffed the dirt. "What's the point of being the good guys if you can't save people?"

Tyler put his arm around Taralyn's shoulder.

"Well, time to shift some bricks. Great to see you, Tyler." They shook hands. "Don't let any man near that girl! Man, she's a beauty!"

Chapter 17
The Light

Gwen had her first bout of morning sickness Saturday, but led Atticus through the footwork of the Morning Meadow. They hadn't spoken much beyond necessity. Busying herself with housework helped. She was just taking out of the oven a squash and chicken casserole when the first elders appeared.

"Peach cobbler!" Beatrice shouted as the screen door slammed.

"In here!" Gwen replied.

"Preacher about?"

"He's at the church, praying."

The look Beatrice gave Gwen was uncomfortable.

"Everything smells so good!" Sara walked in carrying a huge basket of biscuits. She sensed the tension in the kitchen and stopped. Her son Mitchell barreled past and ran into the backyard.

Her husband walked in and took the biscuits. "Why don't we put these on the table? Where's Atticus?"

"He's praying." Beatrice snapped.

"Will you act as host, Larry? I'll go get Atticus." Gwen smiled nervously.

He kissed her cheek. "It's good to have you back, warrior."

"Thank you."

Beatrice and Sara exchanged looks behind her back.

The church glowed with sanctity. Cedar, bees wax, and old hymn books melded their odors, soothing Gwen's jittery stomach.

Atticus knelt at the altar, the light from Jesus on the cross bathing him with colors as if it were a halo from heaven. So lost in prayer, he didn't hear her approach.

She whispered, "Atticus?" But he didn't respond. She reached out a shaky hand and touched his shoulder. Fire arched from his body into hers. She was consumed by it; able to neither move nor speak, she clung to his shoulder and allowed wave after wave of power to fill her.

The baptismal pond shimmered as if it were filled with water.

"Atticus!" She shouted, but it came out a whisper.

"Help me open it," he gasped.

She placed her other hand on his head and centered her thoughts on goodness and light. "I serve the Light, the bringers of Light, and the Light eternal."

The pond rippled like liquid mercury pulsing to match Atticus's heart beats.

"I believe in God the father Almighty," as Atticus recited the Apostle's Creed, the portal solidified into a sterling shield. It held steady until the end of the creed and then blinked into nonexistence.

Atticus slumped against the altar railing and Gwen

gathered him in her arms. "You did it. You've formed a portal of light."

"But nothing happened." He pressed his forehead against her shoulder.

"There was no one on the other side, that's all. No one to walk through. But if there had been, the person would have served the light."

"Are you sure? I was afraid another ukera would come through."

"Only good creatures can enter a portal of light. Only evil ones can enter a door of grief. That's the way it works."

"I'm exhausted." He clung to her.

"It'll be easier each time," she assured him.

"I never want to open a black hole again."

"Then don't." She stated. "It's your choice." She wiped the sweat from his face and stood. "Your elders are waiting."

Slowly, tenderly, he wrapped his arms around her hips and pressed his lips onto her abdomen. "I'm sorry." He kissed her again. "I'm sorry I lost my temper. I'm sorry I scared you into running away. I'm sorry that that bastard betrayed you. But I'm not sorry you're pregnant. And I'm not sorry that I love you. I do love you." He stood, but kept his arms around her waist. "I want to marry you. I want you to love me and be my wife."

"Atticus," she warned.

"But I'll wait."

She nodded.

Chi and Visolela were just driving up as Gwen and Atticus stepped onto the porch. The four friends embraced each other and Chi silently handed Gwen a container of vitamins.

The table was full of food dishes and so were the counters.

"Smells like heaven!" Atticus grinned. "Oh, are you all right, Gwen? You look a little green."

"Get used to it," Chi smirked.

"I'll be right back." Gwen retreated.

She knelt beside her bed and plundered beneath the mattress. For several seconds, she panicked, unable to find the ring. Her fingers curled around the chain first and pulled the ring out. It glowed in the afternoon light.

"Are you feeling all right?" Visolela was peeking into her room.

Gwen slipped the chain around her neck and under her shirt. "Sure. How are you feeling?"

"Like I have to pee all the time."

"Really?" Gwen laughed.

"You wait."

The backyard swelled with people. Gwen greeted each in turn and finally came to an older woman she'd never met. Her hair was silver curls swept up in a loose French twist. She wore a soft cotton blouse and jeans. She had silver rings on her toes and her fingers were adorned with gems and jewels.

"I'm Rawan," she stated, taking both of Gwen's hands in hers. A cool tingling filled her. "Well, preacher, you don't waste any time, do you!"

"Hey!" Gwen jerked her hands away.

"Rawan is a healer," Atticus stepped beside the two women. "She can sense things about a person's physical health."

"Some things are nobody's business." Gwen walked away.

"Let's begin," Atticus called. He continued once everyone was seated around the picnic table. "It seems our timeline has been shortened. We had planned on having at least another year after the warrior's arrival to prepare the complex. However," he shrugged. "In reality, we have about six more months before the refugees start arriving. How will we adapt to this?"

Visolela raised her hand. "It doesn't change the food or supplies. They are being stockpiled now."

"Construction?" Atticus addressed Matthew. "Will we will be ready?"

Matthew took a deep breath. "We could work double shifts, if we hired more workers. Priority can be given to the barracks and kitchen. The church and school can take a backseat." He turned to Taralyn. "How many applicants on the original list passed your screening?"

"There are thirty-four left that are eligible to be hired." Taralyn placed her hands on the table.

"Great. I'll get my foreman to contact them tomorrow, do a revised schedule, and implement the double shift by Monday."

Everyone nodded.

"About the approval list," Taralyn began, keeping

her eyes locked on her fingers.

"Yes?" Matthew peered around Tyler to see Taralyn clearly.

"There is someone working at the site who was never on the list."

"That's impossible," Matthew huffed.

Taralyn looked up at her father.

"Damn," Tyler mumbled.

Taralyn nodded. "His name is Doug Tompkins and at one time, he was a student at Quantico, planning a glorious future in the FBI. Then, about four years ago, he was hired by the Internal Intelligence Agency. IIA was created as a subsidiary of Homeland Security, but was given precedential powers over CIA, FBI, National Guard, and all police and sheriff forces in certain situations. He is still in their employ, but he is working as a hardhat on our site."

Tyler reached over and squeezed her hand.

"How did they find us?" Sara asked.

Atticus held up his hand. "It doesn't really matter. It was bound to happen."

"How do you figure that?" Rawan snorted.

"Well, I would hope that someone somewhere would notice alien soldiers appearing and disappearing in flashes of light," Beatrice quipped.

"Those gangs in malls. The ring guerrilla, the media calls them. Pretty hard to miss them," Larry added.

"And the creatures. The Nazis utilized them during the war. Vile things," Rutger sneered. "There have been two captured in the US in the last decade."

"What creatures?" Mitchell asked.

"Mutated lizards. They can track any person anywhere in the world."

"Ukeras," Gwen glanced at Atticus.

"We used to call them *gestanken*." Rutger said.

"Stinkers?" Mitchell translated.

"Ya. They smelled."

Sara looked around. "I hate to repeat myself, but how did they find us here?"

"Someone was smart enough to connect the dots," Tyler suggested.

"They didn't find you." Gwen stood up. "They found me. They were looking for me."

"Why?" Chi asked.

She took the chain from around her neck. "Because of this."

"What is it?" Atticus squinted as the ruby caught and refracted the sun's rays.

"It's called the Ring of Gothiaren. My battle commander and I found it in some tombs on his world. He brought it to me in March and told me to keep it safe. He said that it is the one weapon his master needs to totally destroy his home world."

"His master?" Beatrice repeated.

"Sanchor is now a Strategia Oscuro. He is lost. He serves the Dark, the Destroyers, and Death."

"You trust this guy?" Matthew asked sarcastically.

"Wait a minute. I think I read this book. Don't we have to carry the ring to the volcano and throw it in?" Taralyn laughed.

"Look, a hobbit!" Mitchell pointed to the forest, giggling.

Gwen, her face flushed, dropped the ring under her shirt and sat down.

"No offense, Warrior." Tyler scowled at the children. "There have been dark soldiers and the like coming and going for centuries. And you've had the ring for months without the IIA stepping in. Ring or not, the IIA is here now. Personally, I'm fond of the boy. But professionally, he constitutes a clear and present danger to us. What should we do about Doug?"

"Jesus told us to pour kindness on the heads of our enemies. If we are at the cusp of an inter-global war, we are going to need someone like Doug and his agency on our side." Atticus looked around at his elders. "Why don't you invite him to church?"

Taralyn and her father exchanged glances. Then they smiled and nodded.

"I need to begin training you as soon as possible. As a matter of fact, I need to begin training as many people as I can."

"The angel showed Atticus that she would train the refugees," Rawan argued.

"So you're just going to sit on your fat asses and let someone else fight for you?" Gwen stood up again. "Atticus says the refugees won't be here for another six months. But the dark soldiers are here now. They're smashing their way through jewelry stores, looking for this," she gripped the ring through her shirt. "The ukeras are here now. There's a dead one in that cemetery, right next to a dark soldier, who was right here in this very yard this week!"

"Gwen," Beatrice's face was clouded.

"You don't know what you are facing. I can train you to at least defend yourselves and your children."

"It's not hard. Gwen showed me some of it," Taralyn offered in light of an apology.

"I've been training, too."

"Preacher, you don't mean you'd kill someone?" Beatrice sat back.

He glanced at Gwen and shook his head. "But I will learn how to defend my flock."

"I'll learn," Sara stated, putting her arm around Mitchell. Her husband nodded.

Gwen looked each elder in the face. "Tomorrow morning at dawn."

Mitchell groaned dramatically.

Matthew raised a hand, "I have an idea." He swallowed. "What if we trained the construction workers, too? They all passed our screening. Well, except the IIA guy. What if you came to the site at – say -- 7 o'clock each morning and we all meet there?"

"Good." Atticus paced. "Good idea. We'll start that Monday."

"What about the IIA guy? Won't he get real suspicious if we start training an army?" Rutger asked.

"The Japanese incorporate exercise in their workday. Tai chi for example. We could say we're doing something similar." Visolela suggested.

"That will work for now. The Morning Meadow is an exercise. The Mountain Wall teaches defensive moves. It will be three months before any of you move on to the killing blows of Lightning Bolts."

"Killing blows?" Rawan gasped.

Gwen growled. "I'm a warrior. I'm not here to crochet an afghan."

Mitchell snorted and covered his laugh with an ill-concealed cough.

Rutger hesitantly broke the tension. "Since the workers will be trained, can you train others? My daughters, for instance."

Gwen nodded.

Atticus raised his hands. "All right, Monday morning at the site. Everybody who wants to be there is welcome. Doubled work force and shifts begin Monday. Be vigilant. Be prayerful. And let's eat!"

Chapter 18
The Twigs

The complex covered four acres on the far end of the cattle pasture beyond the church. The foundations for the barracks, kitchen and dining hall, school, and church were already poured. Pipes and conduits popped up here and there like wheat among the rubble. Gwen eyed the terrain as she would any battleground. *It'll do*, she thought.

Two dozen men in work boots and jeans blinked at her in the morning light. There had been a fluke in the plan to hire more workers, but by Wednesday there should be approximately fifty workers plus the elders and their families to teach.

She held her staff at Dawn and addressed the crowd. "I am Gwen Staff bearer of--" she stopped. She had been Gwen Staff bearer of Sanchor. "I am Gwen Staff bearer of Atticus. You are Twigs of Atticus." She bowed.

Atticus and Taralyn stood at Dawn and returned her bow. The men, women, and children around of them did likewise.

She led them through the opening of Morning

Meadow as she had done for Atticus and had them repeat it while she observed, correcting here, complimenting there.

"Twigs of Atticus, tomorrow I will tell you the story of grandmother spider. Now, Dawn. Lord of Light, guard and guide. Lord of Light, protect and preserve. Lord of Light, direct and defend."

"Amen," Atticus commanded.

"Man, that looks tasty!" The man beside Doug pointed his training rod at the rump of the young woman bowing in front of them.

"Hey, watch your mouth! Keep your eyes to yourself!" Doug puffed out his chest and glared at Juan.

"Doug!" The girl turned. "I didn't see you behind me."

"Oh, sorry." Juan beat his fist against his chest twice. "My bad."

Doug raised an eyebrow and Juan retreated.

"This is great, isn't it!" Taralyn grinned, sparkling with sweat.

"It's a little weird, if you ask me. I've never heard of her style of martial arts before." They walked together and placed the rods in the containers by the field. "What are you doing here?"

"I'm being a twig," she giggled.

He watched her face light up as she laughed. An old man walked up to Taralyn and hugged her.

"Good morning, Taralyn."

"Twig Taralyn!" She corrected him.

"Taralyn Twig of Atticus," Gwen spoke softly from behind the group. "That is the correct title. Taralyn Twig of Atticus."

Taralyn held her empty hands at Dawn and bowed, grinning. Gwen returned the bow and turned to Rutger. "Rutger Twig of Atticus."

He bowed.

She turned to Doug.

"Umm. Doug Twig of Atticus." He curtsied.

Gwen didn't smile. Doug glanced at Taralyn. She wasn't smiling either. He straightened and bowed correctly.

Gwen kept eye contact for several seconds but then turned and walked away.

"Sort of takes this twig stuff seriously, doesn't she," Doug mumbled.

Rutger nodded. "Sort of." He winked at Taralyn and followed Gwen.

Doug scowled. "My bad. My big bad."

"No." Taralyn shook her head. "Gwen just isn't feeling well this morning. Once you get to know her, she's nice. She understands things."

They watched as Gwen and Tyler bowed and then hugged each other.

"Well," Doug shifted his feet. "Tyler and Gwen. I never thought." He glanced at Taralyn with a red face.

"No." Taralyn frowned. She repeated firmly, "No. Not my dad. Never. He still loves Mom."

Doug crossed his arms and whispered, "We all do."

Chapter 19
The Interpreter

"Now, that was cool," Doug dropped his training rod into the cylinder. "Cool story, cool spider exercise. Very controlled with a new age twist."

"Anastasi. Grandmother Spider is a creation story from the Anastasi Native American tribe." Mitchell handed his rod to Taralyn who slid them in.

"Doug, this is Mitchell."

"Hey, Mitchell. I'd bow, but I've relinquished my rod."

Mitchell moved between the two and took Taralyn's hand.

Doug grinned at them. "So, is this Morning Meadow some kind of community get-together? I thought it was just for the construction workers."

"It's for all of us."

"Yeah, I got that, half pint, I was just wondering -- why?"

Mitchell looked at Taralyn and she looked down at him.

Doug frowned. "I get it, not much else to do in this great metropolis. Except--oh, I forgot—we're going to be painting the walls next month. You could come watch them dry."

"There's plenty to do here," Mitchell growled.

"Yeah, and what do you have planned for this afternoon, sprout?"

"My name is Mitchell. And I'm going with my dad to the airport to pick up the scientists from Chechnya."

"Who?" Doug stumbled.

"The scientists from Chechnya. I'm their interpreter."

"What, you speak fluent Chechnya?" Doug hesitated before adding, "Little grasshopper."

"Nobody speaks Chechnya, asshole."

"Mitchell!" Taralyn gulped and laughed.

"I speak Ingushetia -- fluently." He released Taralyn's hand and ran to meet his brothers.

"My bad again. Didn't mean to upset the tiny tyke."

"He," Taralyn looked away. "Mitchell sort of has a crush on me."

"Smart man," Doug spoke seriously.

Taralyn blushed beautifully.

Doug took her hand and walked with her. "So, what do you really do for fun around here?"

Taralyn glanced at him. "Church. We all go to church together. Want to go?"

"Church?"

"Taralyn. Doug. I've got to meet with Matthew for about thirty minutes. He'll drive me home, if you want to take the car." Tyler didn't miss the swift movement of Doug releasing Taralyn's hand.

"You can drive? Thanks for the warning. I'll keep off the roads."

"Dad, I've invited Doug to church with us. Tonight."

Tyler took a deep breath. He held out his hand, "Why not come to dinner at our home first, then we can all ride together."

Doug shook his hand. "I get off at five o'clock. What time?"

"Six." Tyler put his arm around Taralyn's shoulder.

"I'll be there. Thanks!"

Chapter 20
The Forgiveness

Eduviges finished the introit with the flourish and went to sit on the front row beside a distinguished looking black man. His bald head was shiny; a full carat diamond glittered in his left ear. His silk tan suit complemented his skin tones. Eduviges sat beside him and he nodded at her.

Atticus stood at the pulpit with his hands raised. "I welcome you in the name of our Lord and Savior, Jesus the Christ."

"Amen," the congregation murmured.

"Announcements. Sister Pearl is in the hospital again. Ladies auxiliary is planning a bake sale two weeks from tomorrow and front of Piggly Wiggly. Choir practice began last week and will be every Monday night from seven to eight here in the sanctuary. Sister Patsy tells me seven of you wonderful angels will delight us this Sunday with joyful noises to the Lord!"

Atticus grinned while they applauded. "Sister Patsy regrets not being here tonight. She has guests moving into the apartments above her shop and their plane was late."

Doug looked around him, noticing that Taralyn's pseudo-sweetheart Mitchell wasn't there. He rested his left arm on the pew and gently rocked it, triggering the camera mechanism.

"This Sunday, dinner on the grounds following service. Please be generous, we will most likely be welcoming several of the construction workers from next door. I believe Gwen is planning to fix three peanut butter pies, but I can't promise they won't be eaten before the dinner."

Doug found himself grinning. He leaned against Taralyn and whispered, "So, Xena Gwen is the preacher's wife? That's unexpected."

"They're not married yet. I think she's going to wait until after the baby is born."

"Excuse me?"

Tyler leaned around Taralyn and looked at Doug.

"Sorry," Doug mouthed.

"Jesus was asked how many times a person should forgive someone who wrongs him." Atticus wandered away from the pulpit, but his voice carried well. "I always thought that was an interesting question. How many times do I forgive you, if you've hurt me? Once? Twice? Three times if you're really repentant?

"What did Jesus tell the man?"

"Seventy times seven." Rutger's daughter Hetta called.

"Seventy times seven. That's right. Mitchell's not here tonight, but if he were, fabulous graduate of third grade that he it is, I bet he could tell us how many is seventy times seven. We mere mortals that we are will have to use our fingers. And toes. And teeth, probably."

Doug found himself grinning again.

"Or a calculator. Seventy times seven --I looked it up earlier--is four-hundred-ninety. Jesus says if someone wrongs us in any way, we should forgive him four-hundred-ninety times. If he hits us, four-hundred-ninety times. If he embarrasses us, four-hundred-ninety times. If he steals from us, four-hundred-ninety times. If he ridicules us, four-hundred-ninety times. If he says all manner of evil against us, four-hundred-ninety times." Atticus raised his left hand and turned in a circle under it. "Jesus tells us we should forgive people. No matter how they harmed you, and there are worse crimes than I have listed. You know what they are: rape, murder, adultery, drunkenness, addiction, greed, sloth, gluttony. The list goes on and on and on."

He lowered his arm. "It's easy to say, I forgive you. Say it with me."

"I forgive you." The congregation joined him. "Easy. Three little words. Turn to your neighbor and forgive him."

The crowd murmured in compliance.

"Now turn to the person behind you or in front of you. Forgive them."

The crowd shifted and grew louder.

"Easy, right?"

They nodded.

"Saying the words is easy. You can say it once, twice, four-hundred-ninety times! It's easy. I forgive you!"

Atticus stepped down from the altar and softened his voice. "I always thought the man should have asked Jesus, not how *many* times do I forgive, but *how* do I forgive."

He lifted his arms shoulder height. "How do I forgive?" His arms lowered as he searched the faces in front of him.

He continued to look at every congregate until some were squirming. His voice fell on them like snow. "You ask for forgiveness first."

"You empty your sins at the feet of your Lord and you say, look father! Look at these sins. Look at these hurtful things I've done. Stealing. Adultery. Murder. Hate. Lying. Lust. Snide remarks. Distrust. Disobedience. Look. I'm sorry! I'm sorry, God! Forgive me."

Doug swallowed, surprised to find tears in the back of his eyes.

"You trusted me and I blew it! Forgive me, God." Atticus slowly returned to the pulpit. "And He does." Atticus smiled sadly. "And then, you can forgive others."

Doug blinked repeatedly, trying to clear his vision. His nostrils burned with the blinked-away tears. Atticus looked at him. Doug felt skewered by Atticus' eyes. "And once you forgive a man for the wrongs he did to you, you can walk together in that light."

"Amen!" Matthew shouted.

"Sister Eduviges, what's our hymn?"

"Number 23 An Evening Prayer." She moved to the piano.

Taralyn glanced down at Doug, still sitting on the pew. She took his arm and pulled, "On your feet, soldier."

They sang together, side by side, as Doug regained control of his emotions. "If I have wounded any soul today, If I have caused one foot to go astray, If I have walked in my own willful way, Dear Lord, forgive!"

"Before we close in prayer, I want to remind you of our morning exercises at the building site next door. Seven o'clock every morning Monday through Saturday. Now," he raised his hands above their heads. "May the Lord bless you and keep you. May the Lord make His face to shine upon you and be gracious unto you. May the Lord lift up His countenance upon you and give you peace. Amen."

As Doug walked down the aisle toward the Narthex with Tyler and Taralyn, he used the time to nonchalantly take a picture of almost everyone in the church with his wristwatch camera.

"Preacher," Tyler shook Atticus's hand. "This is our friend, Doug Tompkins."

"Preacher," the Doug extended his hand.

Atticus hesitated and then took Doug's hand in both of his. "When you're ready, Doug, God will forgive you. I'll pray with you, or any of my elders will. We'll get this straightened out."

Doug fought the incredible desire to sob and the choking desire to run. It frightened him. The preacher frightened him. Images of death flashed before him. Beth Fogel in the classroom. Beth at home with her family. Beth's decapitated and tortured body. Doug wrenched his hand away. "I'm not much for praying."

Gwen crossed her arms as Doug passed.

"Preacher, this is my cousin Jarmille." The pianist presented her guest.

Doug drew a deep breath and forced the memories away. He felt angry now, like the battle inside him had turned and the soldier was winning. Braver now, allowing his anger to strengthen him, he turned and got a great picture of the pianist, the preacher, and the bald man in the suit. Jarmille shook hands with Gwen next.

"I'd like to meet with you tomorrow afternoon to discuss," Gwen's eyes slid to Doug's attentive face and stopped.

"Business. We will discuss business, tomorrow." Jarmille filled in.

Gwen smiled and pointed, "The parsonage is over beyond the cemetery."

Chapter 21
The IIA

"Rutger Pardulfo." The picture flashed on the screen in front of the agents. Colonel Morgan Forest glanced around the room before continuing. "Came to America in 1946 and changed his name to Perkins. Prior to that, he was an SS officer in Nazi Germany. He was second in command at Gretnagrad, infamous for the war crimes perpetrated there. Especially known for its experiments in genetics, Gretnagrad continued to operate until 1961 under the code name Gretalkinder." The picture changed. "This woman, Kaela Kinski and her three daughters Elke (flash), Milia (flash) and Hetta (flash) were interned at Gretnagrad. The women are fraternal triplets, the result of experiments performed on Miss Kinski, who at the time of their birth was still clinically a virgin. Rutger Pardulfo smuggled them out at the end of WWII."

Flash to a picture taken on the building site. "Mr. and Mrs. Larry and Sara Sveete, originally of South Dakota. Sara Sveete was more widely known as Summer Sweet, the romance novelist. Lawrence Sveete was CEO of Sveete and Moreland,

Incorporated. A successful, happy, all-American dream-come-true family."

The screen changed to an old school picture of a brooding teenager with a shaggy haircut. "Nicholas Sveete, their son."

"No shit," a young man in a FBI crew-cut exclaimed. "Sorry, Colonel Forrest. I didn't mean to cuss."

The colonel in the Armani suit pointed at him, "Care to enlighten us?'

The officer explained. "Nicholas, a straight A student, scored a perfect SAT in seventh grade – got a D in AP Chemistry. He challenged his teacher, who sent him to the office with a discipline referral. The next day, Nicholas blew up the chemistry lab, as well as the lunchroom, and fifty-seven of his classmates."

The screen changed to blurry children. Colonel Forest continued, "Afterwards, the Sveetes moved to Morning Creek and began adopting children. Four of them - James, Patrick, Simon, Thaddeus - go the Blake Primary, where they are considered average students and generally well-behaved." The screen showed a close up of Mitchell. "Mitchell is nine years old, IQ of 161 – on a bad day – and speaks any language presented to him. For those of you who give a shit, the technical term for this protégé is a linguistic savant. And," Forest paused dramatically, "He was adopted privately in Germany, after the Sveetes began going to church with Pardulfo."

The picture switched to a middle-aged woman with frizzy blond hair. "Beatrice Horne. Born 1947, lived her whole like in Morning Creek. Not much on Sister Bea, as she's known by the townspeople. Her son James, however," (another school picture flashed above them) "loaded his pick-up truck with the high school's football team and drove off a bridge."

"Was he on the team?"

Another question followed the first one, "Was it intentional?"

Forest shrugged, "No one knows. He was a likeable jock, made average grades, had no hopes of a scholarship to college but didn't have any ambition to go. He was going steady with one of the girls in his church."

A surly man with gray hair in a sports jacket concluded, "They broke up and he lost it."

"No," Forest shook his head.

"The truck – brakes failed? Bald tires?"

"No," Forest again negated the theories. "He just drove off the bridge. 1987. Sister Bea still puts flowers on his grave."

A picture that at first looked very much like a bear in a hard hat resolved into that of a huge man with a fierce expression. "Matthew Kellerman. Brilliant engineering student at MIT. As an undergrad, he designed a chemical-free computerized laser pest control program. Empty the house of pets and people, aim the laser at the walls, and every bug and rodent in the house is turned to dust. Ten years ago, he was wooed and won by DIA and helped design the Windgate Weapons System which is still in use today."

A young woman interjected, "That's the system that

135

destroys its target on a molecular level, like a disintegration ray."

Forest nodded, so she continued. "You feed in the coordinates, engage the system, and every living creature in a square acre becomes dust particles. Without radiation as a bi-product."

"Four years ago, Kellerman quit, packed up a few belongings, and drove to Morning Creek. He does handy-man jobs and is the construction manager for the complex – which we will discuss later."

The image of Eduviges filled the screen. Her braided hair flowed to her waist; her dress was brilliant orange, yellow and purple. "This woman lives quietly in a four-room wood-frame house in Morning Creek. She gives piano lessons and has about a dozen cats. Her name is Eduviges McGuinna. She was married to Paul McGuinna from 1973 to 1980. Her maiden name is San Rios."

"San Rios? From California?" a young woman on the front row named Cortez suggested.

"The same."

"Who?" a young man with a Tennessee accent asked. He was a senator's son, but very few in the room knew this.

"Offin and Jaleshia San Rios were her parents. Shiloh San Reyes is her uncle. Pili and Nangwaya San Rios, her older siblings. The San Rios and San Reyes are a play on words. Offin was named after the Offin river in Ghana, but his last name was Hamilton – a surname he claimed was given to his ancestors by slavers. In the 1957, he legally changed his name to San Rios. His brother liked the idea of being a king – hence reyes instead of rios."

"Offin, Jaleshia, Pili, and Nangwaya San Rios and Maxwell San Reyes. Weren't they the founders of the Bronze Tiger Militant group from the sixties?" The senator's son redeemed himself.

"Give the boy a star."

"This is incredible," a voice murmured.

"It's numbing," someone else replied.

"When her family resisted arrest and were killed, the team searched the compound and found Eduviges hiding under the steps in the basement. She was six years old. She became a concert pianist, traveled the world, but never spoke another word until four and a half years ago."

"When she moved to Morning Creek?"

"So, this preacher is a faith healer, too?"

Forest took a sip of water. "No, not that I've heard. But there is a faith healer in the group of elders."

The young man coughed to cover a nervous giggle.

"Rawan Collier. We're trying to trace her. We know she has family in various states, but most of them seem to be below the paperwork trail. No socials, no birth certificates, very few have drivers licenses."

"Illegal aliens?" suggested one.

"Gypsies?" suggested Cortez.

The colonel paused and then addressed the tough looking woman, "Why gypsies, Lieutenant?"

"Rawan is a gypsy name. It means *a fine lady*."

Morgan drew a deep breath. "Good. You can help

trace her."

Lt. Isabel Cortez grinned. The expression gave her a feral look, like a glimpse of a wild cat who was trying to fit in as a domestic. She wasn't beautiful, but she was schooled in using her attributes – all of her attributes – to her advantage. She had slept her way into this meeting; she would make damn sure - now that she'd earned the attention of the Lucky Lieutenant - as he used to be known – that she kept climbing up this ladder of power. She set out to align herself with Colonel Forest, and she knew she would do whatever it took to strengthen that alignment. The grin disappeared, masked by a fake look of shy pride.

"We're only halfway through the Elders. This next couple, Dr. Chi and Visolela Abubakar are applying for US citizenship. Originally, they are from Nigeria. Specifically, Ikara, Nigeria, where Dr. Abubakar served as the head of Botswana Medical Corp. Eight years ago, ebola swept through Ikara, decimating the population of fifty thousand people. Within four months, only a handful of citizens were left alive, including Dr. and Mrs. Abubakar. The doctor was nominated for the Nobel Prize for Medicine. Not because he developed a cure for ebola, but because he refused, even at gunpoint, to abandon his patients." He nodded at Cortez, "I believe you were on that mission, Lieutenant."

She reddened, but not from embarrassed pride. She remembered the feel of the trigger, the idiotic look on the Nigerian's face, the desire to kill the man and burn the tainted buildings to the ground. "Dr. Chi

Abubakar was very brave."

The colonel again paused, evaluating the well-concealed lie. To the audience it seemed as though Forest was allowing them to catch their emotional breaths. He changed the slide. "Taralyn and Tyler Fogel. These two were the link between Gwen Hampt and this previously unknown group. Tyler is a securities expert. He retired at thirty-eight from the NSA and opened his own internet forensics and securities business. Taralyn, his daughter, was arrested at seven years of age for hacking into the Guatemalan government site and pasting butterflies all over it. Elizabeth Fogel," the picture changed to a stunningly beautiful woman in uniform. "Married to Tyler, mother of Taralyn, taught hostage negotiation at Quantico."

"Beth Fogel, I'll be damned. She was one of my instructors," a hoarse voice at the table whispered. "Care to fill us in on what happened to her?" The colonel asked.

"She was kidnapped by terrorists. About six years ago. I attended her inurnment ceremony at Arlington."

Forest bit the inside of his mouth, denying his desire to succumb to anger. "Taralyn traced her mother via computer within four days of her capture. She had compiled satellite images of the entire area and vitas on each terrorist involved. At eleven, she impressed the hell out of the Defense Department. The President flatly refused any attempts at negotiation. Tyler put together an insurgency plan, manned with his employees, and one of Major Elizabeth Fogel's favorite students, who is currently our man in the field at

Morning Creek."

Forest puffed out anger and centered himself. "Their transport was refused airspace and was quarantined on the ground, forcefully."

"But then the president rescinded that order." Karl George had been that particular president's Special Agent in Charge. He'd been transferred to the IAT after that incident, but not willingly.

The picture changed to a decapitated and mutilated body and Forest spoke as if he hadn't heard Karl. "Her body was still warm when Tyler's team finally arrived."

"God almighty."

"The Reverend Atticus Jordan." The picture changed to reveal a grinning man proudly holding a two-year old boy in his lap with an arm around a plump and pretty woman. "Presbyterian by faith and ordination. Not much on him. Good student, clean kid, no arrests, no scandals. Not related to any crime families, cults, or wackos. He and his family moved to Morning Creek five years ago."

The group seemed to take a collective breath of relief.

The picture changed to show what looked like a stone barbecue pit beside a stream. A charred small form lay on top of it. The body of a woman sprawled at the base, eyes glazed in death with blood from her slit wrists pooled around her head.

"Martha Jordan left a note stating that God demanded she sacrifice the little boy."

The screen flared to white and black of a handwritten suicide note.

"But that's just a page out of the Bible," the senator's son argued. "It's when Abraham thought God wanted him to sacrifice his son. It's from Genesis."

"Genesis 22 : 1-19." Cortez provided. She continued smugly, "I was raised in a convent."

A few men snickered.

Karl George lamented, "I guess Ms. Jordan didn't find the ram in the bushes like Abraham."

"That's quite a happy little parish you've got there, Colonel." The only man in the room who out ranked him sat furthest away.

Forest nodded at him. "So, into this happy little parish comes Gwen Hampt." The picture showed a happy if plain woman in her early thirties with red hair and a microphone in her hand. "Gwen is a school teacher. She prefers teaching fourth grade, hates teaching kindergarten. Worked in the same school in Wyoming for ten years. Active in church, sang in the choir, taught Sunday school, vacation Bible school, and was president of the women's circle. Never married. No long-term relationships. Three years ago, she disappears. Twenty-eight months later, she reappears and refused to explain where or why she'd gone. She then moves to Tacoma, Washington and gets a job at a discount clothing store. March of this year, she calls 911 and claims there are intruders in her house. Police arrive and find one DOA in the kitchen, and this."

A ukera, strapped to a gurney, appeared on the screen.

"A ukera. Alive, but barely, in her bedroom."

The room buzzed.

"And then Gwen disappeared."

"Poof – disappeared?"

"For lack of a more technical term – no. She jumped over the back fence and ran away."

Forest looked around again. He clicked the computer's remote. A picture appeared of a family in wide-collared shirts and denim dresses once popular in the seventies. "Gwen Hampt is the girl in the middle. Her sisters, Edwina and Winifred on each side. She has her hands on her brother Fredwyck's shoulders. Point to ponder – especially in light of Cortez's take on the meaning of names – all four of the children's names have the same derivative – a friend in time of battle. Her parents behind her are Amanda and Clive, the UK Ambassador to Guatemala."

Click. Yellow police tape ticketed a hotel hallway with a body next to an open door. "The guard." Flash. Bloody sheets pulled back to reveal two adult bodies. "The parents." Flash. A naked teen-age girl stared blindly at the splattered walls. "Edwina." Flash. An open closet revealing a tiny boy held in the arms of another teen girl. Their faces were unrecognizable. "Winifred and Fredwyck."

"Gwen snuck out to go bar-hopping with friends the night her family was killed."

He allowed the mumbling to die down before he switched to the last photo. It was an arrest photo of a young, bald black man. "Jarmille San Rios. Gunrunner. Arms dealer. Marine trained in a Raider Battalion, he later spent three years in Columbia training assassins. Code name, the Consultant. Made a deal with the US government by turning over all he knows or all he said he knew about his dealings in South America."

The screen changed as Jarmille stood next to Eduviges, shaking Atticus' hand. "Illegitimate son of Maxwell San Rios. First cousin to Eduviges. And new member of the church."

His blackberry beeped. "We'll adjourn for lunch. Meeting continues at 1400. Dismissed."

Chapter 22
The Hands

"Dawn," Gwen commanded. She walked through the crowd of sixty twigs who were spread six feet apart from each other.

"Awareness." She touched the shoulder of an older man.

"Awe." She stood still as she watched her army prostrate themselves.

"Surrender." She meandered around, touching three more shoulders.

"Dawn." She held them there longer than usual, inspecting them.

Doug snorted with impatience. She caught his eye. He held her gaze, emptying all emotion to the void. She nodded.

"Spider's Web." She kept her eyes on Doug, ignoring the others.

"Frog in the Pond."

One of the men she'd touched on the shoulders smacked his neighbor in the stomach because he launched with the wrong foot. Gwen nodded again.

"Rainbow." She touched the shoulders of two more

men and a woman who was one of the Chechnyan scientists named Otka.

"Journey."

She stood at the front as the sounds of groans, popping spines, and complaints rolled around the compound.

"Dawn."

As her twigs returned to the beginning, Gwen approached Doug. He eyed her nervously.

"I am Gwen Staff bearer of Atticus." She bowed.

"I am Doug Twig of Atticus." He inclined his head.

"That remains to be seen." The blow she struck against his training rod stung his palms. The people around them gasped and started to move away.

"Dawn!" she yelled. They held still.

The two began a slow circle. She slapped his thigh with her rod. "Mosquito Bite," she explained.

He limped, rubbing his leg.

"Stag in Spring," she warned as she struck his rod three times above their heads.

Looping her rod up between Doug and his rod, she jerked it out of his hands. "Salmon for the Bear."

The rod clattered and rolled as it struck the pavement between Mitchell and his mom.

The crowd murmured. "*Dawn,*" she again demanded.

"You have me at a disadvantage," Doug spread his hands in front of him.

"I don't think so." She feinted with her staff to the right.

Doug reacted smoothly and crouched just out of

her reach.

Juan shouted, "Use the force, Luke," and the crowd laughed nervously.

Gwen galloped three steps forward and popped his other thigh. "Wolf in Winter."

She retreated while he glowered in pain. He crouched again, raising his hands defensively, balancing his weight on the balls of his feet.

She galloped forward again; he stepped sideways and grabbed her rod. Using her weight against his, she pivoted suddenly, flinging him away from her. He rolled to his feet with a fluidity that made her smile.

She stood at *Dawn*. He watched her suspiciously. Slowly, she stretched her arms up to the position of *Surrender*. He attacked; swift kicks and stunning blows with the sides of his hands.

She heard Atticus shouting.

She twisted deftly and flipped Doug onto his back with her rod at his neck, her knees on his chest. She whispered intimately into his face, "I do not need a man who fights like a soldier. I need a man who is a weapon. Are you such a man?"

He stopped struggling. "Yes."

She stood up. He gingerly climbed to his feet.

"I am Gwen Staff bearer of Atticus. You are Doug Feet and Hands of Atticus." She bowed and he returned it.

She turned around, raising her voice. "If I touched you on the shoulder this morning, step forward." The seven people came closer. "You are now Fingers and Toes. Doug will instruct you beginning Monday morning."

She held up her rod. "Dawn. The Lord of Light guide and guard. The Lord of Light protect and preserve. The Lord of Light direct and defend you all."

Chapter 23
The Infiltration

"I sure enjoyed the anthem today, Patsy," Doug shook the huge blonde's hand and smiled lusciously.

Patsy giggled.

"Does anyone ever play those drums?"

"Well, they belong to Beaucephus, Le'Vander's brother. But he'll be in jail for another couple of months. Do you play?"

"Yeah, I do."

Taralyn looped her arm through his. "I didn't know that."

"My mom got me a set when I started middle school. She said it would be better if I hit the drums than my little cousins."

"Therapy drums," Tyler laughed.

"Well, I'll expect to see you Monday night then," Patsy spoke over her shoulder to Doug as she shook Atticus' hand.

Gwen gave her a swift hug and Patsy giggled again.

Taralyn hugged Atticus and then threw her arms

around Gwen's shoulders. "I thought you were going to kill Doug yesterday."

Tyler and Atticus embraced. Then Tyler kissed Gwen's cheek. "You had us worried a bit."

Atticus took Doug's hand in both of his, but didn't speak. The men eyed each other warily. Gwen smiled warmly and stretched out her hand. Doug hesitated before taking it.

"I chose people who needed extra training. They are slower but more deliberate in their movements. Like you, they couldn't extend themselves into the rods to become one with the rod. I thought they would benefit from your teaching. As we grow, I will add more to your team."

"Thank you."

"Can I be on Doug's team?" Taralyn looked hopeful.

"No." Doug, Atticus and Tyler answered as one.

"We need your fingers unbroken, Taralyn," Gwen explained.

Taralyn pouted.

"We need your fingers unbroken," Atticus repeated firmly.

"Yes, Atticus," she complied. "But I'm going to join the choir."

"No fear of broken fingers there," Doug laughed. "Broken eardrums, maybe."

"Hey, I can sing," she growled, as the two walked away together.

"She's got a crush on him," Tyler worried.

"That's natural, Tyler." Atticus put his hand on the father's shoulder.

Tyler sighed, "I'm getting old, Preacher."

Chapter 24
The Mountain Walls

Gwen figured she was five months pregnant the first Monday in August when her army split into two groups: twigs and toes. They had been training for two months and it was time to go from Morning Meadow to Mountain Walls. She had stationed Doug's team on the other side of the dormitory shell for a reason. After Mountain Walls, she would again divide her group into defensive and offensive teams. The offensive team would learn the seven death blows. She wanted Doug fully ensconced as a team leader on the other side of the compound before she began teaching her specialty. He obviously wasn't lost, but he had never declared for the light.

"*Dawn*," she called. Her fifty-two twigs stood and faced her. "You have grown well, twigs. You are now saplings. I greet you, Saplings of Atticus."

They grinned at each other as they bowed.

"Pair up facing each other." She observed while they quickly moved around. "We begin the journey up the mountain walls." She faced the doctor. "Billy goat." They smacked rods in the form of an X, first with her right, then her left at shoulder height. "As you practice this, watch your knuckles. A broken finger can disable you. And try different ways of butting your rods together. Begin. Notice that balance must remain in your hips and toes. Your knees must give and take. The power of the billy goat is not only from his shoulders, but from his ankles, butt, spine, everything. Every part of you should flow into this movement. Don't be afraid to change your footing."

Her saplings began to move around the compound as the cracking sound of rods filled the air.

Several people tripped, but jumped back up and began again. Matthew stood firm, growling low in his chest, while Elke Perkins shoved against his rod with all her might. Her feet slipped in the sand, but she persevered. "Elke, Journey *to shoulders!*" Gwen shouted.

Elke twisted, bringing her rod shoulder high. Matt grunted as the pressure point shifted on his staff so quickly that he lost balance and crashed to one knee. Gwen cheered and held up the staff hand of the little white-haired lady. "*Dawn,*" she spoke proudly. "*The Journey up the Mountain Wall* does not rely on strength but perseverance and cunning. Now, choose another partner. *Dawn. Billy goat.*"

The crowd moved with renewed vigor. Shouts of pain and laughter intersperse the grunts of effort. Gwen smiled and relaxed. Her saplings learned swiftly. She glanced at Atticus struggling against Tyler and felt her heart race. He laughed at something Tyler had said. His face was radiant and his body moved with well-defined muscles. She caught her breath. He was gorgeous.

"Gwen?" Visolela spoke softly and took her elbow. Gwen had forbidden Visoloela to participate at all, but she always came to observe. "Gwen, I think I need my husband."

Gwen looked confused and then panicked. "Dawn! Chi! It's Visolela!"

The doctor's rod clattered to the ground as he ran forward. He placed one hand on her swollen belly and touched her cheeks. "Contractions?"

Visolela nodded.

"When did they start?"

"About four this morning."

"You've been having contractions for three hours! Why didn't you tell me?" Chi bellowed.

"It's too early. I was afraid."

He hugged her to his chest. "Don't be afraid, Visolela. I'm with you."

"Tyler, dismiss the saplings with prayer. Make sure Doug does the same with the toes. Atticus. Give me your keys. Get in Chi's car and drive them to the hospital. I'll bring your truck." Gwen touched Visolela's shoulder, "It's going to be alright."

The woman shuddered and water burst between her thighs.

"Come on," she grabbed Atticus' wrists with crossed arms. "We'll carry her to your car."

Atticus took a deep breath and walked in perfect tandem with Gwen to the car. Visolela moaned again as she climbed into the backseat next to her husband.

Atticus stared at Gwen blankly.

"It'll be alright. Drive carefully." Gwen kissed him gently on the lips. "I'll be right behind you."

Chapter 25
The Ladders

"Six pounds, eight ounces!" Atticus grinned proudly into his congregation Wednesday evening. Most of the pews held more than a scattering of people; the church had swollen to about fifty members this summer. "Visolela's weak, but she and the baby are coming home tomorrow morning."

"Just in time for Morning Meadows practice!" Matthew joked and the congregation laughed.

"Does this little miracle have a name?" Rutger called from beside his wife and daughters.

Atticus nodded, "Kayien. Kayien Promise Abubakar."

"Hallelujah!" Eduviges shouted and began playing *I am a Promise*. The congregation stood and, unable to find it in the hymnal, tried to sing without the words. At the end of the song, Atticus asked them to be seated. "The choir is still growing. I think we have the only choir in the US with more basses than sopranos! But there's always room for more. I understand we're going to have a drummer next Sunday and Sister Patsy has asked anyone who plays any kind of musical instrument to please come forward Monday night at 7:00."

Atticus looked around. "Any more announcements?"

Le'Vander raised his hand beside Patsy. Atticus nodded.

"My mother's been having chest pains all weekend, but she's too stubborn to go to the hospital again. She says she's tired of the hospital."

"We'll keep her in our prayers for health and for her attitude. Maybe Sister Rawan might stop by her house tomorrow morning."

Rawan nodded.

"Welcome in the name of the Lord. Let's stand and confess our faith."

As Doug bowed his head, Taralyn slipped her hand into his. Her hand was warm and tingly. As she prayed, her hand grew warmer and a peace flowed into Doug. He barely noticed that everyone else had begun to sit down. Taralyn sat beside him, folding her tiny hands in her lap.

"I want to talk to you this evening about ladders." Atticus came away from the pulpit. "Ladders are wonderful inventions. I use them to climb up on the roof. We used them to paint the fellowship hall. That light right up there," he pointed. "Blows every year around Easter and I have to use a ladder to climb up there and change it. But ladders in and of themselves are useless. Think about it. Here you have two long poles with small strips of wood in between them. If you want to use the ladder, you have to lean it up against something first. The ladder has to lean against something solid. You have to be able to trust that this thing you lean your ladder against is strong enough to bear your weight. You also have to make sure that this solid, strong thing you lean your ladder against is in the right place at the right time."

Atticus paced around between the altar and the baptismal pool.

"If I lean my ladder against my parsonage, but I need to change this here spotlight," he didn't complete the thought as the congregation chuckled.

"Well, how about I lean my ladder against these pews and try to change the spot light? Pews are good and solid. Pews are in the center of the church, right below the light. But the solid, strong, well-located pews are not going to point the ladder in the right direction."

Atticus stepped down in front of the altar table. "Think about the ladders in your life. The things that help you do the jobs you need to do." He ticked them off his fingers. "Kindness, responsibility, righteousness, love, intelligence, courage, talent. What else do you need to do the things you need to do? Strength? Prayer? Determination? What am I leaving out?"

Atticus stared around his flock.

"Faith." Gwen's soft voice carried well.

Atticus smiled at her and she caught her breath.

"Faith. Think of faith as a ladder." Atticus wandered back up the steps, allowing the listener to absorb the concept.

"Envision your faith as a ladder. Is it spindly and weak? Does it wobble and have splinters? Is it made of durable steel? Does it have all those stupid warning signs on it? What does your ladder of faith look like?"

He stopped behind the pulpit. "What is your ladder of faith pointing to?"

"Heaven," Rutger stated seriously.

"Without a doubt, Brother Rutger. Your faith leads to heaven. But what of the rest of you? Where does your faith lead you? Glory? Honors? Fame? Duty? Heaven? Hell? Does your ladder serve the light? Ladders can lead down into pits of despair, too, you know. Where will your faith lead you?"

Atticus stared over their heads and spoke thoughtfully. "I guess it all depends on what your ladder's leaning against."

He refocused on their upturned faces. "You see, some people lean their faith on principalities, government, loved ones, friends, hates, desires. Some people even try to lean their ladders against themselves. Some lean their ladders against the church. Sounds solid and strong, but it can only lead you so far." Atticus pointed at the roof.

"Lean your faith on God." Atticus frowned. "Don't lean on your government. Don't lean on your principalities. Don't lean on your loved ones. Don't lean on your friends. Don't lean on your hates. Don't lean on your desires." Pausing between each word for emphasis, Atticus admonished, "Don't lean on your church.

"Lean your ladder of faith on God, and He will lift you up to Heaven."

Doug blinked as Tyler stated, "Amen."

"We'd planned to sing *Jacob's Ladder*, but Sister Eduviges, I wonder if you could play *Leaning on the Everlasting Arms* for our hymn this evening?"

Eduviges stepped over to the piano and flipped through the spiral book on the stand. "Number 160," she called and began to play.

As they exited the narthex, Atticus shook Doug' hand. "How's the karate lessons going?"

"Akido. Fine. It'll be fun teaching again."

A man in a beige business suit was behind Doug. He bowed, his palms together at his chest. He began to speak rapidly in another language.

Atticus touched the man's arm and held up a hand. "Mitchell? I need you!"

Mitchell came running and swatted Taralyn's rear as he passed her.

The man repeated his words.

Mitchell translated, "My name is Samir Ahmadinaja. I have dreamed about you. I have spoken with you in my dreams. I have seen this place. I am here. You have need of me."

Atticus nodded pensively while Doug adjusted his watch. It clicked three times before Tyler grabbed his shoulder. Tyler firmly moved him away from Atticus and the Iraqi.

"Tell Samir: come and pray with me," Atticus told Mitchell.

"So, what are you leaning your ladder against, Doug?"

"You know me, Tyler." Doug began to joke, but

sobered as he looked into Taralyn's big eyes. He swallowed and glanced back at her father. His eyes filled with tears and he blinked angrily.

"I do, Doug. You're leaning your ladder against a government that's going to fail you. It failed me, and I lost Beth."

"I don't work for the FBI anymore," Doug blinked.

"How can you lie? How can you lie to us?" Taralyn shouted.

Tyler grabbed her elbow. "Quiet, Taralyn. He's not lying. You know he doesn't work for the FBI."

Taralyn snorted and jerked her arm away. "His words are true; it's the concept that's a lie." Turning on the young man, she sobbed, "You lied to me, Doug." She stomped off to the car.

"She knows?" Doug felt an iceberg settle in his stomach.

"How could that possibly surprise you?" Tyler growled.

"So," Doug looked at his feet and asked, "I guess this means goodbye?"
"We need you, Doug."

"I can't serve two masters, Tyler."

"No, you can't. You need to choose the light. We can save people. We can help others. We can hold back the darkness." Tyler's voice rose.

"Doing what?" Doug spoke with incredulity.

Tyler took a deep breath. "Will you pray with Atticus?"

"No." Doug stepped backward. "Tyler, the man has you hypnotized. Brain-washed. You're talking crazy."

"That's exactly what I said." Gwen stepped between the two men. "I'm still not quite sure it isn't crazy. Maybe we've all gone insane."

Doug took a deep breath and Tyler calmed himself.

"But Tyler's right, Doug. We do need you. We need you to continue telling the IIA about what you see here. Eventually, we're going to need their help."

"Why?"

"I can't tell you that." Gwen pursed her lips. "Not until you pray with Atticus."

"You have to choose whom you will serve, Doug." Tyler put his hands in his pockets and walked away.

Chapter 26
The Capitulation

Doug met with his ex-twig team the next morning and led them to the other side of the building site. He hadn't sent the photos of the Iraqi to Colonel Forest last night. He hadn't slept. When he closed his eyes, he saw Beth's face. He saw Beth's eyes surrounded by Taralyn's face. He felt the fire that stormed through him as Taralyn held his hand. He saw Tyler - crumpled and broken – holding Beth's still-warm headless body. So Doug paced the confines of his apartment and didn't open his email at all.

He could hear Gwen's voice as she trained her saplings, but didn't catch the words.

She was instructing. "The mountain walls defend you against your foes. Begin at *Dawn*, now *Billy Goat*." She wandered, observing, correcting, and suggesting. "Dawn. Push a man off balance and he cannot fight you well."

She pulled Juan forward and used him as part of her demonstration. "Watch." She pushed her rod's end into his shoulder. Juan stumbled backward. "Again." She shoved the butt of her rod into his other shoulder with the same result. "This is called *Picking an Apple*. From *Billy goat* to *Picking an Apple*, step backward on one foot, draw back and aim for the dimple just inside the shoulder and the collarbone. Too hard, and you break the collar bone. Too softly," she pushed Juan gently and his rod automatically came down against the top of her staff.

"Again: *Billy goat* to *Picking an apple*." She allowed Juan to practice on her. "Saplings, begin."

Their laughter turned to groans and complaints as some rods struck harder than expected.

"Dawn," Gwen snapped. "Face forward. *Dawn. Billy Goat. Dawn. Frog in Pond. Dawn. Picking an Apple. Dawn. Frog in Pond. Dawn.* Now, think about what you have just done. Face your opponent, and try to defend yourself as you push your opponent off balance."

Slowly, a few saplings combined *Frog in Pond* as their opponent applied *Picking an Apple*. She allowed them five minutes' practice time.

"Dawn!" Gwen pulled Taralyn forward. "Where else could you pick an apple to throw your opponent off balance?"

Rutger suggested, 'Hips."
Gwen poked Taralyn in the hips and she tripped sideways.

"Oh, I know! Elbows!" Matt said.

"Hold your rod at Frog," Gwen commanded Taralyn. She complied, and then was spun around by the Warrior's picking the apple.

"Knees, definitely the knees," Tyler called out.

"You know, you can come and help demonstrate being the apple, Dad."

Everyone laughed, and Tyler graciously stepped forward as his daughter demonstrated the effectiveness of picking the apple at his knees.

The group practiced various ways to pick an apple for ten minutes, occasionally switching partners.

"Dawn. We will work through *Morning Meadow* now, but as you do, think of ways you can use each step in your role as the *Mountain Wall*."

She released them with prayer.

Atticus helped her into his truck. "Gwen, I gotta speak my mind."

"Shoot." She took a deep breath as she adjusted the seat belt above her swelling abdomen.

He glared at the road ahead in silence.

She reached over and touched his elbow. "Atticus, what is it?"

"I don't like you fighting."

She coughed. "I'm a warrior, dear. Your warrior."

"You're a pregnant woman. I don't like you endangering yourself and the baby," he growled.

She took a calming breath. "How am I supposed to train your army if I can't fight?"

Atticus turned into the parsonage's drive. Shutting down the engine, he gripped the steering wheel with both hands. "I can't bear to lose you, Gwen."

She unbuckled and slid toward him, but didn't speak. After a moment, he glanced at her. Slowly, she placed her hand on his arm. She closed her eyes, centering herself, and began to pray. She heard him take in his breath as she knew the power surged from her palms into him. "Don't be afraid, Atticus," she whispered.

He released the steering wheel and wrapped his arms around her, engulfing them both in power. She moaned and then laughed. Grabbing his hand, she quickly placed it on her abdomen. "She's kicking."

Atticus spread his palm against her, joy spread across his face. "She's so strong. Hey, little one!"

Gwen laughed as Atticus pushed his face closer to her stomach. "Hey, little girl. What you doing? Feels like *Frog on the Pond*."

Gwen absently ran her fingers through his hair.

He closed his eyes and Gwen felt the power of his prayer. "Lord of Light, guide and guard this little girl. Lord of Light, protect and preserve my little girl. Lord of Light, direct and defend our little girl."

"Amen," Gwen sobbed.

Atticus glanced up and saw the tears streaming down her face. He sat up and pulled her into his arms and rocked her gently. "I love you, Gwen. I love you."

"I love you, too," she whispered.

He kept her in his embrace, as if he hadn't heard, then opened his door and helped her out of the truck from the driver's side. His arm encircled her waist as they made their way up the porch.

The phone rang.

"I'm going to sit on the porch for a while," Gwen sat down. She heard him answer on the third ring.

Atticus came out drawing on his Navy sports coat, a striped tie hung loosely around his neck.

"Le'Vander's mother was just rushed to the hospital. I've got to go."

Gwen stood and helped straighten his collar. His hands grasped her elbows. "What can I do to help?"

"You can love me," he kissed her forehead.

"I do." She cupped his cheek and stood on tiptoes to brush his lips with hers. "I do love you, Atticus."

He kissed her nose, her eyelids, her cheeks, and then her parted lips. She felt weak in the knees. The phone rang again, jarring their embrace.

"Can you answer that? I've got to go. Call the elders, too. Let them know about Le'Vander's mom." He hurried down the steps.

"I will."

Atticus glanced up and dashed back up the steps for a light kiss. He grinned and patted her abdomen, "By, Baby Girl. By, Love."

Chi was on the phone, advising her that Le'Vander's mom had just arrived at the ER with congestive heart failure. Gwen phoned the rest of the Elders, requesting prayer.

She stayed busy cleaning and baking. She started out with a chicken divane casserole, but the recipe on the back of the container of sour cream caught her eye and she made a dish of clam dip. The clam dip was cooling in the fridge when she realized she had the makings for chocolate cake and while she got out the mixer, she thought she might as well make some bread loaves, too. She was very productive, but she'd find herself standing dazed, remembering her feelings for Atticus.

Pearl McAfee was laid to rest Sunday after church. The construction workers, who hadn't known the feisty mother of Le'Vander, left the church to get into their trucks and cars. The rest of the congregation walked solemnly out to the waiting cemetery. Atticus kept the ceremony short and comforting.

Le'Vander stood, looking bone-weary, beside an older man. Beaucephalus, pronounced the Southern way - Bo-see-fus - or Big B as the townspeople called him, had been let out of jail for just these twenty-four hours. Big B had seemingly spent his freedom making up for lost time – he reeked of cigarettes and whiskey and swayed in a non-existent breeze. Pearl's favorite Bible verse, surprisingly enough, had been John 11:35, "Jesus wept." Patsy stood by the open grave and sang Pearl's favorite song, *Wind Beneath my Wings*. Le'Vander's face and shirt were shiny with tears. As the casket was lowered into the grave, Patsy slipped her hand inside his. He leaned against her and she let him. The congregants sang *Abide with Me* and then, after a gentle closing prayer, wandered away, leaving Le'Vander to mourn, with Patsy by his side.

Doug walked beside a silent Taralyn. Her sandals made little slapping noises against the soles of her feet. She hadn't spoken to him since Wednesday night. Her silence was like a wound festering inside him. She stumbled and he grabbed her hand. "You OK?"

She glared and nodded, her face pink with embarrassment.

"This looks like a grave. See how the grass covering

it is new, and the dirt is still soft.   Wonder why there's no gravestone." He glanced at Taralyn. She looked panicked, her mouth half-open as if to answer him. "What?"

"Nothing." Taralyn dropped his hand.

Doug looked back at the sandy oval outline and saw another unmarked grave next to it.

Chapter 27
The Ground

"Samir Ahmadinaja. Import-export businessman specializing in antiquities." Forest flashed the three shots Doug had taken on the screen. "His father disappeared under Sadam's reign. His wife was stoned to death for giving directions to a male foreigner and her scarf slipped. His daughter was kidnapped, raped, and de-handed when he refused to smuggle artifacts out of the country during Desert Storm. Both sons were killed in active duty. He's here on a buying trip visa – short term, but he applied for American citizenship yesterday. He has purchased a building in Morning Creek – in cash – and plans to open an antique shop."

"New member of the church?" Lt. Cortez smirked. She could allow herself the smirk because her flirtations with Forest over the last few months had been increasingly accepted and sometimes returned. It wasn't that she liked him, nor did she particularly find him attractive – too muscular for her tastes – but he was definitely the alpha male, and so she'd made it a goal to take advantage of whatever power he might bestow.

"Joined last Sunday." Forest switched the slides to a black and white of skeletal remains. "Our agent in the field suggested we have a look-see in two patches of disturbed ground in the cemetery. "Using satellite telemetry and radar imaging, this has been identified as a male human, covered in metallic armor – breastplate, helmet, shin guards. An empty sheath at his waist; we assume used to contain a sword. This one," new image," is the remains of a ukera."

Low whispers filled the room.

He watched Cortez – she wasn't looking at the ukera; she was watching her peers. Her competitiveness worked in her favor as an investigator for the IIA. But she was not well-liked. He was right to choose Tompkins as the field agent over Cortez.

Chapter 28
The Battle of Shergoque

The door of despair darkened a half-mile down the hill. They had the high ground, but the door forming below them was abnormally large – enough for four or five to come through at the same time.

"Steady." Sanchor's voice rumbled around the hill and his soldiers took courage from the sound. Five hundred Feet under Eolocal. Two-hundred-fifty Swords under Ricean. Five hundred Staff Bearers under Gwen. Two hundred fifty Archers under Ybib. All fought for the light and followed Sanchor.

Gwen took a deep, calming breath.

"The darkness emerges," Ricean shouted the warning as soldiers began to come through the hole. "Steady. Make them come up to us. We want them breathless before we begin to dance."

Gwen shifted balance, her hands felt sweaty on her staff at Pine Tree Rest. She glanced down and was shocked to see how vastly pregnant she was. "Sanchor!" she called out. He turned to face her, his white cloak shadowing to black.

"Do you still love me, Gwen?"

Gwen sat up gasping. Her face and hair were shiny with sweat. She choked back a sob.

"Gwen?" a light tap sounded on the door. "Are you alright?"

"Atticus," she sobbed.

The door flew open. He fumbled for the light on the dresser.

She groaned as pain gouged a path down her sides. "Atticus!"

He was beside her, stroking her hair away from her face. "What's wrong? You're burning up!"

"It was a nightmare. The Battle of Shergoque. Just a nightmare." She clung to him and groaned again.

"You're sick, Gwen. I'll call Chi. Just lie back down."

"No!' She grabbed at him. "Don't leave me. Don't go."

He perched beside her and held her shaking body against his. "Baby Girl is fighting hard tonight." He smoothed her swollen belly and felt an elbow or a knee rub its way across the expanse underneath his fingers.

Gwen tilted her head back and wailed. He rubbed her back and held her until she quieted. He pressed her back against the mattress and stroked her face until her eyes closed and her breathing calmed.

"Do you want some water?" he whispered.

"No. Don't go. Don't leave me." Her eyes flew open and she grabbed his hand.

"I'm right here." He pulled her hand to his lips and kissed it. "Gwen, I won't leave you."

Tears trickled out of the corners of her eyes and she cried softly.

"The Battle of Shergoque. What happened there?" He lowered their hands to her pregnancy and gently massaged through her cotton gown.

"They came through a hole of despair. Wave after wave of them. We fought, but inch by inch they drove us up the hill and onto the plateau. Eolocal fell and then Ybib. The entire Hand of Sanchor tried to surrender, but the Dark soldiers just kept beating them. Dark soldiers usually welcome surrenders, they sell the captives and torture them until they turn. But these didn't let - They were all beaten to death. The Swords of Sanchor tried to flank the Dark soldiers, but they were set on by spikes. Their bodies were hoisted above the battlefield, still alive; skewered on those massive pikes. Bermerk, who was Eolocal's second fell, and then Tumley. Sweet Tumley."

"Shhh," Atticus crooned. "It was just a dream."

"They all died. All but a handful of us."

"It happened long ago," Atticus whispered soothingly.

"But they all died."

"Gwen." He gripped her hand firmly. "Look at me."

She wiped her face.

"Greater love has no man than this – to lay his life down for a friend."

Her breathing stilled and she squeezed his hand. "Sanchor was lost that day. He lost himself to despair and grief."

His thumb traced the outline of a leg through her abdomen.

"In the dream, I was pregnant. Bigger than I am now, if you can believe it."

He smiled as she tried to laugh.

She lay silent for a minute. Quietly, as if to herself, she said, "I don't want to lose you, Atticus. And I don't want to lose our little girl."

Joy swept through him: our little girl. "You won't lose me to despair or grief, Gwen. I've already fought that battle and I chose the light."

She raised his hand to her lips and kissed his palm. "I'm so sorry your son died."

Atticus bit the inside of his lips and slowly nodded and then he stood up. "He was a good boy. I'll get you some water."

"No." Again she clung to his hand. "Don't leave me."

"Gwen?" Atticus asked.

"Just lay beside me for a little while. Please?"

He held her back against his chest, legs spooned together, and they fell asleep.

Chapter 29
The War

"Otka says she doesn't want to go back to Chechnya," Mitchell held the woman's hand and peered up into Atticus' face.

The scientist spoke again.

"She wants to stay here and help you complete the compound."

Atticus glanced sideways at the young woman. Her face was pale with a pinched mouth. Her hair was pulled back in a tight mousy-brown braid. Her slender body was boy-like. Her eyes were pleading.

Atticus' voice was gentle and calm. "Why?"

Mitchell translated fluidly. "I have lived my whole life surrounded by war. It never sleeps, it only eats. It eats my family and friends. I smell it on my skin. It is a part of me. War is also a part of Gwen Staff Bearer of Atticus. And a part of Doug Hand of Atticus. But it is not a part of you. You will not recognize it when it comes. You need me. You are preparing all of this for a war. I feel it in my soul. Let me stay. Let me help."

"Do your other colleagues feel the same way?"

"No."

Behind them, Gwen called out the stations of *Morning Meadow*. The battle staffs had arrived. Six times heavier than training rods, they were challenging to the saplings.

Atticus took Otka's hand in his and placed his right hand on her forehead.

The Elders on the field paused, drawn spiritually toward the power they felt surging nearby. Gwen gasped as her baby stretched within her.

Chapter 30
The Killing Blows

August slipped into September and the humidity lowered to the eighties. Jarmille had picked a dozen people, including Otka, for weapons training. They met in the back woods, concealed from everyone except IIA.

Doug had led his group through the basics and moved on to striking blows.

Gwen had taught her saplings the *Mountain Wall* sufficiently so that they could defend themselves in a skirmish. It was time to pick her Staff Bearers. She paced them, observantly. They had a right to know what would be expected of them. They had a right to choose. She touched Tyler's shoulder as he crept his spider back up to *dawn*. He seemed to know instinctively what she was asking of him. He glanced at his daughter beside him and then turned back to Gwen and nodded determinedly.

Juan blinked when her hand fell on his shoulder. He was standing at *surrender* with a smile of utter contentment on his face.

She passed by Mitchell and his brothers. Mitchell

would never choose the path Gwen had, but his brother Thaddeus might in a dozen years. She laid her hand on Sara's shoulder. A mother has no qualms about killing to protect her children.

Nathan who was a finish carpenter grunted in surprise as Gwen touched him. Samir tripped during *Journey* and gaped at her as if her fingers burned him. Her saplings came to *dawn* at the end of *morning meadow*. "Pine trees at rest," she commanded.

She searched their faces. She needed one more. She couldn't decide. She centered herself and closed her eyes, searching the crowd with her heart.

The saplings murmured softly. They shifted, making room as someone walked forward.

"Gwen Staff Bearer of Atticus."

She opened her eyes and looked up into Matt's face. Tears filled her eyes, but she stretched out her hand and touched his shoulder.

Taralyn's voice rang across the ground, "Saplings of Atticus. May the Lord of Light guard and guide you. May the Lord of Light protect and preserve you. May the Lord of Light direct and defend you. Amen."

Everyone left quietly, unsure of what had happened, but sure that something crucial had taken place. Gwen looked at the six people who had formed a semi-circle in front of her.

"You know there will be a war."

They glanced at each other and nodded.

"The enemy kills only when every ounce of terror and pain has been sucked from your marrow. Their blows are meant to break but not kill. To maim but not kill. To torture but not kill. They thrive on grief and they will use everything in their power to push you to the edge of despair in the hope that you will be lost and join them."

Atticus walked up beside her but remained silent.

"We do not take pleasure in such darkness. When we strike, we kill."

She met each face and saw understanding and acceptance. "Tomorrow, Taralyn will continue training the saplings. You will become Staff Bearers. I will teach you the seven lightning bolts. The seven killing blows." Atticus glowed with power as he prayed silently beside her.

"Tomorrow morning, I will greet you. If you cannot kill, then you will remain honored saplings. If you can kill, swift and merciful, you will name yourself as Staff Bearer."

She bowed at *Dawn* and they returned it before wandering thoughtfully away.

The next morning, all six of her chosen named themselves Staff Bearers.

September drifted into October.

Chapter 31
The Strategia Oscuro

The door of grief flickered and solidified. Gwen stood at Pine Tree Rest, her Staff Bearers spread behind her. Her belly strained against her tunic, her baby's elbows and knees plowing around underneath her skin.

A helmet poked through the hole, black and charred, covering the Strategia Oscuro's face. He stepped through, his black cape flowing in the breeze, the seven-point star embroidered on his shoulder sparkling in the light.

"Steady," she called over her shoulder.

The Strategia Oscuro stepped forward and bowed to Gwen at Dawn. She bowed in return.

"Do you still love me, Gwen?" Sanchor's voice hissed intimately from behind the mask.
Gwen groaned as her baby jabbed her foot into her kidney, but couldn't answer his question.

"You know what I've come for," Sanchor's voice echoed from behind the mask.

Gwen's hand pressed against her womb, protecting her unborn child as well as the children her people had with them. "You will not take them."

*"I've fought beside you. I taught you everything
you know. Do you really think you can keep me from
that which I desire?"* He lunged forward with Stag in
Spring *and she countered with* Bear on the Mountain.
She side-stepped Picking an Apple *that was aimed at
her shoulder and used her rod to dent his thigh shield
with* Wolf in Winter.

"Give the children to me." Billy Goat *shoved Gwen
backward. Sanchor paced in a circle.*

*"No." She brought her staff low, protecting her
child.*

"Then I'll have to kill you." He lunged, Chopping
Wood. *Gwen felt her ribs crack and her skin burst
open.*

"Gwen!" Atticus was shaking her. The forty-watt
bulb flickered as the lamp continued wobbling where
Atticus had knocked it onto the floor while turning it on.

Gwen choked back a cry as reality swam into
focus. She burrowed her face into Atticus' chest,
clinging to him and sobbing.

"Gwen," he stroked her back and held her.
"Gwen, it was just a dream."

"So real." Her body trembled. "It was so real."

"You're burning up again. Let me call Chi."

"No. It was just a dream. I'll be alright." She sighed
and relaxed against him.

"Was it the Battle of Shergoque again?"

She curled his fingers into his pajama shirt as if trying
to be as close as possible. Her voice was muffled
against him. "After Sanchor was lost, I met him in

battle. We were protecting a dozen children, trying to find them sanctuary."

"Children? What happened?"

She gently pushed away from him, as if she didn't want the memories she had relived in her dreams to cling to him. "I'll take a shower and cool off."

He held her arms. "What happened?"

"I knew what they would do if they captured the children. But I couldn't kill him." She shrugged. "He broke my ribs and left me for dead. But the children made it to safety."

He wanted to kiss her. He wanted to toss her on the bed and do everything in his power to make her forget Sanchor. But he could not.

She looked at him, but her eyes weren't focused on his face. "I couldn't kill him. How many have been lost because I couldn't kill him that day?"

Sweat pasted her cotton gown between her breasts and along her ribs. She threw back the tangled sheets and moaned as she sat up.

"Gwen, what's this?" Atticus touched a bloody patch on her gown just below her left breast.

"Ow!" She snatched his hand away and looked down in surprise.

He stood. "I'm calling Chi."

He got off the phone and heard the shower running. The bathroom door was open. Gwen's plump form showed behind the opaque curtain. He could hear her sobbing.

Atticus reached in and turned off the water, then wrapped a towel around her trembling body and helped her to his bed. He toweled her hair and slipped a clean T shirt over her head. As if she were a child, he helped her into jogging shorts. She stared at the wall, afraid to close her eyes, but she took his hand and drew it to her lips, pressing a tender kiss into his palm before releasing him.

After Chi examined Gwen, he met with Atticus in the kitchen.

"I want her to stay in bed. Three days minimum."

"What happened, Chi?"

"She has got an abraded contusion on her ribs. Not fractured, somehow, but they will cause her some discomfort. She refused a sedative."

"She said it was a dream."

"Has she been having nightmares?"

"Yes. Every few nights, I hear her call out. Once or twice, I have to wake her up because she's yelling."

Chi took a deep breath.

"I can't stay in bed for three days."

The men turned from their places at the kitchen table to stare at Gwen.

"You'll do as the doctor says," Atticus warned, anger flickering in his voice.

"It's closer now. The war. It's coming and we're not ready yet."

"We'll be ready for the refugees," Atticus assured her. "Here, come sit down."

She leaned against him as he wrapped his arm around her shoulders and led her to the table.

"You have a slight temperature, Gwen. I have only

made a cursory examination, but I would say that you are suffering from post-traumatic stress disorder. I want you to take it easy. For the baby's sake, Gwen." Chi spoke slowly.

"I have to finish training the Staff Bearers."

"Tyler can take over tomorrow. He's trained men in hand-to-hand combat for years." Atticus gently massaged her shoulders. "Yes?"

"No."

Atticus placed a hand on her head and rocked it up and down. "Yes. For three days."

Gwen smiled. "Yes. But just three days."

"Who hit you?" Chi asked.

"Sanchor." Gwen swallowed from Atticus' coffee mug. "In a dream. He was going to take Baby Girl and I wouldn't let him."

Atticus crouched beside her. "It was just a dream."

Tears filled Gwen's eyes and she nodded.

"Now, go crawl in my bed. I'll change your sheets. I'll check on you in a minute."

Chi frowned, but waited for Atticus to return to the kitchen before voicing his concerns. "You told her it was just a dream, like dreams are not real."

Atticus blinked.

"The Angel of the Lord comes to you in a dream, and he is real." Chi spoke deliberately. "Whatever struck her was very real. I dreamt of you, and you are real. You dreamt of the Warrior, and she is real. She is dreaming about Sanchor, and that dream was so real that if the blow had been lower, she could have lost the baby."

Atticus stared at Chi in shock.

"Did it not occur to you that there are others who have this ability to appear at will in the dreams of others?"

Atticus's shrug turned into a tremble. "But I don't injure anyone. In a dream – I couldn't."

"You could not. Obviously, Sanchor can. And possibly will again."

Atticus' face filled with fury.

Chi help up his hand, as if calming the storm. "How do you keep someone safe from a dream?"

"Prayer." Atticus answered immediately. "You pray."

"Then we better pray without ceasing, Preacher."

The men walked together to the door, where Chi paused. "I would like to examine this dreaming more closely. How is it you learned to do this?"

Atticus frowned, strangely displeased by the idea of sharing this knowledge. "I have always been able to do it, even as a young child. I don't know if you can learn."

Chi hesitated, and then embraced his friend and walked to his car. As the door to the house shut, Chi turned back, strangely displeased with the idea that Atticus might have been lying to him.

Atticus crawled in beside Gwen and wrapped her in his arms. His hand slid over her shorts, caressing the skin rippling with stretch marks. Baby Girl pressed against his fingers.

Atticus began to pray.

The third day of rest ended Friday night, and Gwen felt better for it. She felt safe in Atticus' bed and no nightmares disturbed her sleep.

Her saplings and staff bearers greeted her cheerfully Saturday morning. As she observed, Taralyn leading the saplings, Tyler the staff bearers, Doug the fingers and toes, Gwen was relieved at how well they all were doing.

Trucks began to roll into the compound as they closed in prayer. The workers hustled away from practice to unload the bunk beds and toiletries into the completed barracks, and food supplies and pots and pans into the cafeteria.

"Elders' meeting after church tomorrow," Atticus called over the noise.

"Covered dish?" Sara asked.

"Absolutely!" Rutger shouted.

Chapter 32
The Portal

Atticus hummed with power. His parishioners, over ninety-five members now, including ten teachers, three doctors, seven cooks, four nurses, and most of the construction workers, gladly squeezed together on the pews. His church would hold two-hundred some-odd people, so although it wasn't crowded, it felt full.

After the end of the service, he watched them drive away and then turned to the elders. He stated, "It's time."

Their eyes widened. They breathed sharply. But they wrapped their arms around each other's shoulders and began to pray.

Gwen saw the shimmering circle first. "Open your eyes. Concentrate on the light. Surrender yourself to it and at the same time, pull it open."

The portal formed on the top edge of the altar steps. It glowed like a sunrise, building white on white until it blazed like silver.

"Hail Mary Full of Grace, the Lord is with you. Blessed art thou among women and blessed is the fruit of thy womb, Jesus. Holy Mary, Mother of God. Pray for all sinners now and at the hour of our death." Sara intoned the rosary. At her side, Samir quoted from the Koran. Matt sang the Twenty-third Psalm.

The silver crackled as a form tumbled backward down the steps. He lunged to his feet, sword held head-high, parallel to the floor. "Whom do you serve?" the boy's voice cracked with adolescence.

Gwen stepped forward. "We serve the Light, the Bringers of Light, and the Light Eternal. We offer you sanctuary."

The teen gawked at her and then dashed back into the circle of light.

"Steady," Atticus warned. "Keep the light steady. Don't let it close."

Three children were pushed through the hole and tumbled down the altar steps. They crouched in fear and then ran to the sides of the church as more children began flinging themselves through the portal of light.

Dozens of children flowed in and gathered around the elders, touching their arms and backs, adding their prayers to the group.

Backsides first, soldiers came through, swords pointed back into the portal. Bloody, dirt-smeared, ragged, the soldiers stumbled their way into the sanctuary. Last came a woman with blood gushing from a skull wound. Her sword jabbed back into the circle and came out dripping with gore. She backed away, carefully descending the three steps. No one followed her through the light. The woman nodded and glanced over her shoulder at the elders. Her twenty-seven soldiers and nearly one-hundred children filled the church, pressing their hands on each other's shoulders. She raised her sword above her head and shouted, "Amen!"

The portal winked closed, leaving a ghost of blue circles in their eyes.

The children and soldiers collapsed to the floor and pews. The elders swooned against each other. The woman's eyes searched the crowd.

Gwen stepped forward. "I am Gwen Staff Bearer of Atticus. Welcome to a place of refuge."

The woman blinked bleary-eyed in the dim light. "Gwen? Of Atticus? I knew a Gwen of Sanchor."

"Ricean?" Gwen's hands folded around her abdomen protectively. "Ricean Sword of Sanchor? Whom do you serve?"

"Fool child! I serve the Light. I just stepped through the light. Have you learned nothing?" Ricean sheathed her sword. "Partmos, count the Swords."

An old man reported, "Twenty-seven, Ricean Sword of Jol."

"And children?"

"Ninety-eight, Ricean Sword of Jol," the first young man who had come through the light shouted.

"Injuries, over there." Ricean marched forward, pointing at the back of the church. "We'll need water and bandages, Gwen Staff Bearer of – Atticus? And a healer, if you've got one."

"We have two. Chi, Rawan, where do you want the wounded?"

They glanced at each other before Chi answered,

"Move them into the fellowship hall. Visolela, go bring me my bag. Rawan, you'll do triage. Look out for internal bleeding."

Sara shouted, "Bea, come with me to the kitchen. We've got two drawers of tea towels we can use for bandages. Mitchell and Tyler and Taralyn, gather the children who aren't hurt and let them lie down." Eduviges grabbed Rutger by the elbow. "You got that case of bottled water in your truck?"

"Ja." In his excitement, his German accent emerged. "Was going to deliver it to the compound this afternoon. Glad I waited."

Matt and Samir helped drag in the bottles. Mitchell handed one to a child a little smaller than himself. "Here, water."

The boy took the bottle upside down and stared at it.

"No, open it. Like this." Mitchell took another from Matt and twisted the lid. He tilted his head back and let the water pour into his mouth.

The boy dropped the bottle and scooted backward until he bumped into the wall.

"What's wrong?" Matt asked. The children all dropped their bottles to the floor and backed away.

The uninjured soldiers stepped between the elders and the children, warily fingering their sheathed swords. "Gwen!" Taralyn yelled.

Gwen wobbled forward.

"They're terrified," Taralyn gasped.

"I just wanted to show them how to drink the water," Mitchell explained.

Gwen bent over and picked up a bottle off the floor. She eyed the children and smiled. "They've never seen a plastic bottle. The rich have tiny glass bottles, most people have one or two clay jars, but water is carried in skins." She knelt awkwardly in front of the teen who had first come through.

"Water for water." She held the bottle out to him and pointed at the skin bag hanging from his belt.

The adolescent glared, but then handed her his bag. "The water of life, I give freely."

"The water of life, I receive from the hands of a friend." She lifted the bag to her lips and squeezed three drops into her mouth. It tasted stale and dirty, but she swallowed. "The water of life, I give freely."

The boy took the bottle, glanced at all the people staring at him and untwisted the lid. He lifted the bottle to his lips and poured a small amount into his mouth. He lowered his face, still glaring, and swallowed.

Gwen handed him back the bag. "I know it doesn't taste like water but it is. It's clean, from a spring."

"I am Ormed Sword of Ricean. Gwen Staff Bearer speaks truly. This does not taste like water, but it quenches my thirst." Ormed swallowed another mouthful without breaking his glare. When he did not drop dead of poison at the hand of this stranger, he nodded to the children around him.

"Gwen!" Atticus shouted for her from the fellowship hall.

She followed his voice and found him standing next to Ricean. The Sword of Jol stood with her arms crossed, her eyes blinked slowly at the ceiling and she swayed on her feet. "She won't let Rawan or Chi near her."

"Of course she won't." Gwen snapped. "Her Swords are wounded. And some of the children, too. She won't allow any medical attention to herself until her Swords are seen to."

Atticus raised an eyebrow. "Any reason you didn't think to tell us about this?"

"Any reason you couldn't have figured it out for yourself?" Her lips quivered with an ill-concealed smirk.

The familiar tinge of anger crept into Atticus' cheeks.

"Ricean Sword of Jol, this is Atticus Priest of God."

The woman's focus lowered and she gazed at him. "Truly?" she whispered.

Atticus took her left hand; her right still gripped her sword hilt. "I am Atticus. The Angel of the Lord told me to prepare for you. He knew you were coming. He said that, with Gwen, you will hold back the dark." Ricean took a deep, unsteady breath. "Gwen Staff Bearer of Sanchor and I have held back the darkness before."

"I am of Atticus," Gwen corrected her firmly.

"Of Atticus." Ricean nodded. "Sanchor is lost."

"Sanchor is a Strategia Oscuro."

Tears fell down the soldier's face. "Many were lost at the Battle of Shergoque."

"And more were saved." Gwen turned to Atticus. "Ricean's husband was also Sword of Sanchor. He was killed on the plains of Shergoque."

Chi stopped next to Ricean. "Is she going to let me sew up that wound now?"

"Are my swords and children tended?"

"Yes. No deaths, but some are serious. Rawan and I have seen to all of them."

Ricean nodded and sank to her knees with Atticus still gripping her hand to help her down.

"What are those?"

Atticus looked up over his shoulder where Ricean was pointing. "What?"

"Those." Ricean grimaced as Chi began suturing. "Atticus Priest of God, those planks that swirl in the ceiling of their own accord."

"Fans. The electric fans?" Atticus scowled.

"Thalectric fans." Ricean murmured.

"Gwen?" Atticus stood. "Is there something you might want to share with me?"

The smirk returned, not concealed at all this time.

The injured were loaded onto trucks and cars, but the majority of the band of Jol walked the two miles to the compound.

Quick-thinking on Visolela's part had started a phone chain which provided twelve workers for the cafeteria, and a warm meal of bread, eggs, and ham for the refugees. The visitors ate with ravenous abandon, and then began to talk and visit with each other and the cafeteria workers. The children began to play and run around.

Ricean took a deep breath and surveyed the café, nodding to herself.

"If you are refreshed, Sword of Jol, I would like to show you your tents."

The soldier followed Gwen across the compound into the barracks. Ormed flanked Ricean as an honor guard and Mitchell escorted Gwen.

"It is cold in here!" Ricean exclaimed.

"Air conditioning. Like the fans, we use it to keep us cool." Gwen spoke softly. "Permit me to show you a new tool."

Ricean snorted nervously, but nodded.

"These are called light switches." Gwen touched the panel. "Push one up, and the lights come on."

The teen yelled in fright and drew his sword.

"Push them down and they go off." Gwen repeated. "Up is on. Down is off."

"Miraculous. No wonder you have to keep your houses so cold, if the light can come and go as you wish." Ricean tried them for herself.

"That's a nice sword," Mitchell commented. Ormed reddened and sheathed it.

Gwen led them into the first room filled with a dozen bunks. "You are welcome to find rest anywhere, but we would be pleased if you found rest on these beds. Mitchell, show Ormed how to climb onto the top bunk once Ricean turns on the lights."

The boys scrambled up. Grinning, Ormed flung himself up and down on the mattress. "Blankets, Mother. They are soft and warm."

"I didn't know you had children." Gwen smiled.

"I had children." Ricean growled. "I have one son now."

Gwen held her gaze without emotion.

"I see you are with child. This is new. Last time I saw you, you were panting after Sanchor."

Gwen's cheeks blushed. She rubbed her belly. "We haven't chosen a name yet, Atticus and I. But he was told by the Angel that she will be a girl."

Gwen chided herself. It wasn't a lie, but it evaded the truth, which was no one's business but her own.

Mitchell and Ormed climbed back down. "Your people can take this wing on the first floor. Now, our world has another gift to show you." Gwen led them into the bathroom. "Mitchell, take Ormed into that side and show him how to use a toilet."

"What?" he squeaked.

"On the world Ormed came from, they dig a hole and squat over it. Then they use leaves."
"Ew!"

"Mitchell, please show Ormed the proper way to use a toilet."
"Yes ma'am. But don't tell my mother. Come here."

She did the same for Ricean who was speechless with amazement. The showers delighted her, though. "Ormed! Come here!"

The boys charged back into the ladies' room. "Look! A waterfall within the house. And soap that bubbles."

When they returned to the cafeteria, Ormed circled his sword above his head, signaling immediate silence and Ricean began to speak. "It is forbidden to light fires in our new tent."

Chapter 33
The Refugees

"You're the Hand of Atticus," the voice of a young girl spoke softly just behind Doug where he sat eating his lunch. He turned around but couldn't find the speaker.

"Where are you?"

"Is it permitted?" the disembodied voice came again, this time from his right.

"Is what permitted?"

"Is it permitted to speak to you? Or should I ask your wife first?"

A blue eye haloed by corn-yellow hair peeked above the cement blocks and disappeared just as quickly.

"I don't have a wife. So you are permitted to speak to me because I say so." He raised an eyebrow, curious to see the rest of her.

She was no taller than four feet and about twelve years old. She was too thin, but her eyes were beautiful.

"Hi," he waved.

She drew a wooden sword out of a sheath at her

side and held it in both hands before her at Dawn. "I am Gilga Knife of Jol."

Doug stood slowly, brushing off his jeans. He grasped his fists together in front of him and bowed. "I am Doug Hand of Atticus."

"I know," she giggled.

"Are you one of the refugees?"

She nodded, suddenly shy.

"Where are you from?"

"Teletha." She beamed. "It is by the Algan Sea. My family were net-makers."

Doug clicked two shots of her on his watch.

She glanced down at the bottled water and sandwich. Doug's heart skipped a beat at the sudden expression on her face.

"I was just starting lunch. Would you like some?"

"I would be honored to break bread with the Hand of Atticus."

"Your English is very good." He motioned her to sit beside him and handed her a plastic bagged sandwich.

She stared at it, squishing the plastic between her fingers. He unzipped his and she suddenly smiled with relief and copied him. He watched as she nibbled the sandwich with a squeamish look on her face.

"I guess peanut butter and jelly isn't a favorite in Teletha."

She shook her head. "Fish. We only ate fish. Every day. Every meal. But I wish I could have set a fish or two aside on the exile."

"The exile?"

She took a bigger bite. "When the dark soldiers came. All of the children were forced into exile. You know what the soldiers would have done to us. So for three years, we stayed in exile." She took another bit. "I liked the caves of Mandor. We stayed in there several moons."

Doug nodded as if he knew exactly what she meant. He did know what soldiers sometimes do to children, but the geographical references were new to him. "So Gilga Knife of Jol, is there a husband somewhere I should have asked permission from?"

"Oh, Ormed doesn't mind if I am spoken to."

Doug sputtered. "You have a husband?"

She blushed fiercely. "Ormed is my husband, but we are not married yet. The healers say I am too young."

Doug gaped at her.

"What are those?" She pointed at the bunch of grapes.

"They don't have grapes in Taletha?" He broke off a sprig and handed it to her.

Her eyes twinkled as her yellow hair swayed from side to side. "Only fish." She stared at the tiny purple spheres in her palm and bit her bottom lip.

"Here." He plucked one from the bunch, placed it in his mouth and crunched.

She copied him. Her eyes burst wide in glee. "These are wonderful!"

"Here, take the whole bunch." Doug felt like Santa Claus.

"Gilga Knife of Jol, do not bother the Hand of Atticus."

Taralyn and Mitchell walked hand-in-hand beside the boy who had spoken.

"Hey squirt. How's third grade? Got those capitols memorized yet?" Doug childishly enjoyed upsetting Mitchell.

"I'm in the fourth grade. But I can see how difficult it must be for you to count that far."

Gilga and Ormed froze in the act of tasting grapes together. Ormed put his hand to his sword hilt and moved Gilga behind him. Without noticing, Doug turned on Taralyn. "And you. Does your dad know you're skipping school?"

"Who died and made you God? I'm here with my father, thank you very much."

Mitchell looked thoroughly pleased.

Doug frowned, feeling stupid. He turned with a flourish, "Gilga Knife of Jol, may I introduce Taralyn Sapling of Atticus."

Taralyn held her hands out and bowed. Gilga stepped from behind Ormed.

"And this half-pint of pudding is Mitchell Sapling of Atticus."

"With Dawn, life returns," Mitchell bowed.

Gilga blushed. "I am honored. This is my husband Ormed Sword of Jol."

"Husband?" Taralyn gasped.

"They're husband and wife, but they're not married yet. Like Atticus and Gwen," Mitchell explained.

"Oh," Taralyn blushed.

"Ricean said that our two clans may not share the same customs." Ormed held out his hands. "Just as the Jol have never seen a thelectric fan, there are things you have never seen from our world."

"World?" Doug repeated.

"But surely love is love, no matter where we are. Gilga and I love each other. We have been friends forever. For the thousand years our people have held back the dark, we never knew which day might be our last. You know the scriptures, 'The door opens; the dance begins.' So we don't waste time. Gilga and I love each other. When she is able to have children, we will get married. For every soldier of the light who falls or becomes lost, a child must be born."

"Isn't your world the same?" Gilga asked.

"Yes," Taralyn agreed.

"Does someone want to explain this different worlds concept?" Doug was ignored.

"But we don't get married until we're really old," Mitchell added.

"Doug," Matt hollered from beside the building. "You planning on getting paid today?"

"Yeah, I'll be right there," Doug growled.

"May the Light bless you and keep you, Hand of Atticus," Ormed bowed and took his child-bride's elbow. They walked away.

Mitchell crossed his arms.

"Scram," Doug commanded. "I need to talk to Taralyn alone."

"Today would be nice, Doug!" Matt hollered again.

Mitchell glowered but followed Ormed and Gilga.

"Tonight." Doug grabbed Taralyn's shoulders. "I'll pick you up for choir. And then you and I are going somewhere quiet and have a good long talk."

"I'll tell you anything you want to know, Doug." She took a step closer to him. "As soon as you pray with Atticus."

He ground his teeth. She smelled of oranges and cinnamon.

"You're one of us, Doug." She stepped closer still, placing her hand on his ribs. "You're just too stubborn to admit it."

Her mouth. Her lips. Her scent. Doug bent his head, following his heart.

"What the hell do you think you're doing?" Matt grabbed Doug by the collar and flung him two yards away from Taralyn. "I ought to fire your ass on the spot. She's just a kid, for God's sake!"

Chapter 34
The Confidence

Taralyn met Doug at the door wearing khaki walking shorts and a loose cotton top. Her hair was spun behind her head and a light pink blushed her lips and cheeks.

"Hi," she bounced.

"Hi." Doug entered the house, trying to ignore her perfume.

"I'm ready; just let me grab my purse."

"Actually," Doug nodded to Tyler who was ignoring them from his chair in front of the TV. "Here's my keys. You go on to choir. I need to talk with your dad. If that's alright, Tyler?"

Tyler glanced between his little girl and his friend and switched off the TV.

Taralyn was speechless. She took the keys, looked to her father for permission, and headed out the door.

Tyler stood slowly. "You want some water or iced tea?"

"Sure, water's good."

Doug followed Tyler into the messy kitchen. Handing Doug a cold bottle from the refrigerator, Tyler asked, "Is this a kitchen table talk, or a rockers on the front porch talk?"

"I don't know."

"Well, mosquitoes are bad for October, but the table's got tonight's dishes on it. Your call."
Doug picked up plates and cups and placed them in the already full sink.

"Problem solved." Tyler sat.

Doug paced and then perched on the wooden chair opposite his friend. "I kissed Taralyn today."

Tyler just raised one eyebrow.

"It wasn't a full blown kiss, but if Matt hadn't attacked me, it would have been."

"You know she's seventeen? And you're twenty-five?"

Doug blew out a breath, gulping and nodding his head. He stood again. "When I used to spend the weekends with you and Beth, you were the closest thing I had to a family." He perched again and held out his cupped hands. "I used to call her Taralittle. Smart as a whip, gangly as all get out, but she," Doug paused and started again. "I loved her. Not in some sick perverse way. I used to pretend that she was my kid sister. She was about the same age as Leta was the last time I saw her."

"Leta?"

Doug stopped. "I thought Beth would have told you."

"Beth never broke a confidence." Tyler glanced away from the young man, trying to cover his irritation.

Doug seemed stunned. "Leta was my twin sister.

She disappeared on her way home from school when we were ten. They never found her body."

Tyler reached across the table and gripped Doug' wrist. "I'm sorry, son."

It was the first time Tyler had called him son. Doug blinked and took a deep breath. "From that time on, I knew exactly what I wanted to do. I wanted to track down bad guys."

Tyler nodded and withdrew his hand.

"After Leta disappeared, my family fell apart. My older sister got pregnant. My mom got religion. My dad started making mistakes at work and got fired so Mom threw him out." Doug gulped his water. "I didn't think anyone would ever love me again."

"And then you met Beth."

Doug jerked as if he'd been slapped. He tried and failed to meet Tyler's gaze. The men were silent for a moment.

"Beth and I weren't happy, when you came into her life. We loved each other, but we hadn't been happy for quite some time. But I think you knew that."

"I guessed it."

"We were married right out of college and had Taralyn the first year. Beth was so driven in her profession; she wasn't interested in having more children. I was. It was a bone of contention between us." Tyler tossed his empty bottle toward the trash can and missed. "The spring before you showed up in her classes, she had a miscarriage. I thought she'd just shrug it off. But she didn't."

Doug stared at his fists on the table. He kept his

voice soft, unsure of revealing a dead woman's confidence, even to her widower. "She felt she was being punished. That God had judged her and found her lacking.

Jealousy swept across Tyler's features, but he let it roll off of him and took a calming breath. "So you two had a lot in common."

Doug nodded slowly, frowning at the bottle in his fists.

"Taralyn grew up pretty much on her own. Pre-school, private school, afternoon care, nannies at night. She's seventeen now, and legally a minor, but she has a maturity about her that is remarkable."

Doug silently agreed.

Tyler got two more bottles out of the fridge and handed one to Doug. "Did you notice, she's got her mother's eyes?"

"Yeah."

"So, when you kissed Taralyn this morning," Tyler looked down at Doug. "What's the chance you were really kissing Beth?"

Chapter 35
The Dream Walker

The breeze rippling the pool of Meshapa was refreshing. Gwen tossed her head back and let it dry the sweat that pearled her neck. Around her, children played with puppies and in the distance, horses galloped and had mock battles, piercing the air with cries of joy and freedom.

She looked around, fond memories of this place of peace and refuge filled her thoughts. She sighed and stretched out on the marble slab that overhung the edge of the pool just outside of the waterfall's mist. The sun was warm without the danger of burning her freckled skin.

"Momma, Daddicus! Watch me!" A red-haired child dove from the banks into the icy water and surfaced a third of the way across the pool.

"Daddicus?" Gwen repeated.

"I love it when she calls me that." Atticus was by her side, stretched out languidly, his arms above his head, his chest and legs bare and tanned.

Gwen smiled and laid back beside him.

"This was always your favorite place here on my

world," a tall man with large ears stood between them and the pool.

"Do I know you?" Atticus stood.

"Sanchor," Gwen sat up.

He was dressed in tan linen robes, his feet shod in leather sandals, a battle staff was slung over his shoulder and his jet black hair was cut short. He ignored Atticus and dropped down beside Gwen. "Do you still love me?"

"Leave my wife alone," Atticus growled, reaching toward his tunic as if to pluck him up. Sanchor stood and focused his attention. The sky darkened and snow began to swirl. The puppies and children ran howling away. The horses reared and screamed in terror.

Atticus stepped back. The form in front of him mutated into a tall ugly man in a black cloak with a seven-point star embroidered on the shoulder. "She doesn't love you. She loves me. She'll never marry you, because I'm going to kill you."

Sanchor's sword pierced Atticus an inch to the left of his navel and punched a hole through his kidney.

Gwen sat up gasping silent shrieks. The bed beside her was empty. Atticus wasn't home yet. She wobbled to the phone and punched in a number. "Visolela, Atticus is hurt. Is your husband home?"

"No, I thought he and Atticus were in the clinic at the compound. What's wrong?"

"It's Atticus! He's been stabbed. Sanchor stabbed him in my dream," Gwen was yelling into the phone.

Visolela's end was silent.

"The phones haven't been set up at the compound yet. Does Chi have a cell?"

"Yes," Visolela answered and gave her the number. "Call me back when you speak to Chi."

Chi patted the arm of a young boy lying in a bed in the clinic and turned to Atticus. "Most of them are suffering from malnutrition. A few have festering wounds caused by unsanitary, stressful conditions, much the same as you would see in any refugee or internment camp. Some, like this boy, have injuries from that battle they escaped."

Atticus smiled.

"Why do you smile?"

"Sorry. Sometimes, maybe it's the same with you and Visolela, sometimes I feel like Gwen is thinking good thoughts about me."

"Dreaming of you? Yes, Visolela and I have shared such moments, also."

"Will the clinic be sufficient to meet their –" Atticus yelped and bent double, clutching at his stomach. Blood splattered between his fingers, freckling Chi's white coat. Atticus' eyes rolled and he collapsed on the floor.

Gwen stumbled into the church just as Taralyn was coming out. "Take me to the compound. Atticus has been hurt. He's there with Chi, but Chi isn't answering his phone. And Atticus has the truck!"

Taralyn took her arm and led her to Doug' mustang.

When Taralyn turned the engine, it faltered and stalled. She cranked it again. "Sorry, this belongs to Doug. Long story. I'll tell you later. Tell me how Atticus got hurt."

"It was in a nightmare. A Strategia Oscuro stabbed Atticus with his sword."

"A dream?" Taralyn turned right onto the main road.

"Some dreams are real. This one was." Gwen grabbed the seat belt crossing her chest with both hands, suddenly nauseous. "What were you doing at the church?"

"Choir practice."

"Alone?"

"No, choir ended about thirty minutes ago. I stayed behind to pray."

"Thank God you did."

Taralyn turned right and headed down the gravel road to the complex. She handed Gwen a small plastic box. "Chi is *7."

Gwen flipped the phone open and pressed the keys.

"It's just ringing again. No voice mail even."

"Keep it ringing. When we get to the clinic, we can follow the sound."

Gwen smiled in relief. "You're brilliant."

"That's what they tell me." She pulled into the compound and screeched to a halt at the double doors of the clinic. "Lights are on."

They dashed through the doors, listening to *Ode to Joy* as it played in the distance.

"Chi!" Taralyn yelled.

"Atticus!" Gwen panted.

A new member of the church, Dr. Thomas, poked his head out of a room to their left.

"Where's Atticus?"

"Gwen, calm down. Dr. Abubakar has him in triage."

"Where?"

Taralyn restated, "Which way?"

"Come." The older man took Gwen's arm and led them to the back.

"No, Chi's phone is ringing on that side. He hasn't answered it. Chi has to be with Atticus."

Dr. Thomas peered down at Gwen. He held out his hand for the phone and closed it, cutting off the music. "He took his jacket off when – he left his phone in his jacket when he changed jackets."

He led them into a huge white room divided into four sections by curtains. The back left section was closed; the other three were empty.

"Chi, Gwen's here." Thomas called softly.

Chi stepped through the curtains and took Gwen's arms. She pushed him aside and shoved through the curtains.

Atticus lay pale and unconscious on the examining table. His jeans were soaked with blood and his shirt was off. A fresh scar puckered his flesh just left of his navel.

"Atticus?" she whispered, taking his hand in both of hers and kissing his brow. "Atticus."

His eyes opened. He looked around in confusion.

"What happened?"

"I was hoping you could tell me." Chi stood beside the table.

"You and I were talking, and then I felt this incredible pain right here." Atticus jerked his head, trying to see what his fingers had discovered.

"Gwen," Chi's frown deepened. "Care to enlighten us?"

"I was dreaming. Oh, Atticus. I didn't know he could hurt you. I didn't know he was a dream walker."

"Sanchor did this?"

Gwen nodded. "He stabbed you in my dream."

"But I wasn't asleep. I was wide awake, talking to Chi."

"How much damage did the sword do?"

Chi shook his head. "None. He has an entry and an exit wound, completely sealed with scar tissue, and he lost what at the time seemed to be a great deal of blood. He passed out from the pain. But he seems fine now. I was about to do a sonogram to determine if there is any internal bleeding."

"Hop us here next to me, Gwen. We'll let Chi do your sonogram at the same time." Atticus grinned, trying to allay her fears.

Gwen giggled and then burst into tears. Atticus pulled her against his chest and rubbed her back.

Chi stepped through the curtains as Taralyn was putting away her phone. "I called Dad, and he's going to call Visolela. She's probably frantic that you haven't answered your phone."

"Thank you." He asked Dr. Thomas to proceed with

the sonogram and took Taralyn's arm. They walked in silence until they entered his office. "Taralyn, what is a dream walker?"

"It's someone that can enter someone else's dream-state and manipulate the dreamer's thoughts. Like Atticus. He would be considered a dream walker."

"That is what I thought. I have been studying this dreaming phenomenon. Many peoples have this ability in their culture. Some peoples have dream walkers who are benevolent, guiding and fore-warning their family members about future events. For some, these dream walkers appear simply as ghosts or unfamiliar visitors, passing through without effecting anything." Gwen interjected, "But some dream walkers are evil, and can kill people in their sleep."

"Do you truly believe this is so?"

Gwen tilted her head, pensively. "Yes. I think so." Chi nodded. "This Sanchor, he can injure the dreamer. He severely bruised Gwen's ribs last week. And now Atticus."

"I'm sure we can find out more about dreaming. You know – how to protect the good guys." Taralyn paled slightly, "How to stop the bad guys."

Chi nodded wearily. "I have seen many things in my life, but never anything like this."

"You dreamed of Atticus, and he was real. I did, too. All of us elders did. So it shouldn't be a surprise that there are others out there that can do the same thing. As a matter of fact, I wondered if we could learn how."

"Why would you want to enter someone else's

dreams?" His cell phone began playing *Ode to Joy* again.

"Well," she pointed at his phone. "To improve communications, in emergencies."

Chi scowled and answered his phone.

Chapter 36
The Date

Taralyn's father opened their front door. She hugged him, "Everything's alright. Sorry I'm late."

"I'm glad you were there to help."

She bobbed her head sheepishly.

"Well, forget the exciting stuff, how was choir? Did they miss me?"

"Doug, oh my gosh! I've got your car." She held out his keys.

He handed her his watch, took his keys, grinned, and left.

"He gave me his watch?"

"Doug made some decisions tonight."

"Decisions? What decisions?"

"Whom to serve."

Taralyn's mouth gaped open.

"We prayed, after talking a great deal."

"You prayed with Doug."

"I think two men who love the same women should pray together."

Her head jerked as if she'd been slapped.

Tyler placed his hands on his daughter's shoulders.

"As long as you live in my house, you will live by my rules."

Taralyn opened her mouth to speak, but shut it again.

"You have a date with Doug March the seventh."

"That's six months from now."

"I know."

"I turn eighteen on March the sixth."

"I do recall your date of birth."

"This is so lame. So archaic. So third-world chastity-belt male dominance crap!"

"My house, my rules."

A light glimmered in Taralyn's eyes. "I can still see him at the complex and at choir and church?"

"Yes."

"Well," Taralyn hugged her dad. "OK."

"OK?" Tyler stepped back. "Just like that, OK?"

"Sure, Dad. Your house, your rules." She shrugged innocently and headed to her room. "But you know I'm going to dream about him."

"Well, sweet dreams, kitten."

"I love you, Dad."

"Love you, too."

Chapter 37
The Things Which Change

Doug sat ready at the drums Sunday morning, trying to wipe away the cobwebs of the most wonderful dream he'd ever had. He and Taralyn sat side by side on a porch swing. They did nothing other than that, but he had his arm around her shoulders and she rested her head against him. They stayed that way, talking about all sorts of things, but Doug couldn't remember what, exactly.

Taralyn walked in with Tyler and sat on their pew. Mitchell, Ormed and Gilga sat beside them. Taralyn smiled shyly at Doug, as if she knew what he was thinking and feeling. The whole church faded away as he drank in her smile.

Mrs. Perkins with a violin, Matt with a trumpet, three clarinet players and a woman with an English recorder sat together on the front row behind the piano. Eduviges glanced at the musicians. She held up one finger; two; three. They began to play *How Great Thou Art* for the introit.

The refugees filled the pews, sidling in next to the regular attendees. People nodded at the strangers with friendly curiosity.

Atticus stood and raised his hands. "I welcome you. I welcome all of you, in the name of my Lord and Savior Jesus, Bringer of Light. I welcome you in the name of our Father, who is the Light. Who made the heavens and set the planets in order. May you find what you seek here. Peace, joy, love, sanctuary. These things are gifts freely given within this place. You can have them, if you so choose."

Patsy stood at the presbytery and led the congregation in *Sweet Sweet Spirit*. Doug closed his eyes and played the drums as if he felt every note in his soul.

Atticus stood again and began to preach. "Changes. We face them every day. They didn't have the cornflakes that you liked at the grocery store, so you had to try something new. You liked the new brand of cereal so much that your waist has changed and your pants are tight. Children come into families, and that's a change. Death causes changes, too. Take a look in the mirror each morning, and you will see changes there; we age. The way we look at the world changes. Look at the changes computers have made in the last twenty years. Pluto used to be a planet when I was growing up. We had the technology to land on the moon, and then that changed, and we lost that knowledge. A thousand years ago, Galileo put forth an idea which changed the way we looked at the universe. Two thousand years ago, a man willingly allowed himself to be crucified and that changed the way we look at life eternal."

He stepped away from the pulpit and pointed into the body. "Last Sunday, long awaited visitors arrived, and changed the way we perceived our place in this church, in this world, maybe even in this universe. And we definitely changed the way they looked at their world." He smiled warmly.

Glancing at a pale and swollen Gwen, sitting behind the ad lib orchestra, knowing that she had slept very little in the last six days, Atticus grew serious. "Things change. Ironically, change is a constant characteristic of life. Birth, love, marriage, generosity, adventure, sanctuary, friendship, trust, sacrifice – these are good changes and lead to times of glory and light. Death, betrayal, victimization, ruin, hatred, despair – these are bad changes and lead to dark times.

"There's not a soul in this place who hasn't experienced both kinds of change." Atticus turned back to the pulpit, giving them time to think.

Slowly enunciating each word, Atticus stated, "God changes not."

"Selah!" Ricean spoke out.

"There was a horrible accident last night, just this side of Atlanta. Maybe you heard about it. Two busloads of children crashed and none survived. What a horrible change for every family, friend, church, and school touched by this tragedy. But it didn't change God. He is the Word. He is the beginning. He is the End. He changes not."

Atticus paced. "Be still and know that I am God. That's what He tells us to do when we question Him. Why did this happen, God? Why did this death occur?

Why did this act of hatred persist? Why did the evil act triumph? Why war? Why rape? Why famine? Why pestilence and disease? Why, God, why?"

He drew a deep breath. "And God answers, 'Shhh. Hush now. Be still.'"

"But it's not fair!" Atticus wailed. He stepped down from the altar and whispered, "Hush, child. You weren't with me when I formed the heavens. Be still. You didn't see the architectural plans I designed for the vast oceans and underground rivers. Sh, you weren't with me at the beginning, and you won't be with me at the end. You can't see what I see."

Atticus sighed, "But God, it's not fair. And God, who doesn't change, puts His hand on your heart and says, 'Peace, Doug. Be still, Ormed. Know that I am God, Atticus. I will be revered by nations, Rutger. I will be exalted over all the earth," he looked directly at a man in the back, "Morgan. For I will not leave you, Gwen. Nor forsake you, Children of Jol. Until I have done that which I have spoken to you of."

"Be still and know that I am God, for I change not. I will keep my promises, through all the wonderful changes, through all the wars and famines and evil changes. Because I don't change. I already AM." Atticus nodded at Patsy and Eduviges and sat behind his pulpit.

Patsy gestured at Taralyn as Eduviges adjusted her music. Taralyn stood, suddenly pale, and walked up the steps to the presbytery. She looked over her shoulder at Doug and smiled fleetingly at her father. Drawing a deep breath, Taralyn nodded at Eduviges, who began to play.

Taralyn's voice was light and crystal clear, "Why should I feel discouraged, why should the shadows come? Why should my heart be lonely, and long for heaven and home? When Jesus is my portion, my constant friend is He; His eye is on the sparrow, and I know He watches me. His eye is on the sparrow, and I know He watches me."

As Taralyn began the second verse, "Let not your hearts be troubled," Doug' vision blurred. He heard a soft plink on the drums and glanced down, surprised to see tear drops on the head. Doug fought back his tears until, during the third verse, Taralyn sang, *when hope within me dies*. He buried his face in his hands and surrendered.

Eduviges swirled her arm around her head after the third verse and everyone repeated the chorus. "I sing because I'm happy. I sing because I'm free. His eye is on the sparrow, and I know He watches me."

Doug felt a hand on his shoulder and knew Atticus was praying for him. It was like nothing he'd ever felt before. His sinuses seemed to open as if he were about to sneeze. Then his scalp tingled and the sensation swept down his spine and he shivered. Gasping for breath, hoping that sneeze would climax, shaking uncontrollably, Doug felt Atticus' grip tighten. Focusing on the sensation, fighting it, Doug almost regained control of his emotions. Almost. Doug's ears popped, and he felt as if a great pressure had been equalized between the outside world and his internal self. Doug stopped shaking. Atticus relaxed his grip, giving his shoulder one soft pat before he returned to the pulpit.

The congregation settled back down as the music faded. Taralyn beamed and sat next to her father. Doug was by her side in an instant and everyone shifted to make room for him. He put his arm around her, just as he had done in last night's dream and whispered, "You make me believe in angels."

Atticus stood before them, solemn and powerful. "We stand on the brink of change. Every day, we stand at the cusp between light and dark, between life and death, between good and evil. The people of Jol have a saying, *The door opens; the dance begins.*"

As a whole, they responded, "Selah!"

"When the change comes, how will you choose?"

Doug gripped Tyler's shoulder on the other side of Taralyn and took her hand. Matt stood up with his hands lifted in praise.

Atticus stepped down and held out his hand to Gwen, who joined him at the front. "Whom will you serve?"

The Jols replied with Gwen as one, "I serve the Light, the bringers of Light, and the Light eternal."

"Another way to say that – for those who believe – I believe in God the Father almighty, Maker of heaven and earth, and in Jesus Christ His only son, our lord." Most of the congregation joined him to complete the Apostle's Creed.

"If you serve the light," Atticus raised his hand. "If you serve God, then you know that where God is, is holy. This is holy ground, and nothing, neither life nor death, nor principalities, nor things present nor things to

come - to sum it up – nothing that changes – can separate us from the love of God." Atticus glowed with power. "Stand. Take the hand of your fellow servants. Sister Eduviges, *This is Holy Ground*!"
She began the chords immediately as the church body began to sing. They sang it through three times.

"May God the Father, God the Son, God the Holy Spirit; God the Light, Jesus the Bringer of Light, and the Holy Spirit of Eternal Light be with you, now and always, and bring you peace. Amen."

Eduviges began *Onward Christian Soldiers* as the congregation filed past Gwen and Atticus at the door.

Outside, the sun had never seemed so bright to Doug. The fresh October air burst with a crispness he never recalled before. He embraced Atticus and then Gwen. Tyler took one elbow and Taralyn the other and led him into the parking lot.

Colonel Morgan Forest straightened from where he'd been leaning against Doug's Mustang. "A word, alone," was all he said.

"Change," Tyler spoke the word softly. He took Taralyn and they moved just out of earshot.

"We haven't received a report from you in a week. We were worried." Morgan stood balanced before the much younger man.

"Gee, how sweet. I didn't know you cared." Doug glanced around him for hidden shootists.

"I don't give a flying fuck about you. You've been compromised. You're useless here. Pack up and hope that there's a job waiting for you when you return."

"No. And I'll thank you to mind your language."

"What?"

"No, sir." Doug saluted. "I have a job here."

"With this bunch of lunatics?" Morgan snorted.

Doug shook his head, "Chief of Security for Tyler's business."

"Pretty girl," Morgan slanted his eyes. "As I recall, her mother was very beautiful, too."

Doug swallowed his unspoken retort.

Both men's faces contorted in reaction to a hideous odor.

"Ukera!" a child of Jol screamed. "Ukera!"

Swords flashed in the sunlight and long staffs suddenly swirled about people's heads.

"Staffs of Atticus, to me!" Gwen yelled.

"Swords of Jol, to me!" Ricean shouted.

"Hands of Atticus, to me!" Doug commanded.

"Weapons to me!" Jarmille ran into the fellowship hall to unlock the weapon's closet.

"Get the children into the church! Anyone without a weapon, get into the church. Now!" Atticus' voice carried above the bedlam.

"They come!" Ricean pointed at the dirt road leading to the sanctuary.

The ukera came first, with its featureless head, wobbling as it searched out the children's heartbeats. Ten paces behind the creature came a band of one-hundred men dressed in flowing black capes, burnished breast plates and cockaded helmets.

"Taralyn," Atticus shouted, "Take the Saplings and form a circle around the sanctuary. No one gets inside, no matter what."

"Yes, Atticus!" She had pulled her battle staff out of her car and positioned her fifty saplings around the church.

"Visolela, you get inside and barricade the doors and windows. Don't let them inside!"

"Yes, Atticus!" She yelled over Kayien's squalls.

"Healers, stay alert! Help anyone who falls."

Rawan, Chi and Thomas and a half-dozen nurses shouted they were ready.

"Swords, flank from the north. Crush them into Gwen's Staffs. But stay out of the way of Jermille's weapons." Atticus stood in the center of the parking lot, the general on the field. "Doug, take your Hands and mix in with the Saplings. They defend, you kill."

"Yes, sir." Without a thought, Doug led his Hands away from Morgan.

"Jarmille, kill the ukera, but don't hit its head."

A volley sounded from the roof of the fellowship hall where Jarmille and his six trainees were kneeling. The ukera stumbled backwards as his chest exploded.

Something flashed from the dark soldiers and Jarmille cussed in surprise. A silver bolt had imbedded itself in his stomach. He fell sideways off the roof and sprawled dead on the sidewalk.

Morgan looked at the encroaching army and then at the poorly trained civilians around him who were desperately trying to protect the children inside the church. In an instant, everything changed for Morgan. He chose. Sprinting to the fallen man, he jerked the AK47 from his grip and, scrambling up a trellis the others had used for a ladder, vaulted onto the roof. "Alright you bible-thumping Baptists, automatic weapons won't pierce the armor of these guys. I know – we've tried! So, aim for the soft spots and target the ones carrying crossbows," he commanded and the Weapons of Atticus obeyed. The bullets bounced off the armor and helmets but found purchase in the exposed necks. As seven archers fell, the dark soldiers were too close to the citizens for Morgan to risk any further weaponry. "Look for chances to pick them off individually, but do not chance killing a civilian."

Ricean's swords attacked from the north and fought hand to hand against the Dark Swords. Her twenty-seven Swords were pitifully outnumbered, but she drew them away from the church as much as she could.

Gwen grew still, centering herself as the Dark Soldiers came within range. She didn't recognize any of them; for that she was thankful. She called over her shoulders, "They will enjoy hurting you. And what they will do to the children is unspeakable. You cannot let them through us. Kill swiftly. Kill with every blow you give. They will not show the children mercy."

Matt growled deep from his chest.

The soldiers fell on them, but the Staffs of Atticus held.

Doug pummeled his opponent to the ground and bent double to catch his breath. He heard a woman cry out and knew instantly it was Taralyn. A soldier shook her tiny body above him, one hand on her throat, the other ripping his claws down her chest. Doug sprang across five fighting pairs and grabbed the man by his chin and the back of his head. With a grunt, Doug snapped his neck. He put his hand on Taralyn's throat, feeling desperately for a pulse. "Medic!" he screamed.

He stayed by her unconscious form and fought.

Atticus surveyed the battle from his spot in the parking lot. There were too many of the enemy soldiers. There were too few of the Jols. His people were too inexperienced. The preacher felt the world shift, as he often felt when deep in prayer, and looked at the battle as if from above himself, far away. The Angel of the Lord stood beside him, observing the slaughter. Sometimes the Angel looked like a child, other times, the Angel was a woman. A few times, the Angel had been bent with age. Now, in the blinding light which always surrounded him in the Angel's presence, Atticus thought he saw a huge white buffalo with a horned mane and massive hooves standing next to a young girl. The Light infuriated him. "Tell me what to do!" Atticus raged.

"Don't you know?" The Angel's voice was tender, calm, soothing.

Atticus became angrier still. "No! Tell me! You brought me here, now use me. Tell me what to do."

The Angel's voice lingered as the brilliance faded. "Pray."

On the parking lot, Atticus fell to his knees. The elders sensed it immediately and added their strength to his. In the center of the soldiers, a white circle formed. It shimmered in the afternoon light and grew larger until it was the size of a door. The color became too brilliant to look at directly, but men began to tumble through it from wherever the other side was.

Shouts of, "Whom do you serve?" filled the dirt road. And dark soldiers began to fall.

As Morgan watched from the rooftop, occasionally picking off an isolated soldier, he saw what couldn't be real – again. In combat, Morgan had learned to act first, react later. He filed away what he saw; he would consider the fantastic events after he survived the day.

"There's another one," Eduviges pointed.

The circle formed behind the enemy, almost to the main highway, but this circle was black.

"It looks like someone punched a hole into night," Vargas commented.

"It's a hole back to their world," Eduviges surmised aloud.

"Are more soldiers gonna come through that black hole, like they did the white one?" Le'Vander squeaked.

Morgan made a decision. "Aim for the black hole. Don't let anyone in or out."

"Out of range!"

"Follow me!" Morgan led his small group off the backside of the fellowship hall, around the south of the church and stationed themselves between the fighting and the hole.

Three dark soldiers made a run for the portal and were hit. A gauntlet reached from the other side of the portal and clawed at the air. Eduviges fired round after round from her M16 into the blackness. Lighter than the AK47, with much less of a kick, the smaller bullets were still extremely effective against the invaders. A dozen more dark soldiers retreated toward the dark door and were eliminated by Morgan's team.

Crossbolts flew out of the dark opening. "Down!" Morgan warned.

"Sweet Jesus," Vargus pitched forward, grasping at a silver bolt sticking out of his shoulder.

"Medic!" Morgan shouted. He pointed at Le'Vander. "Don't let him pull that out."

Two more soldiers were at the edge of the hole, scrambling to leave this world. It was only big enough for one man at a time, but they fought each other, each trying to go first. Morgan fired, hitting both of them. One fell backward to the road. The other fell forward into the darkness. The Door of Despair winked for a moment and then disappeared.

For three heart beats, Morgan looked around him. They had won. What few soldiers were left were being dispatched by the people with swords. The preacher was getting to his feet. The people with sticks were standing facing out with their sticks shoulder high, but parallel with the ground. Moans swirled around him, along with cries for medic and healer. Dead soldiers and church members spread before him.

He heard the preacher's voice. "Rawan, set up a triage in the fellowship hall, like you did before."

Before? Morgan wondered.

"Rutger, organize transportation of the wounded to the clinic. Chi and Thomas will meet you there. Saplings, help carry the wounded into the hall." Atticus took a deep breath. "No! Don't open the sanctuary yet. Not until we're sure they won't come back. Once the wounded are at the clinic, we'll transport the children to the compound. Visolela! Do not open the doors yet."

"Yes, Preacher!" came a shaky voice from inside the church.

"Hands, Staffs, Swords, and Weapons," He pointed to each group. "Hold your positions."
Patsy squatted beside Doug and Taralyn. He held her in a fierce embrace. "Is she OK?"

Doug nodded, unable to find the words.

"I just got knocked out," Taralyn whispered hoarsely.

"Well, I hate to take you out of the arms of such a good-looking man, but preacher said all wounded go to the fellowship hall."

"No, I'm fine. I'll stay here."

"No," Doug turned her face up to his. "You'll do as you're told. Atticus said it. Do it."

Taralyn gulped painfully. Doug kissed her for what seemed the tenth time, since the fighting had stopped and then helped her stand. She wobbled on her feet and Patsy helped lead her away.

"Hands, Weapons, clear the road," Atticus commanded.

The two teams sprang forward, dragging the dead off to the sides. Morgan and Doug's teams met in the middle. Morgan helped Doug carry a corpse off the road. "I want answers."

Doug grinned mischievously. "I think you found your answer, Colonel. What you want are details."

Morgan frowned and then nodded.

"You're not alone. I have no idea what just happened here. I'd hate to be in charge of our debriefing."

Morgan groaned and rolled his eyes.

The two men stepped aside as four pickups made their way to the highway, loaded with wounded.

"Come on, I'll introduce you to Atticus and Gwen." Doug glanced back at his team. "Stay with the Weapons. Keep vigil. We'll be back."

Atticus and Gwen held each other while surveying the battle field. "Gwen, Atticus, this is Colonel Morgan Forest. He works for IIA and is in charge of the project that I used to -- I spied for." Doug' voice drifted away as he watched Morgan squint at the preacher.

Atticus said nothing.

Morgan snorted and then peered at him again. "You look different now. Different from the pictures I've seen of you. Different from this morning even, in the church." The colonel took a step closer. He wanted to say, *I know you.* He wanted to confess, *I dreamt of you. You used to sit next to me and talked to me in my dreams when I kept vigil beside my wife's hospital bed.* Morgan shook his head and remained silent.

As if the preacher could read his thoughts, Atticus nodded gently. "When you're ready, Morgan, we'll talk again."

"I know you, Colonel." Gwen offered.

"I tried to interview you in Tacoma."

Gwen nodded and then shook her head. "No. It's more than that. I can't remember exactly, but we've met before."

Morgan straightened and looked her in the eyes. "You threw up on my shoes eighteen years ago."

A tall muscular blonde man stepped forward. His skirt was soft leather, his chest bare. He carried a staff and a wooden sword. "You opened the door into my world."

Atticus nodded.

"I am Shallon of the Faleavers. These are my brothers." He pointed at the three dozen men behind him. "I serve the light."

"As do we, Shallon of the Faleavers. I am Gwen Staff Bearer of Atticus. This is Doug Hand of Atticus. The woman over there with black braids is Ricean Sword of Jol. This is Atticus Priest of God."

Shallon peered at them all. "We were out hunting. And the circle of light appeared."

"Thank God you were there, to come here and fight," Gwen commented.

"The door opens, the dance begins. It has always been this way." Shallon shrugged. "But, Atticus of God, what have you done with the moons?"

"The what?" Doug asked.

"The moons: the Three Sisters." He pointed above the church's roof line. "It is autumn now, and the moons are all together in the sky until the first spring rains. But they're not there now."

Morgan exhaled with a chuckle. "Change. Things change, Shallon of Faleavers." He put his hand out to the confused man. "I am Morgan Forrest. I guess I'm Morgan Weapon of Atticus."

Chapter 38
The Dead

The wounded had all been attended and those who needed it were in the clinic on the compound. The children and church members were eating in the cafeteria. The elders sat together at the back table with Ricean, Shallon, Doug and Morgan.

"What do we do with all the dead?" Rutger asked. Ninety-nine dark soldiers lay inside the shell of what was to become the new church. Tarps, sheets and blankets covered their faces.

Matt supplied an answer. "We use the bulldozer to dig a mass grave."

"They had souls," Gwen growled.

"We'll give them a proper burial." Sara assured her. "But we better do it tonight. There's a hundred bodies out there."

"There's more. Some of our own died, too." Tyler looked around.

Doug slid his hand over Taralyn's under the table. Atticus sighed, "The bodies of our friends were brought here. The doctors will fill out death certificates to be legally filed. We'll bury our friends in the cemetery

Wednesday just before church."

"I have a suggestion," Tyler raised his hand. "There are four of us to be buried. If we have a common funeral for our soldiers during the evening service, with internment thereafter, and then everyone came back here for a meal, that would be about all we could handle – emotionally."

Atticus gritted his teeth and looked down.

Sara spoke gently. "Pete Vargus and Mandy Reeves are from Morning Creek and all their families are here. One of the Swords of Jol died, and Jarmille. So the only one who might have family to travel here is your cousin, Eduviges. Is Wednesday too soon to set his funeral?"

Eduviges blinked and focused as if she'd been far away. "We're not much on family reunions. Our gatherings tend to attract Feds and other lowly creatures."

Morgan glanced askance at Doug, but acknowledged Eduviges's remark with a nod.

"I'll notify my uncle, but he'll agree with the arrangements I make."

Morgan took a cell phone out of his pocket and opened it with feigned innocence. "Eduviges, if you'll give me Uncle Shiloh's phone number or maybe his street address, I'd be more than willing to contact him."

"Hey," Gwen snapped. "We lost family here today. You may not know what that's like, but you need to back off."

Atticus held up his hand. "Morgan knows what that's like. He's not being insensitive; he's just trying to hide the pain of memories."

Morgan turned beet red and glared first at Atticus, then the ceiling. After a silent moment, Eduviges stated, "I forgive you."

Morgan cleared his throat and reached to shake her outstretched hand. She snatched the phone and flipped it closed. "But you're not getting his phone number."

The elders chuckled.

Gwen stretched and rolled her head on her shoulders. "We have so much to talk about. But most of it needs to be set aside for the time being. Ricean Sword of Jol, would you show Shallon of the Faleavers and his brothers to the barracks and teach them how to live safely within it?"

"I shall do so with honor."

"Tyler, we need the security system up and running tonight."

"After what I saw today, proximity alerts are useless if the door opens inside the compound."

Doug interjected, "But we can post guards."

"Whatever it takes, I want this compound secure by nightfall."

"Yes, ma'am." Tyler promised.

"I can help. I can get twenty-five sentries posted here within the hour." Morgan offered.

"No." Atticus spoke without looking up. "No strangers inside the compound. Tyler and Doug can secure the facility. Morgan may get his men to patrol outside the perimeter. If we find anyone inside the fence who doesn't serve the light, they will be killed."

Morgan shrugged as if Atticus' threat meant nothing. "You're the boss."

"Yes, Morgan," Atticus speared the colonel with a look that brooked no insolence. "I am the boss. I am Atticus of God. If we find anyone inside the fence who doesn't serve the light, they will be killed."

"And that includes me."

"Does it? Whom do you serve, Morgan?" Atticus held Morgan's wrist in a tight grip.

Morgan felt like he couldn't breathe, like he was underwater and the surface with its waiting oxygen was too far above him to be of any use. He looked at this man, this Atticus of God. He found he had gotten to his feet while all the others gaped up at him in alarm. Morgan shivered and felt his ears pop, readjusting to some barometric change within him. He heard himself say, "I am Morgan Weapon of Atticus. I serve the Light."

Doug cheered, the rest of the people at the table seemed pleased. Morgan sank to his chair again, exhausted, and drew a deep breath.

Releasing Morgan's wrist, Atticus looked at Gwen. "What time is it?"

"Six twenty-five."

Atticus stood slowly. "Time for church."

The elders gawked at him.

"Church. Then we come back here to bury the dark soldiers. Matt, do you mind skipping church tonight and get started with the bull dozer?"

"I'll do it, Atticus. There's a nice stretch of pasture land at the bottom of the compound. By tomorrow morning, it'll just look like a newly plowed field."

Juan stepped forward from a nearby table, "Can I help?"

Matt blinked and for some reason blushed. "Sure."

"Atticus Priest of God," Ricean held up her hand. "This is your land. These are your people. This was your battle and your victory."

Atticus didn't respond. Her words were like spears of guilt in his heart; he didn't want her to see that. She was used to battle and victory and death; he didn't want to own the weight of it all.

Ricean paled. "There are many differences between our people. I have no desire to offend you."

"I get one-third," Shallon declared.

"Have you no respect? This is not your land." Ricean growled.

"Atticus gets one-half of the weapons. Ricean gets one-fourth of them as does Shallon." Gwen settled the matter. "Elder Rutger and Elder Mitchell will divide them."

"What do a child and an ancient bag of bones know of weaponry?" Shallon snarled.

"Rutger may not know swords, but he knows the hearts of men. Mitchell hears the words you speak, but listens to your soul." Gwen spoke firmly.

The looks Shallon gave Rutger and Mitchell were equally nervous and appraising. "Agreed."

"I will not have us profit from killing," Atticus growled.

"It's not profit, not like grave robbing or anything. These people hold back the dark. They need to replace and replenish what weaponry they have."

"Why bury a perfectly good sword, that is what I say," Shallon added.

"Money, jewelry, personal items – they remain with the deceased," Atticus stated.

"Unless the jewelry is a weapon, too," Ricean bargained.

"How could jewelry be a weapon?" Shallon asked.

"Oh." Ricean calmed her features into a look of innocence. "Like a wedding band."

Shallon laughed and then bent double to laugh harder. Ricean smiled with her lips only.

"Atticus," Gwen began. "Atticus of God, we should collect all of their personal items – including jewelry – to help build the compound."

Atticus glared at her and noticed Ricean was holding her breath. "All right."

"Then the Faleavers get a full portion of the weapons, since –"

"Shut up," Rutger pointed at him. Shallon bristled but fell silent.

"It's past time for the evening service," Atticus rubbed his face where his five o'clock shadow as darkest.

Tyler asked, "Couldn't we hold the service here, Pastor? We're all here and we're coming back here." Atticus sighed and nodded.

"We could meet on the exercise field."

Atticus nodded again.

Gwen took her time standing up. "Spread the word. Fifteen minutes, everyone to be on the parade ground except Elder Mitchell, Elder Rutger, Shallon of the Faleavers, Ricean of Jol, and Matt and Juan, Staffs of Atticus."

"Amen," Eduviges clapped her hands.

Sara's husband leaned into her ear, "Are we going to have to call everyone by their full titles from now on?"

They walked away, but Atticus remained seated. Gwen put her hand on his shoulder and leaned against him.

"No, don't touch me." He pulled away. "I'm unclean. I stink of death."

She placed her hands on his cheeks and turned his face to look at her. "You smell of battle, fought and won. We all do. Now, they're waiting on you to tell them they fought bravely and killed for the right reason."

He took a shuddering breath, "I'm going to be sick."

She nodded, "Come on, the bathroom's not too far."

He stood and took her elbow. "No, I'll be alright." He pressed his hand over her abdomen. "How's the baby?"

She pressed his hand and walked with him outside. Men, women and children stood before him in the dimming light. He looked at each one while they swatted at mosquitoes and waited for him to speak. Finally, Atticus looked at Gwen and raised his hand. "You fought well today," he told them. "You lost friends and family today. You stood and faced the darkness and defended the light."

He lowered his hand and began to pace. "You fought well. We knew the war would come here. We prepared for it. We're still preparing for it. And I don't know about you, but I plan to pay much better attention tomorrow morning during our exercise."

"Amen," someone called out.

"Because of you, these children were safe. Because of you, and Pete Vargus and Mandy Reeves and Jarmille San Reyes and Siskret of Jol, these children have a chance to grow up."

Atticus cupped Gilga's face. "Jesus said that a man would be better off if someone tied a millstone around his neck and dropped him off into the deepest ocean -- better off – than if he hurt a child. Gwen tells me, uh, that's Gwen Staff of Atticus to you. Gwen tells me that the Dark soldiers would rather steal a dozen children than a thousand adults. She won't tell me what they do to children, but perhaps it is better – tonight – not to dwell on such things. Jesus knew the evil that is done to innocent children, no matter what world. He was very firm about it. We're a mite far from the ocean, so we're dropping the dead bodies in a hole. Elder Matt is digging back yonder."

A few people shuffled nervously.

"This has been a terrible day. War has reared its ugly face. We've been waiting for it, dreaming about it, preparing for it. But today, it came." Atticus cleared his throat, struggling to remain calm. "And it will come back."

"Gwen, my lovely wife-to-be, will train you well, but

don't put your trust in her."

Several people jumped in surprise.

"Don't. She's a woman. She's flesh and blood. Don't put your trust in her."

Gwen stared at the top of her belly, frowning.

"I used to think guns could blast through anything. But they didn't. The armor the dark solders wore was impenetrable. If it hadn't been for excellent marksmanship of Jarmille's team, and Morgan, we would have suffered more losses today. But don't put your trust in their marksmanship, or their weaponry.

"Ricean and her Swords gave as good as they got. But don't put your trust in her or her swords.

"Same goes with our new friends, Shallon and his three dozen brothers. They were there when they were needed, and fought for our side, and the day would have been lost if not for them. But don't put your trust in them.

"Doug and his Hands, Taralyn and her Saplings. These children right now would have been suffering the vilest tortures and inhumanities you could ever imagine if not for their courage, their strength. Your perseverance." Atticus touched Doug and Taralyn as they stood arm in arm. "But don't put your trust in them."

Atticus turned and looked between the buildings at the setting sun. He turned back to face them, eyes cruel with anger. "And don't you dare put your trust in me."

Not a few people shifted uncomfortably, fingering their weapons.

Atticus began to sing. "Turn your eyes upon Jesus. Look well in His wonderful face. And the ills of the world will grow strangely dim. I can't remember the rest of the words."

"In the light of His glory and grace," supplied a few voices.

Atticus changed tunes, "Trust and obey, for there's no other way, to be happy in Jesus, but to trust and obey. That's another one. And this one: A mighty fortress is our God, a stalwart never failing. You know what a stalwart is? Me neither. Doesn't matter." Atticus swatted at a bug. "Today was just a taste of what is to come. If you don't put your trust in God, we'll never survive. We were – each one of us –sent here to hold back the Dark. The only way we can do that is to put all of our faith and hope and trust in God Almighty, Maker of Heaven and Earth."

Atticus' voice broke and he stopped.

From the middle of the group, Eduviges began to sing, "Amazing Grace, how sweet the sound."

Patsy joined her in the next phrase, and soon most of the Earthers were singing and the off-worlders were humming or wordlessly singing along. Those who weren't singing were crying. The verses ended and Atticus raised his hands in blessing. "May the Lord bless you and keep you. May the Lord lift up his countenance upon you, and give you peace."

Everyone responded with either *Amen* or *Selah*.

"Now, we're all going into the new church and work together to take the dead to their graves. And when they're all in there, we're going to pray over them, because they had souls."

They drove the two short miles home in silence. Atticus pulled into the drive and a light rain began to fall. He went straight into the bathroom, leaving Gwen to lock up and turn on the lights. She peered into the pantry and fridge, but couldn't find anything of interest to her. She woke up on the couch when she heard Atticus finally exiting the bathroom. All the hot water had been depleted, but she'd bathed in plenty of cold lakes the three years she had spent on the other world. After her shower, she put on a cotton gown and crawled in beside Atticus. He usually tucked himself around her, but tonight he lay flat on his back, staring blankly at the ceiling.

"Good night, Atticus."

He grunted in reply.

When she awoke, she wasn't sure what the sound was. The bed trembled and heaved while a soft mewling filled her ears. Gwen sat up and reached out for Atticus. The sounds were emanating from him.

She pulled him to a sitting position and grabbed his face. "They fought well. They won the day."

"They died." He pushed her away, but she came right back.

"What did you think would happen?"

"They trusted me." He sank his fingers into her arms.

"Yes, they did. You're their pastor; they're supposed to trust you."

"But they died!" he screamed.

"Won't we all?" Her soft words startled him. "Isn't

that the end of this journey we call life? We all die.
And then we go on."

Atticus gulped between sobs. "I know that. But –"

"Mourn each death, but do not despair. That's a
scripture on Gith. Mourn each death, but do not
despair."

"I loved them," Atticus pleaded.

She kissed his cheeks, "Hush Atticus. Of course you
loved them."

"They trusted me."

She kissed his eyelids. "Of course they did. We all
do."

"I could just have easily been you who died." His
fingers dug into her flesh.

"It may be me the next time. And you will mourn
be, but do not despair." She kissed his lips. "I am
eternal, only this body will die."

"Don't die," he kissed her back. "Don't die, Gwen."
"I love you, Atticus." She straddled his lap and
surrendered to his kisses.

"Love you, Gwen," he mumbled passionately
around her lips.

She heard her gown rip and couldn't stop her
hands or his as they stroked and fondled their way
around each other's bodies. It was awkward at first,
because she was six months pregnant, but she found
her way. He was inside her as she rocked in his lap.
She soared, gasping, and coasted through the clouds.
He came quickly, but held her and caressed her until
she was complete in him. He cradled her in his arms as
she fell back down to earth.

Chapter 39
The Contractor

"What's an ebenezar?" Mitchell forced himself between Taralyn and Doug as they walked together to breakfast after the morning exercises.

"An ebenezer?" Taralyn repeated.

"Yeah. I know who Ebenezer was, but not want an ebenezer is." Mitchell took their hands.

"How was it used?" Taralyn asked.

"Juan said that Atticus looked like he'd been raising his ebenezer."

Doug stumbled.

Taralyn's face grew red, "It's a song. A hymn. It's from (she sang the tune) Come thou fount of every blessing."

Doug coughed and choked.

"It's a hymn?"

"Yep," Doug agreed, "It's definitely a 'him'-thing."

"Oh." Mitchell gave them both a suspicious look.

Doug shouted, "Hey Juan, cayote tu boca circumlo los ninos. Me compredes, Ebenezer?"

"Yo hablo espanol, moron," Mitchell kicked Doug. "I'll just go ask my mom."

"Yeah, you do that," Doug stopped to rub his shin.

"No, don't!" Taralyn turned red again, but didn't elaborate.

"Oh." Mitchell glanced back and forth between Taralyn and Doug. "There's a hymn about that? Gross!"

Tuesday afternoon, Atticus swung by the compound to check on the progress. The men were finishing their lunches and shouted greetings to him. He smiled and waved.

"Matt, can I have a minute?"

Matt pointed toward a piece of ply board across two sawhorses that served as the blueprint table.

"Come thou fount of every blessing," Juan's deep baritone rolled over the work site and his fellows joined in, "Tune my heart to sing thy praise."

"Knock it off!" Matt hollered, hands on hips.

Atticus' expression questioned Matt's unprovoked irritation at an old hymn.

"The community center, church and fellowship hall – and the school will be completed by Thanksgiving."

"That's wonderful," Atticus began.

Juan began again, "Rise up, ye men of God!"

"Shut up!" Matt was blue in the face.

His workers roared with laughter.

"Anything else?" Matt took a calming breath.

"Uh, no." Atticus glanced up at Doug, who had tears rolling down his face from laughing so much. "Um, I want the Elders to escort the families at the funeral tomorrow."

"Sure," Matt answered, but he was squinting his eyes up at Juan.

"Is everything alright, Matt?"

"Fine," he growled. "Just fine."

"Stand up, stand up for Jesus," Juan began one more time and Matt took off running. Juan squealed and ran the opposite direction with cries of "Lo siento! Lo siento!" as the construction workers burst out laughing again.

Chapter 40
The Lucid Dreaming

"See, then you tie this here, and pull it through the loop." Doug was showing his best friend how to tie a fly and weight onto their fishing poles.

A tall man in jeans, a white shirt and boots walked into the yard, stopping just in front of the steps leading up to the porch. The latest litter of puppies – fourteen of them – yapped and rolled and tugged around his feet. There were always puppies at Doug' house. Doug grinned down at the stranger. "Hi, Mister!"

"Hi," the stranger had a gentle smile. "I'm looking for Doug."

"I'm Doug!" He pointed proudly to himself.

Beside him, his best friend gasped, "Atticus?"

The stranger squinted, as if he couldn't see her very well. "Taralyn? What are you doing here? And why are you both six years old?"

Doug' best friend jumped to her feet, and as she stood, she grew from the six year old tomboy in cut offs and skinned knees to a really pretty teen-ager. Her cut offs switched to a short skirt and then flared out and down to her ankles. "Hey, I know you," Doug pointed up at her.

"Doug, we need to talk, but as adults." The stranger's voice and face were familiar. Doug trusted him.

"OK." Doug agreed, and instantly grew into the young man Atticus recognized. He stared in confusion at the fishing pole he held. He looked at the two people standing in front of him on the porch. "Taralyn? Atticus? This is a weird dream."

Atticus' face bore the marks of fury as he looked at Taralyn.

"It is a dream, Doug." Taralyn kept her eyes on Doug, ignoring Atticus. "It's a lucid dream."

"It seems so real."

"Parts of it are real. You, me, Atticus. We're real. We're in your dreams because," but she hesitated.

Atticus snorted, "I'm in your dream because I needed to speak with you. Alone. It's time."

Doug was so confused. "We were going fishing."

"We'll go fishing tomorrow." Taralyn took the pole from him and leaned it with hers against the railing.

"How did you do this?" Atticus' voice rumbled like thunder through Doug's dream.

Taralyn straightened her shoulders and was somehow older, taller, braver. "The same way you did. I learned how to dream walk."

"It's not something you can just decide to do." Atticus' jeans and shirt metamorphosed into a flowing white robe. Lightning streaked across the sky behind him. "It is a gift from God."

Taralyn crossed her arms. Her fingernails shaded to purple and her blond hair braided itself into a black

Nordic-like helmet. "It's not a gift from God. It's a talent, like singing or playing the piano. Or like preaching. I wanted to learn, so I googled it and read all I could about it and then I taught myself."

"Who do you think you are, playing with people's minds?" Atticus roared.

"What?" Doug shouted and the winds died down. "I'm dreaming, but you two are walking around in my dreams?"

"It's not like I'm trespassing. You like me being here."

"Yes, Taralyn, it is exactly like trespassing. You're violating my innermost privacy."

"I thought you liked it," She shrank to an eleven year old.

Doug had a look of horror on his face.

"You had no right to do this, Taralyn." Atticus stepped onto the porch.

"Wait! And you do?" Doug shook with outrage. "Everyone thinks you're God's chosen one. And it's nothing more than mind tricks a stupid teenager could learn."

Taralyn jerked backwards as if slapped.

"What's next? You going to part the Red Sea?"

"Don't talk to me that way," Atticus' body seemed to fade slightly.

"I'll talk to you anyway I want to. To both of you! Get out of my dream. Both of you! Get out!"

Doug bolted upright in bed, drenched in sweat and flipped on the bedside lamp. He looked at his wrist, remembering too late that he'd given his watch to Taralyn. He rubbed his face and got up. "What a bizarre dream," he mumbled to himself.

"Hey." Doug caught up with Taralyn the next morning. "I'll buy you a cup of coffee."

She glanced sheepishly at him. "You don't mind?"

He grinned and slung his arm around her shoulders. "Why should I mind?"

She shrugged, embarrassed.

"Hey Tyler," Doug beamed. "I was just going to buy this lovely little girl a cup of coffee. Why don't you join us?"

"Thanks." Tyler stepped in line. "You OK this morning, Taralyn?"

"Yeah. Sure." She nodded quickly. "Fine."

"Is something wrong?" Doug peered down at her. She shook her head.

"She had a nightmare last night and cried for a long while." Tyler explained.

Doug squeezed her shoulders. "Must have been a night for them. I had a horrible dream about us arguing. I can't remember why we were so mad, but it was just a dream." He kissed the top of her head. "They fade away with the morning."

Tyler pierced Doug with a look of warning. "There wasn't anyone named Ebenezer in either of your dreams, was there?"

"Good morning," Atticus stepped beside them and the three cracked up laughing. "What?"

"Sorry," Doug held out his hand. "Sorry, inside joke."

"Really sorry, Atticus." Tyler adjusted his glasses. "Nothing. How are you?"

"I need to talk to you, Taralyn, but I think Tyler and Doug should listen. My office won't be finished until Thanksgiving, but we can go back to the parsonage."

"I promised to take Mitchell and his brothers to the mall in Ithica Springs."

"You can call from my house and cancel it."

"That's not fair. Sara and Larry have been looking forward to a day alone." Taralyn crossed her arms, scowling.

Tyler and Doug exchanged confused glances.

"Do you want us to discuss it here?" Atticus' voice stayed low and calm.

Taralyn remained surly, but silent.

"Discuss what?" Tyler asked. "Atticus? Taralyn? What?"

The young woman's nostrils flared and she glared at the floor.

"Here or at the parsonage?"

"Fine!" Taralyn stomped away.

Gwen was toweling her hair as the door opened and the four walked in. "Hi!"

"Gwen, would you mind fixing another pot of coffee?" Atticus kissed her cheek.

"I made sweet rolls. I'll warm those up." Gwen smiled at the guests, who frowned in return.

"Have a seat." Atticus offered. Taralyn and Tyler took the couch, Doug the ottoman and Atticus the armchair.

"Taralyn, you need to tell us what you did."

"I didn't do anything wrong." Taralyn crouched at the edge of the couch.

Tyler put his hand on her arm, protectively.

"I didn't say it was wrong. I told you to explain your actions."

"You said it was wrong last night," she stabbed him with her words. Tyler paled as Doug reddened, both of them fighting their vivid imaginations.

"I got angry." Using that still small voice, Atticus continued. "You have to maintain an incredible amount of control in dreams. If you don't, it can be disastrous."

"Dreams?" Tyler asked.
"Nightmares," Doug concluded intuitively.

"If you don't tell them, I will."

Gwen leaned against the doorway between the living room and the kitchen, listening.

Tyler looked at Doug for support. "You can tell me anything, baby, you know you can."

"Absolutely," Doug agreed.

Taralyn lifted her head and straightened her shoulders. "I'm a dream walker."

"What's a dream walker?" Doug asked.

"It means I can enter someone's dreams and talk to them."

"May I just speak for those of us who haven't read *Twilight*, that's not possible," Doug scoffed.

"It is possible." Tyler assured him. "Atticus can do it. That's how I knew to come here. When Beth died, I went through the house and threw out every bottle of booze I had. And I had a lot of them. Did you know I was an alcoholic?"

"I knew you drank," Doug shrugged.

"It was more than that. Much more. I thought when Beth died I'd just crawl inside a bottle and die, too. But I didn't. I looked at Taralyn and chose hope instead of despair."

Taralyn squeezed his hand.

"And then I started having these really weird dreams. This man told me he needed my help. And he needed Taralyn's help, too."

"I convinced him to move here."

"In your dreams?"

"Yes." Tyler replied.

"And you can do this, too?" Doug asked Taralyn. "You can crawl around inside someone's head while they're asleep?"

Taralyn nodded and hung her head.

Atticus nodded.

Tyler cocked his head, looked back and forth between Taralyn and Doug, and then growled.

"My dreams?" Doug jumped up. "You've been in my dreams? I swear, Tyler, God! I swear, I never touched her! It's not my fault! I didn't touch you, did I? For God's sake, I was asleep!"

"Sit down," Atticus commanded.

"Taralyn, tell your father. I never touched you." Doug perched on the ottoman. "For God's sake, you're just a kid."

Taralyn gaped at Doug, shock vying with anger and hurt on her face.

Gwen quickly sat down beside Taralyn and took her hand. "Doug didn't mean it, Taralyn. If he really thought of you as a child, he wouldn't have panicked in his urgency to assure your father about your virginity."

"Virginity?" Tyler's face was purple.

"Well, that's what you three are so worried about, aren't you? You men can figure out what might happen when a woman wanders around in some man's dreams. Taralyn wasn't seeing the big picture. She just found a mystery, solved it, and used it to spend time with someone she obviously cares about."

"That's not the point," Atticus stated.

"I think that's a very valid point," Tyler contended.

"We were going fishing," Doug remembered.

Taralyn nodded.

"And we sat rocking on the porch, all night, just talking and making plans."

"That was Saturday night. I couldn't dream walk Sunday, because of the battle, but Monday night, you mentioned hiking in the woods, so I thought about it and the next thing I knew, we were hiking in Montana." Doug smiled, "Tuesday we went to the beach. It was beautiful. Crystal clear water, not a soul for miles."

"I saw a picture of Long Boat Key in Florida a few years ago. I've always wanted to go there. So I thought, why not?"

"Wednesday, you weren't in my dreams."

"I was too sad after the funeral."

"Thursday, we sat on the porch swings again, but it was different. We were old."

"I thought about what you'd look like in twenty

years. Suddenly, we were both old. So Friday night, I wondered what you were like as a little boy."

"And I taught you how to tie flies on fishing poles."

"See, Tyler. Sweet and innocent dates," Gwen grinned.

Doug stood and paced around the ottoman. "Who else? Who else's dreams have you visited?"

"No one."

"You better not."

"Don't yell at me.

Atticus raised his voice. "Sit down. Hush up, both of you. Is the coffee ready yet?"

Gwen's eyes narrowed.

"What I meant, love of my life, is that your sweet rolls smell delicious and I could really use a cup of coffee."

"Why of course, my manly hunk of burning love." Gwen scowled, but went into the kitchen.

"In one week of chance happenings, you've learned how to control your dreams incredibly well." Atticus leaned his elbows on his knees. "You said last night that it was a talent, like singing, and you could improve your skill by practice."

Taralyn nodded.

"Can you teach someone how to do this?"

"I think so." Taralyn licked her lips and took a cup of coffee from the tray Gwen carried.

"How?" Tyler asked, taking a cup as well.

"I center myself, like I'm about to pray. And then, I focus on who I want to see. All the energy we pull from the universe when we pray, I just channel it and concentrate on seeing Doug, and then I'm there, with him."

"It sounds like astral projection," Gwen offered.

"How did you know what to do?" Tyler asked. "I didn't know. But I believed it could be possible. After Atticus was attacked by the guy in Gwen's dream, I practiced every night, trying different things."

"It only took you six days to learn how to dream walk?" Atticus shook his head. "And another short week to master it."

"Master it? I'm still just playing around." Taralyn glanced up at her father. "Learning. Practicing. I meant to say I was still practicing."

"You changed your appearance and that of Doug. You manipulated your environments. At will. It's more than I can do."

"You just haven't explored it, because you don't think you're allowed to use it for fun."

"Fun?" Tyler puffed. "Atticus dream walks as a means to an end. For good. He takes it seriously while you're joy riding."

Taralyn did that cocked head shake that only teen girls can do. "What's your point? In case you hadn't noticed, there's not a lot of joy around here. We train for battle every day. We just fought aliens from another world. And we killed them all. And this is just the beginning of this war. Ormed and Gilga haven't known anything BUT this war. They love each other and are going to get married as soon as they can, because they may be dead soon. You won't let me date Doug until I'm eighteen."

Doug held up his hand, "That was my decision, Taralyn. Your father agreed to it, but I decided when we'll date."

Taralyn squared her shoulders. "Well, I didn't like your decision. You never asked me. So I made up my own mind and took you out on dates. We had fun and we didn't do anything wrong or illegal."

"Foolish!" Atticus growled and stood, "Foolish child!"

"Have you ever made puppies? I made them. Doug wasn't allowed a dog when he was growing up because his twin sister was allergic, so I made puppies for him last night."

Atticus jerked his shirt up from the waist, exposing his stomach. A scar puckered the skin to the left of his navel. He turned around and pointed at the scar from the exit wound. "This came from a dream, and I wasn't even asleep. Gwen was dreaming and the bastard who fathered her child is a dream walker."

Gwen's head jerked up. She stormed into the kitchen. The people in the living room heard the outer door slam.

Atticus rubbed his forehead and groaned. He sat back down, straightening his shirt. "The man who did this is a Strategia Oscuro. Not only can he walk through a sleeper's dreams, he can manipulate them sufficiently to affect the waking world, too. Taralyn, I believe you have the ability to do this, too."

Taralyn sipped her coffee for lack of something to say.

"I want you to teach us how to do this. All of the elders. And Doug. But first, I need you to teach Gwen how to shield her dreams."

"I don't know how to do that."

"You must. You threw me out last night."

"But I didn't."

"I did," Doug spoke softly. "I was angry and I shoved you out of my mind."

"Tonight, I want to meet with you both in the dream world. We'll practice together."

"I don't like this." Tyler objected.

"I'll keep her safe." Doug met Tyler's gaze. "I swear it. I'll keep her safe."

"We've got an Elder's meeting this afternoon. Doug, it'll need to be voted on, but I'd like you to consider joining the Elders."

Doug nodded.

"Now, if you'll excuse me, I have to go apologize to Gwen."

"We'll let ourselves out," Tyler stood.

Gwen was dancing with her staff in the back yard. She plunged and twirled, slashed and twisted. She was magnificent. Atticus stood and watched her as her breath puffed white in the cool morning air. She turned, and his heart leapt into his throat; her cheeks were streaked with tears.

She grounded her staff at Pine Tree and wiped her eyes.

Atticus slowly approached her and stopped only when his chest pressed against her staff. "I'm sorry."

She didn't look at anything other than her staff.

"I had no right to divulge that information."

Her features wrinkled in anger.

"I got carried away and betrayed your confidence. I had no right to do that."

Fresh tears slid over her eyelids.

"I hate him. I hate what he did to you. I hate," Atticus stopped as Gwen looked at him.

"I'd forgotten," she whispered. "I'd forgotten this baby wasn't fathered by you."

"Gwen." Atticus put his hands on hers.

"I thought you loved her. I thought she belonged to you."

"I do. She does. She's my daughter. Now. Always. I'll never think otherwise."

"But you did."

"I'm sorry."

Gwen shuddered, trying to catch her breath.

"I love you, Gwen."

"Because the Angel of the Lord told you to."

"No." He cupped her face. "No. It has nothing to do with that. I love you. I want to marry you."

"So ask me."

"What?"

"For six months, you've told me we were going to marry, but you never asked me."

Atticus blinked. Slowly, he sank to one knee in front of her. "Gwen Hampt, would you marry me?"

Gwen choked back a half-laugh/half-sob and nodded vigorously. "Yes. Yes, Atticus."

Chapter 41
The Maxwell's Demon

"Well, what a week," Rutger handed Gwen a tuna fish casserole.

She sighed, smiling. "Keep your coat on, the temperature's dropping."

The Elders sat around the picnic table as Matt built a fire in the pit.

"Let's join hands and open with a prayer." Atticus stood and held out his hands. "God Almighty, it has begun. We're not ready, but we trust in your power and omniscience. Use us, Lord. Give us eyes to see opportunities that would normally have gone unseen. Fill us with your strength and don't leave us. Stay by our sides, God. Lead us to your victory over the darkness. Amen."

"Man," Doug wiggled his fingers. "Do you always feel that when you pray?"

Taralyn nodded.

"No wonder they sing songs about Ebenezer."

Tyler smacked the back of Doug's head, but Sara and Larry who'd overheard, giggled.

Atticus looked questioningly at the elders. "What?"

Gwen touched his elbow, "I'll tell you later."

Rawan grinned, "I'm sure you will."

Sara and Larry tried to cover their smiles.

"Don't think I don't know that you two have been singing hymns today, too." Rawan pointed at the couple. Sara blushed.

"Make a joyful noise to the Lord," Rutger quoted.

"Hallelujah," Eduviges laughed.

"Does this have anything to do with the hymn *Come Thou Font of Every Blessing*?" Atticus questioned them.

"Why do you ask, Pastor?" Matt opened his eyes in mock innocence.

"It's just – people burst out laughing any time that hymn is mentioned. All week long."

"It's nothing, I'm sure." Gwen spoke softly.

"Then why are you blushing?"

Gwen turned crimson, determined not to look at the elders. "It's just the nearness of you."

"Isn't that a song?" Atticus frowned.

"It's amazing what can be said in a song," Bea said sweetly.

"Y'all need to grow up!" Mitchell declared.

The elders roared with laughter.

Gwen reached over and kissed away Atticus' looks of confusion. "Along those lines, Atticus and I are getting married."

They spent the next five minutes hugging and kissing everyone.

They began with the treasurer's report, which reflected the cost of construction, labor, and supplies. "Add back into the pot the one-hundred-thousand or so from the returned PCs and we're doing extremely well."

"Why did we return the computers?"

Taralyn answered Atticus. "We were going to use the computers in the schools, but they're useless now. The people of Jol don't possess a written language. The concept of an alphabet is completely foreign to them. I hadn't considered that. We'll have to begin with a much more traditional education framework and eventually work up to computers."

"We'll buy a few at a time and incorporate them into the children's classrooms." Bea insisted. "But I don't think the adults will ever adjust to a written language. They can barely fathom electricity."

"Thealectric fans," Doug repeated a word that only now made sense to him.

Matt spoke up. "Shallon's people are a little more advanced technologically. They know how to forge steel. The only way the people of Jol came to use metal swords was by finding them."

"Funny, they are space travelers with less technology than us. Never would have thought of that." Rutger shook his head.

"It's not like they came in a shiny space ship," Sara rolled her eyes.

"How did they get here?" Doug asked.

"The doors," Eduviges offered. "You saw them Sunday. One white, one black."

"So, who opened the doors?"

"I did." Atticus replied. "I opened the white doors. One of the soldiers must have opened the black one."

Gwen corrected him, "No, no. Doors are the black ones. Portals are the light. That's a very important distinction."

"Again, just for clarity's sake, how did you open them?" Doug tilted his head.

"I prayed."

"Just like that?" Rutger asked. "I know that I was part of the first door – sorry, portal; but I was just caught up in the power. I didn't know what we were doing." Bea pulled her sweater closer. "You just prayed and the portals opened?"

"Maxwell's demon." Mitchell's high voice silenced every other word.

They all stared at him.

"Honestly, it was so obvious a reason, I had no idea you didn't know." Mitchell shrugged.

"Mitch," Doug peered around Sara and Larry to look at him. "I've never heard of Maxwell's devil."

"Demon," Mitchell corrected.

"Missed that day in the fourth grade, did you?" Taralyn smirked.

Mitch smiled with adoration at Taralyn. "In 1867, a Scottish physicist named James Clerk Maxwell wanted to find a situation where the second laws of thermodynamics would fail."

The elders blinked and nodded like they understood.

"In normal situations, molecules in an enclosed space will remain in constant motion." He saw his father squinting at him and rephrased it. "In a glass of tea, the sugar and tea are constantly moving around, right?"

The elders relaxed a bit.

"Suppose you've got a jug of tea, and you put this wall right down into the middle of this enclosed space, dividing these molecules into two equal sets. Maxwell came up with an idea that in the middle of this wall, there might be a door, which only lets slow molecules through to one side and fast molecules through to the other side. Eventually, one side of the – the jug of tea would be filled with fast molecules – hot tea, and the other side with only slow ones – iced tea."

The adults blinked soberly, which Mitchell took as acquiescence, if not complete understanding.

"Other scientists argued that the gatekeeper – named a demon for lack of a better term –couldn't possibly exist because it would require too much energy to perform this function, and so the theory of thermodynamics would remain constant."

The adults blinking rate slowed.

"Well, it's simple. The demons use the energy of Atticus' prayer to let through the like-kind of energy."

"Good prayer, good people," Doug grunted.

"Bad prayers, bad people." Rutger warned.

"Despair," Gwen spoke. "The black holes are called Doors of Despair. Emotionally dark places can open them."

"The bus wreck in Atlanta Sunday morning," Bea's voice quivered. "All those children."

"That might have been where they came through," Rawan guessed. "It would take them a few hours to march the sixty miles here."

"So why have we not heard about this before?" Chi asked.

"We have," Rutger supplied. "Wars, tragedies, natural disasters, all had legends about strange creatures or missing people. In the midst of the Battle of Thermopolis, a foot solder wrote about soldiers in strange uniforms who killed all in their path. Berserkers fell into the midst of Norse battles. Valkyrees – winged witch-like creatures – were supposed to be drawn from Valhalla by the sounds of battle. Whole battalions of ships have been gobbled up by black holes. Every generation has its tales of vicious creatures and missing people."

Larry held up his hand, "The Ninth Legion."

"What?" his wife asked.

"Rome's Ninth Legion. It was stationed along Hadrian's Wall in Britton. Gone."

"Gone," his wife's eyes narrowed.

"They disappeared and although there are many theories about it, no one knows the truth – maybe they marched into a portal and never returned."

"Yeah, but nobody's ever described a black or a white hole just opening up and swallowing people." Bea rubbed her arms to ward off the cold.

"Halloween," Rawan added. "Originally, it was a night when the door between the dead and the living was opened. And the door is often described as a black mirror or a shimmering spot in a dark lake. Maybe a Maxwell Demon was responsible for that, too."

"OK, dead people, bad guys." Matt trembled.

"Why haven't we heard about the good doors – sorry – good portals?"

"We have." Atticus spoke. "Second Kings 2:11 says that Elijah went up by a whirlwind into heaven."

"You cannot be serious." Chi snorted. "One would hear about it. People do not just disappear."

"Yes they do," Doug stated. "My sister did."

Taralyn put her hand on Doug's. "I'm so sorry." Sara added, "Hundreds of children go missing all the time. Maybe they're not all snatched or run-aways."

Rawan tisked, "Many's the time my people were accused of stealing children."

"Your people?" Gwen asked.

"Gypsies."

"Stolen by gypsies," Rutger quoted.

"Or," Bea added, "Ran away with the circus."

"So, children and adults disappear every day, and some through doors or portals." Matt got up to stoke the fire. "Do they ever come back?"

"I did." Gwen stretched out her hand. "I was praying, deeply praying in church one day, and a white circle appeared and then expanded. I stepped through it and found myself in a different world. And then two and a half years later, I came back to Earth the same way."

"How wide spread is this phenomenon?" Visolela asked. "I mean, Atticus prayed and the people of Jol came through. But the next time he prayed, the people of Faleavers came through and they are from a different planet than the Jols. Where did the dark soldiers come from? Are they from one planet and they are slowly conquering their way through the universe?"

The elders stared at each other without answers.

"So you and Gwen can open one of these good portals?" Tyler spoke slowly. "And when the portal opens, refugees come pouring through, is that the plan?"

"Part of it."

Tyler continue, "Once you learn how to open these portals, you can come and go between the worlds." Atticus nodded.

"You could bring people here, train them into an army, and then send them back."

Atticus nodded again.

Visolela gasped, "So the war is not going to take place here!"

"Not unless they find out what we're doing," Rutger mused. "But if the dark side ever found out where we are and that we're training soldiers from all different worlds to fight them," he left the phrase unfinished. "What about some kind of spiritual cloaking device?" Matt fidgeted uncomfortably.

"Oh!" Taralyn gasped. "Or a force field. A way to keep the Maxwell demon from letting them through!"

"Yes," Atticus nodded gravely.

"I've used crystals to focus and channel energies," Rawan mused. "If I could find the exact combination of crystals and gems, Tyler could rig it into his security system. Project a – OK Matt, I'll use your term – project a cloaking device over the compound. That might work."

The movement of Gwen grabbing the ring around her neck caught Atticus' attention. He patted her knee and shook his head with the barest of movement. She dropped her hand and nodded.

"I guess I'll have to fire our teachers. Soldiers aren't going to need much in the way of reading and math," Bea frowned.

"Of course they do," Rutger argued. "Depending on the age of the student, reading and math are much greater weapons than swords."

"We'll send them back to the worlds with skills that didn't develop naturally within their civilizations," Matt worried. "That's wrong."

"How?" Taralyn questioned. "How is it wrong to prepare them to win the war?"

"You can't just hand a caveman a grenade and say, go win the war."

"We're not going to use grenades," Eduviges scoffed.

"Why not? We used automatic weapons Sunday. Why not just toss a grenade inside every black door as soon as one opens. Or a nuke?"

"Matt," Atticus began.

"Or, I know, I developed this really cool bomb, destroys every living creature in a two acre radius." Matt stood up, shaking.

Atticus jumped up and gathered the huge man in his arms. "Matt, we're not going to do that."
Tyler and Doug exchanged glances, which obviously asked, *why not?*

"We'll use everything within our power to keep the compound safe. But there are other things that we can teach our army. Other than weapons."

Taralyn sat up straight. She turned and saw Gwen put a single finger to her lips.

Chapter 42
The Puppies

The church was packed to standing room only Sunday.

Doug winked at Taralyn from his place at the drums. The three of them had met last night on the front porch of his childhood home, but he didn't learn much. He watched Taralyn and Atticus shape shift into a dozen different animals, but mostly he sat on the steps and played with the puppies.

Atticus opened the service with an invocation and the Apostle's Creed. Then the choir stepped onto the altar and did a moving rendition of *Love Lifted Me*. Doug lost himself in the joy of the drums. After the hymn, he took Taralyn's hand and sat beside Tyler, but he couldn't concentrate on the sermon. His thoughts were on the puppies. They had silky ears and ice cold noses. The smell of a puppy was like no other scent in the world. Doug closed his eyes and inhaled the memory.

Taralyn leaned against him, "Are you thinking about puppies?

He grinned sheepishly. "Yeah."

"I could see them." Taralyn leaned closer. "Doug, I could see your thoughts."

Doug's heart raced. He put his lips against her ear, "How long before March sixth?"

Monday morning, Atticus stood before the entire compound; the children huddled under blankets worn like cloaks. "Today, we begin to train. Gwen will train Staffs. Doug will train Hands. Ricean will train Swords. Morgan will train the home guard. The children will also begin training. They may choose how they want to train physically, except with the home guard. The elders are here to being the spiritual training. We will be walking around the field. If we touch your shoulder, please stop what you're doing and listen to us.
That's exactly what they did. They began with the adults, touching them one at a time and praying. Very few of the adults resonated with the power of the elders in prayer, but the names of those who did were marked down on the clip board each elder carried. The children were much more responsive. The names of them were written down, too.

The elders met in the cafeteria after morning exercises to discuss their findings.

"Divide these into eight students for each one of you. Tomorrow morning, pull your group aside and set up a practice time three or four times a week. Teach them how to pray with power."

"So, like Wednesday before church?"

"No," Gwen objected. "Not unless you're planning

on telling Patsy why she can't have your children in her choir."

"Heaven forbid," Perkins rolled his eyes.

"I want them ready by Thanksgiving."

"Ready for what, Preacher?" Bea asked.

"I'm going to open another portal as soon as the compound is finished. We have one-hundred-fifty-nine refugees today, but room for over a thousand. For three months, I plan to open a portal once a week and see who comes through."

"And then?" Sara asked.

"By then, you'll each have learned how to open a portal yourself."

"With thirteen of us opening holes on other worlds, it'll seem like the rapture over there," Bea cackled.

"Fourteen," Atticus spoke softly. "Fourteen of us. I'd like you to pray about Doug. I'd like to nominate him for position as an elder."

They nodded.

"Where is the boy?" Rawan asked.

"He's gone with Morgan for the day, to discuss security measures and weaponry for defense."

Eduviges spoke without looking away from her coffee. "What about Morgan?"

No one responded.

"How much do we share with him? How far do we trust him?"

"Not far," Atticus advised. "I've prayed with him, so he is one of us. But there is a strain of resistance in him. Until he overcomes that, no lengthy conversations about portals or prayers or dreams. I've already cautioned Doug to keep silent about Mitchell's demons."

"Maxwell's," Mitchell frowned.

"Well, I've got visitation to do." Atticus took their hands.

"Atticus," Gwen interrupted. "The children – they only have a few clothes each, and Ricean and Shallon's groups are not much better prepared for a Georgia winter. I was thinking, a few of us could go into Morning Creek to the Salvation Army and the thrift shops and buy some clothes for them"

"Cash only," Larry warned.

"Drop Gwen off at our house. Larry will have the funds and I'll drive." Sara glowed with excitement.

"I want to come," Visolela's face lit up.

"You're not going to the Catholic thrift shop without me," Bea assured them.

"Ten o'clock?" Gwen smiled.

"Let's pray." Atticus squeezed her hand.

"Jeans, T shirts, sweat shirts, socks," Gwen itemized.

"Dresses for the girls," Sara insisted.

"What about shoes?" Bea asked. "They never have many children's shoes at the thrift shop."

"The Jols don't wear shoes." Rawan added, "They think they are horrible."

"What about sandals? We wore sandals when I was on Gith." Gwen suggested.

"Oh!" Sara perked up. "Oh! I have an idea. The Iraqi shopkeeper. He could import hundreds of sandals from his country. We could buy them cheap."

"I'd forgotten about Samir. But Atticus must have brought him in for a reason." Gwen nodded.

"Road trip!" Sara stood up. "Last one in the van's a Maxwell's demon."

Chapter 43
The Prayer Warriors

Mitchell sat on the floor of an unoccupied dorm room and looked at his eight students. Ormed and Gilga sat with their shoulders touching. Tishel sat beside Gilga and kept her arm around her brother Harl. Harl didn't speak, but Mitchell felt the boy would be one of the first to open a portal; he was so powerful. Uvat and Sapwu were from Shallon's group. They stared respectfully at the floor. Completing the circle were Seng, a sour looking teen boy and Rosam, a pregnant girl not much older than Gilga.

Mitchell took a deep breath. "Think about everything that's going on around you. Listen. Do you hear your heart beating? Ignore every other sound around you except for my voice and concentrate on your heart. No other sound exists. Just the bearing of your heart."

Mitchell observed their faces and shoulders relax. Their breathing steadied.

"Now, think about everything that happened today. From the time you woke up, went to morning exercise, breakfast. Some of you started school today.

Others helped on the worksite. You talked to friends. You played games. Take all of those things and roll them up like a blanket and tuck them away." Mitchell waited while their faces twitched with the mental activity.

"What's left of today is us sitting here. We're safe. We're warm. We're among friends who all serve the light."

They each relaxed further.

"Think of the person to your right. Close your eyes, but see that person's face in your mind. Smell their scent. See the clothes they wear. Now, think about hugging them in friendship."
Smiles flitted across lips around the group.

"Do the same for the person to your left. Picture them as completely as you can. Now hug them."

"Now think of yourself. In your mind, look at your feet, your toes, your knees. Look at your hands. Pretend you can see your face. Look at each feature. Take your hands and cover your face. No! In your mind, not really." Mitchell grinned in embarrassment. "In your mind, push away all thoughts of your day. Shut out all thoughts of the people around you. Ignore how your body feels. Imagine you are being hugged – not the way grown-ups hug, but with the comfort, safety and love of God. Cling to this hug, and absorb it within your being. Let everything around you fall away except for this feeling of contentment. This is your connection to God. Now focus that feeling smaller and smaller in size, but with the same intensity and power. Take a deep breath and let this feeling block out everything else. The only thing in the entire universe is this feeling at the center of your being. Just you and God." Mitchell paused, relishing this next step. "Now, hug God."

The room blazed with power. Harl and Ormed were brightest, then Rasom who seemed to have a second glow emanating from her belly. Sapwu's glow flickered brilliant to flat and back again. "You are now centered. If I ask you to center yourself, this is how you will go about doing it. When you're ready, release God and return to this world."

Again Mitchell paused until the power dimmed and his students opened their eyes in delight. "Practice doing this four times a day for one week. Do not do this while you are handling weapons or tools. Atticus was really strict about that. And don't hold anyone's hand to practice this, not yet anyway."

Chapter 44
The Plans

Atticus awoke with a grunt.

"Kicked you out again, did he?" Gwen rolled over, trying to get comfortable.

"I just don't see how he does it." Atticus sat up.

"Did you ask him?"

"Of course I have. He doesn't know. He just pushes and here I am."

"Why don't you try it on me?"

"What?"

"Dream walk. Dream walk in me. Teach me how to do it. Between the two of us, we can work it out."

"No." Atticus turned his back, searching the floor with his feet for his slippers.

"What do you mean 'no'?"

"I mean no. I'm not going to walk through your dreams. And I'm not teaching you how to do it."

"You didn't teach Taralyn, but she learned how."

"Taralyn isn't my wife."

Gwen barrel-rolled to a sitting position. "What's that supposed to mean?"

"It means I have control of my emotions when I'm with her."

"Whereas, with me, you lose all sense of reason."

"Sort of," Atticus hesitated.

"I drive you beyond reason."

"No. Don't put words in my mouth." Atticus stood up.

"Don't put words in your mouth. Don't upset the elders. Don't sing too loud or pray too hard. I'm the warrior the angel sent you, and that's all I'm supposed to be."

"What? I've never said any of those things."

"Really?" She stood with her hands on her hips. She seemed abnormally huge tonight.

"Honest."

"Then walk in my dreams."

"It wouldn't be right."

"But it's alright to walk in that child's dreams?"

"She's hardly a child." He knew before the words stopped that he'd said the worst thing possible. "Gwen."

She picked up her pillow and clutched it to her chest. "Every night, we lay down together and I can't wait for you to touch me. But you can't wait to dream walk with her."

"You can't," he began. "Gwen, dream walking isn't like that."

She glared at him and turned to leave the bedroom.

"Gwen, come back to bed. This isn't like you. You can't honestly be jealous of Taralyn."

"Everyone loves Taralyn. Why should you be any different?" She marched through the living room into the kitchen and outside, but her voice carried well. Atticus followed her. "Doug is in love with her. Mitchell is, too. And Matt. His heart rips itself open every time he looks at her."

"Why is the sun shining?" Atticus looked around.

"So why should it surprise me that you love her, too."

"Gwen," Atticus pointed to the large pool beneath a waterfall that grew out of the trees in his backyard. "Where are we?"

"The Pool of Meshapa," as if it were natural they should be there.

"We're dreaming. Together."

"Don't change the subject." She threw her pillow down and it became an elongated slab of granite beside the pool.

"This is the subject. This is exactly the subject. I can't dream walk with you because we are too intimately linked. I don't know where you end and I begin." Atticus reached out his hand and projected them back into bed. He was surging inside of her, her fingernails racking his shoulders. Their orgasm rattled the windows. Something crashed. They rolled as one and his back lay on the sun-warmed rock slab beside the cool waterfall of Meshapa. Children played around them, chasing butterflies and each other. At the edge of the yard, puppies yipped and tussled with each other while a yellow lab watched with pride. Gwen sat beside him, a white gauzy shift pulled down exposing *her plump breasts. An infant suckled at one of them noisily. Her face was lifted up to catch the sun; her eyes closed in utter contentment. This was heaven.*

After church the next Sunday, Atticus gathered the elders in the sanctuary.

"By Thanksgiving, when the church is finished, I want each of you to be proficient in opening a portal. You do so by focusing and purifying your prayer. But every time one of us opens a portal, we need to be prepared for someone to come through."

They nodded, excitement mixed with concern.

"Eventually, you will become the teachers. The prayer groups you've formed – you will teach them how to open portals."

Matt raised his hand. "You know, you're talking about seventy-seven people being able to open portals. The compound was built to hold only one thousand. If we're not careful, we could have seven hundred people pour through in an hour or less, every day."

"How do we *be careful*?" Tyler asked.

Atticus looked at them. "First. Only one of us opens a portal at a time. The others observe and support. Secondly," here he paused. "Secondly, we start sending the adults back."

The elders started.

"They stay with us long enough for medical treatment. They'll be well-fed physically and spiritually. They'll be shown the school and told our vision – to raise an army to hold back the dark. And then they'll be sent back to their worlds to spread the word."

Eduviges raised her hand. "What word would that be, Preacher?"

"That this is a sanctuary for children. Here, their children will be safe and well-fed. They'll be educated in trades and trained to fight."

"You said we'd be training an army," Bea scowled. "You never said they'd be children."

"And they're just going to give us their children?" Larry growled.

"We did," Rutger's voice carried. "In Germany, the Jews sent their children to the US and England to be safe. The British parents in London sent their children to the countryside rather than lose them in the bombings."

Rawan's nostrils flared. "I've read what became of those kindertransport."

"That's because there was nothing prepared for the children who were sent away. We're prepared to take care of the children."

Atticus nodded approvingly at Rutger. "They stand a better chance of survival here – away from their families – than on their home worlds."

"Why?" Taralyn seemed surprised by her own question. "Gilga and others have mentioned that the Dark soldiers are especially drawn to children. But no one has ever told me exactly what they do with children."

Atticus turned to look at Gwen. She cleared her throat and rubbed her belly. "I've told you that Dark soldiers prefer to maim and torture rather than kill outright. It's not just that they enjoy doing so – because they do – but because their aim is not to destroy the light, but to turn it. Anyone can be turned to the darkness by despair, grief, rage; you know what these emotions are. Children. Well, they need to rebuild their armies, just like we do. We are building an army of children – using safety, food, medicine and education and hope that the children will remain in the light. They turn the children first, using methods specifically designed to create the utmost despair. Torture, rape, from what I hear, those are just foreplay to the methods used to turn a child." Gwen couldn't continue. She felt her throat burn.

In the silence that followed, Matt raised his hand. "We have enough acreage for two more barracks."

Atticus grinned and held out his hands. "Let's begin."

Seven people crawled through the portal Bea opened on Thursday. They were horribly burned. Two had died by the following morning and the other five would be spending weeks in the compound's hospital. Two old women tumbled through Eduviges's portal Saturday. They were frightened, their hands gnarled with arthritis, they eyes clouded with cataracts. However, these women could pray with a power that rivaled the elders. Ten children ran through Matt's portal the following Tuesday.

An elder tried every morning after exercise, with varying success. By Thanksgiving, they all knew the spiritual paths to opening a portal, but most were opened and no one came through.

Chapter 45
The Thanksgiving Feast

As exercises ended Thanksgiving morning, Atticus raised his arms and everyone gathered around him on the huge field. "In six hours, we are going to gather in the cafeteria for our feast. Everyone is invited. But before we do so, we need to," Atticus stopped. He cocked his head, as if listening. Taking a deep breath, he continued. "We need to form two circles. Elders on the inside, everyone else form a circle around us."

The elders joined a tight circle as they had planned to do, all facing the empty space between the church and the cafeteria. Atticus broke between a pair of parishioners and asked one to walk all the way around the inside of the huge ring, doubling the circle. He then reached across the couple between him and his original partner and took her hand again.

"Those of you who know how, center yourself. Those of you who know how, pull down the white light and let it flow between you. Those of you who know how, surge this light into me and I will focus it to form a portal of light." Atticus began to pray. The elders prayed for him and with him. The area between the two buildings began to glow. A golden circle formed in the air, expanding and filling in with molten silver. For a full minute, the portal shimmered and then a hand grabbed empty air from the other side. It withdrew and a face peered through. The face was filthy and fringed with coarse brown hair and a beard. His mouth dropped open and jerked back to the other side. A younger woman, filthy and bedraggled, peered through and spoke to someone behind her. She said something to them, but no one heard her. She stepped through and stood trembling before them. In a shaky voice, she asked, "Whom do you serve?"

Shouts of "the light" and "God the Father" rang around the field. The woman looked incredulous and then jumped back through the portal. Almost immediately, adults and children began pouring through. They'd stumble and stare gape-jawed at the people in front of them, only to be shoved on the back from people trying to come through behind them.

Gwen joined the hands of Visolela to her left to Eduviges on her right and eased her way under the joined hands of the people around her. She approached the strangers and bowed. "I am Gwen Staff of Atticus. Welcome to a place of sanctuary."

One-hundred thirteen people came through that day. They were shepherded by the elders and Ricean and Shallow. They were amazed by the miracles in the barracks. Those who needed it were escorted to the medical center. By noon, the new refugees began to claim the second floor and discovered the joys of hot water and clean Sally-Ann clothes.

The cafeteria was filled with people from various worlds. They feasted on turkey, ham and fried chicken, green bean casserole, stuffing, sweet potatoes soufflé, mashed potatoes, olives, pickles, beets, ears of corn, field peas, biscuits, rolls, and cornbread. Pecan and pumpkin pies vied for attention with spiced apples and peach cobblers.

Children danced and ran around, spilling over with laughter. Adults glanced suspiciously at the other strangers, but smiled generously, too.

People visited in small groups, strange musical instruments colored the silences, and singing broke out sporadically.

Atticus stared around his flock, a worried look on his handsome face.

"You look tired," Gwen filled his tea glass from the pitcher on the table.

Atticus frowned, "Too many dreams, not enough sleep."

"I hear that," Doug yawned.

"I'd like to table our experiment for two weeks," Atticus spoke softly.

"Gladly." Taralyn agreed. "I can't remember the last night I slept without being pestered by one or the both of you."

Tyler blinked, frowning.

Gwen grinned, "You know, taken out of context, that statement could be used to incarcerate both these men for life."

Neither Tyler, Atticus, nor Doug returned her grin.

"Matt! Hi!" Taralyn waved and smiled at the huge man walking toward the table, a full plate balanced on one hand, a glass of tea in the other. He nodded and smiled. Juan walked up to him, and Matt blushed.

"I'll be right back," Atticus stood, gesturing to Matt. Matt handed Juan his plate, admonishing him not to steal his food and followed Atticus out the door.

The night was crisp, promising frost by morning. "Let's go into my new office."

Atticus pointed to a couch which Matt half-filled, and sat across from him in the fresh-leather armchair. "We're about the same age, Matt, but I want you to think of me as an older brother right now."

Matt nodded.

"There have been a lot of changes around here this year. And every single person involved is vital."

Matt squinted, but he nodded again.

"We have to be more than a team; we have to be one body, acting for the greater good. Do you understand?"

Matt nodded and leaned forward on the couch, studying the rug between them.

"I won't presume to butt into your private feelings for anyone."

Matt glanced worriedly at Atticus and looked back at the carpet.

"But I don't have to tell you that jealousy is a vicious weapon, one that could destroy us all, not just the three of you."

"The what?" Matt sat up.

"I know you've never said anything to Taralyn, but

you attacked Doug, and I can't," Atticus took a deep breath. "You can't let that happen again. No matter how you feel about Taralyn, you can't let it divide us." Matt snorted.

"Believe me, I know jealousy. It is a cancerous monster."

Matt bit the inside of his cheek and nodded.

"In time, I think you'll see, and so will Mitchell, that Taralyn and Doug have always loved each other."

"I know they do." Matt sat back, relaxing.

"So, you're alright?" Atticus stood.

Matt stood and grinned, "Never better. Thanks, Preacher."

Back in the cafeteria, Matt sat next to Juan. "Did you eat my coleslaw?"

"Naw, it tasted funny." Juan pressed his knee against Matt's. "What did the preacher want?"

Matt glanced at Juan's plate, comparing it to his. "He wanted to make sure my heart wasn't broken."

"Que?"

"He thinks I'm in love with Taralyn and might be jealous of Doug."

Juan turned to glare at the unsuspecting couple behind them. "Are you?"

Matt's elbow brushed Juan's. "What do you think?"

"Well, I know what I thought," Juan glanced behind him again. "But now I don't know. What did you tell Atticus?"

"I told him, 'fish gotta swim, birds gotta fly.'"

"Que?" Juan squinted. "Verdad?"

"You gonna eat that coleslaw?" Matt picked up his fork and hovered it over the plates.

"It's from the song," Juan sang softly, "Fish gotta swim, birds gotta fly."

Matt crooned, "I gotta love one man 'til I die."

"Can't help loving that man of mine," Juan finished.

"So, Juan, about the coleslaw?" Matt leaned against him.

Juan scooped a forkful of the white stuff and gently placed it between Matt's lips.

Chapter 46
The Dance Begins

"So, before we began building the other two dormitories, we wanted your opinion of the ones you're in." Matt nodded at the crowd of adults and teens and sat back down.

They looked at each other, waiting for someone to speak up.

Orwin stood. "The barracks are wondrous tents. We are grateful for them."

Atticus paced. "What would make them better?"

The Jols bowed their head, studying the floor tiles. The Faleavers glanced at each other, warily silent. The others – the Yseluta, the Shadeziah and Eurnied as relative newcomers – kept silent and stared at no one. Atticus looked at the elders for help.

Mitchell stood up. "Guests are pleasant distractions which have no permanence. They are like plates beneath the feast. Family is the meat and gravy of the feast."

The Jols laughed.

"We are asking if the feast would be better with a pinch of salt, or more pepper. Not which fork to set beside the plate."

The crowd murmured appreciatively as Mitchell sat down.

"There are too many people in each room," Tishyn spoke up.

"No privacy," said another.

"The beds are too narrow for more than one person and too difficult to move side by side."

"No one cleans up underneath. We all clean our areas, but the big communal areas," the speaker shivered and made a face.

"Like the bathroom," agreed the person to her right.

"If a toilet overflows, we don't know how to fix it."

The suggestions continued, one spilling over the next. Sara and Bea wrote furiously while Atticus pointed to each speaker. Finally, after forty-five minutes, the crowd's comments dwindled.

"Anything else?" Atticus looked around the conference room.

Ricean stood. The room stilled. "Atticus, Priest of God." She waited.

Atticus hesitated before stating ceremoniously, "Ricean Sword of Jol."

"We would like to hold the Feast of Winter's Night."

Atticus blinked and turned to Mitchell.

The boy stood up. "From what I understand, the Feast of Winter's Night is called many things on different worlds. It is the longest night of the year. The time when the planet turns back to the light. Even here on this world, we celebrate it as Christmas and Yule and many other names."

Atticus bowed, "We would be honored."

Gwen stood up, struggling with the shape of her body. "Ricean Sword of Jol, I will dance on the Winter's Night with Atticus."

The Jols whistled.

Ricean bowed. "Anyone who wishes to dance at Winter's Night is welcome. Let me know if the decision sits well with you now, or dance when the music begins."

Atticus turned to Gwen and raised an eyebrow. Mitchell covered his face and giggled. "Let us know if you need any assistance with the planning," Atticus spoke hesitantly.

Ricean straightened her back. "I would ask Tyler Staff of Atticus for assistance."

The crowd murmured.

Tyler stood, "Sure. Glad to help."

Olmed whistled.

Gilga stood. "I will be dancing with Olmed."

The room cheered.

Tyler frowned and leaned toward Mitchell, whispering behind his hand. Mitchell shook his head and Tyler sighed in relief.

Shallon stood, "May my people dance?"

"You have brought no women with you," Ricean noted without judgement.

Shallon crossed his arms, "No, nor do we wish to dance with any woman here."

"Oh." Ricean looked at the floor, thinking. She repeated herself, "Anyone who wishes to dance at

Winter's Night is welcome. Let me know if the decision sits well with you now, or dance when the music begins."

"Then I will dance with Maynao."

The man named grinned and leapt to his feet. "I will dance with you Shallon of Faleavers." The brothers of Shallon stomped the floor, smiling.

Matt held his breath, hope beating in his chest.

Atticus raised a hand; the room stilled again. "I would like to confer with my wife, but I believe I understand the gist of the Dance. We have learned that there are many differences between our peoples, but since we are all soldiers of the light, we can adapt to these differences."

Chapter 47
The Tower of Babel

Mitchell sat between Samir and Sara, translating. "Samir says he can get you one gross water bags of sheep's stomach."

Samir interjected two words, which Mitchell repeated in English, "The finest sheep's stomach water bags."

Gilga sat across from them, staring.

"And Samir would like to borrow Maynao's bolo for a while."

"Why?" Sara asked.

Mitchell asked Samir, who shrugged and said something as if it were not important.

"He wants to make a pattern of it."

Sara frowned. "A pattern? So he can make replicas and sell them?" She straightened. "He wants to copy their weapon and sell them? Absolutely not."

It didn't take Mitchell's words for Samir to understand. He streamed forth a slew of syllables loudly, gesturing angrily with his hands.

Suddenly, Gilga was holding a knife at Samir's throat. "You will apologize to Sara Staff of Atticus,

294

Mother of Mitchell Prayer Warrior of Atticus."

Samir asked her a question.

"Of course I understand you, peddler. Apologize for what your faithless lips allowed to pass as words."

Sara was standing, her hand clenching Mitchell's arm. "Gilga, what are you doing?"

"He said foul things about you. I grow weary of his breathing." She tightened her grip. "Apologize."

Samir babbled a humble apology. Gilga released him with a grunt of disgust. Samir bowed and rubbed away the drop of blood on his neck.

"How did you know what he said?" Mitchell asked.

Gilga frowned. "I heard his words. How else would I know?"

"But he was speaking in Arabic," Sara stated.

Gilga looked from Mitchell to Sara to Samir. "He speaks words. Words are words. Are they not?"

Samir spoke quickly.

Gilga replied, "Yes, I understand you. I understand every word you speak. Why wouldn't I?"

Mitchell looked at Samir, who asked the boy a question.

Mitchell spoke in German. Gilga replied, "Yes, I understand you."

He asked her a question in Russian.

"Of course, your words sound no different."

He tried again, forming words that sounded beautiful, filled with elongated vowels sounds and few consonants.

Gilga looked confused. "Mitchell told me to tell both of you that he is speaking one of the Inuit languages and that he has never met anyone else who speaks it. But that he read it in a book and thinks his pronunciations might be correct."

Samir looked incredulously at Sara.

"I understood you, Gilga, but not the words my son said. Ask Samir if he understood you."

"He sits right here," Gilga pointed.

Mitchell spoke to Samir, who nodded and pointed to Gilga.

"What does this mean? How is it you don't understand each other," the child asked.

Mitchell drew a deep breath, "You see, there was this Tower in Babel."

"Atticus." Samir stated.

Sara nodded. "We need to tell Atticus."

Chapter 48
The New Sanctuary

Atticus looked around the new sanctuary in amazement. The stained glass window behind the altar was a replica of the rose in Chartres Cathedral. The baptistery pool was twelve by nine by three feet and hidden beneath the floor behind the choir loft. Two rows of men, one row of women and three rows of children – one dozen in each - filled the choir loft. They were dressed in light purple robes with white V stole collars. Eduviges sat on the bench of the grand piano. Various instrumentalists, including Doug at the drums and Matt with a trumpet, Rutger's wife with a violin, and several non-Earthen woodwind and strings filled a small square between the choir and the piano. Patsy, her golden hair pinned in a tall profusion of curls, sat with the musicians. The pews were filled with construction workers, warriors, townspeople, and many children. There was a loud hum of excitement filling the sanctuary.

Across the top half of the back wall, the one everyone would look at while they exited the sanctuary, was the scripture: *Trust in Him at all times; ye people, pour out your heart before Him: God is a refuge for us. Selah.* **Psalm 62:8**

Atticus knelt to pray.

Chapter 49
The Orange

"Chi, do you have a moment?" Atticus called to the man from across the cold practice field. The doctor kissed his son and placed the baby into Visolela's arms.

"I will meet you in the cafeteria," he told his wife.

Atticus led Chi into his jumbled office and offered him a seat on the couch.

"It's about Gwen."

Chi nodded, waiting politely.

"I think there's something wrong."

"How so?"

Atticus laughed and looked sideways. "She won't stop cleaning. She has even mopped the walls."

"It is called nesting. It is normal."

"Martha never did that." Atticus growled.

Chi drew in a deep breath. "It is normal that you would think of your late wife and child at a time like this."

Atticus pursed his lips.

"How is Gwen's appetite?"

Atticus shrugged. "She eats a little now and then,

299

not much at meals, but she has snacks during the day, and drinks a glass of milk or has a bowl of cereal before bed."

"And her sleep? Is she sleeping well?"

"No. She gets up three and four times a night. She paces or she sits in the arm chair, reading."

"Nightmares?"

"None that she's mentioned."

"And you? Are you having nightmares?"

The men stared at each other. Atticus dropped his head and nodded.

"This is why you have stopped dream-walking with Doug and Taralyn?"

"Yes." Atticus growled and rubbed his face. "No sense in dragging the two of them into my nightmares."

"I understand." Chi sat with his hands folded.

Atticus fidgeted and stood up to pace around his office.

"Pastor, what would you think about Taralyn and Doug training other elders to dream-walk? You needn't be there."

Atticus halted and squinted out the window.

Chi continued softly, his voice reasonable, "We can each open portals now with relative success. We need to begin training our prayer students how to do so."

Atticus nodded. "I was going to suggest that at our next elder's meeting."

"And once we all can open portals, then what?"

Atticus' nostrils flared, but he didn't reply.

"We will need to be able to communicate once we travel through the portals." Chi kept his voice soft.

Atticus returned to the armchair and sank down. "Was it that obvious?"

"Who will you send?"

"I don't know yet. The angel," Atticus blanched and glanced at Chi. "The angel hasn't spoken to me since the battle."

The men looked at each other. Chi sat back. "You think the angel has stopped speaking to you for a reason."

Atticus shrugged uncomfortably. "It's possible."

"Because of Gwen."

Atticus nodded.

"Because you are having sex."

"Not recently, but yes. We became intimate the night of the battle and continued until Thanksgiving."

"You were careful not to injure her or the baby?"

"Of course I was." Atticus reddened and his voice was raised.

Chi held up a mollifying palm.

Atticus blew out an angry breath. "But I shouldn't have become intimate with her. We're not married."

"So, the angel has become silent because you have become intimate with Gwen."

"I think so."

"You have become intimate with the woman you love."

Atticus blinked.

"You love the woman the angel told you he would send to you."

"I love Gwen, yes."

"The woman the angel promised would become your wife."

"But we're not married yet." Atticus sat forward. "It's wrong."

"Right and wrong. Who defined these words?"

"What do you mean? Right is right, wrong is wrong."

"Oh? So the Angel of the Lord has turned his back on you because you make love to the woman he promised would be your wife."

"She's not my wife yet. That makes this wrong."

Chi nodded. "When I was a little boy, my father promised that when I was old enough, he would give me a grove of orange trees. I loved oranges you see. And coming home from my aunt's house one day, I saw the biggest orange in full ripeness, dangling from the tree in my father's grove. So I took it. I ate it. It tasted delicious. The most delicious fruit God had ever created. But then, I worried that my father would be displeased with me. You see, I lived with my mother and aunts and only saw my father occasionally. And even though he had promised me a grove, it was not my grove yet. I had stolen the fruit. I hid from my father the next time he came to our village. And the next time, too. I hid from him, because I had done wrong."

"But you had done wrong. You stole something that was not yours."

Chi leaned forward, placing his elbows on his knees. "My father never returned to our village after that. He was murdered by thieves who beat him and left him to die alone beside an unfrequented road. I never got to tell him I was sorry I stole his fruit. I never gave him the chance to forgive me."

After a moment of silence, Chi stood. "Thank the Lord you do not have thatched roofs in Georgia. My mother used to have them replaced every time she came near to labor." Chi squeezed Atticus' shoulder and let himself out of the office.

Chapter 50
The Warrior's Daughter

*"Atticus, why are you here?" The voice sounded
from far away. Far in time. Far in distance. Far in
eternity. It was the Angel of the Lord.*

*Atticus kept his head bowed, his eyes closed, his
hands clenched together in front of him.*

*"Atticus," the Angel said again. "Why are you
here?"*

"I'm here to pray."

*"You can pray anywhere. Why are you here?" The
voice sounded farther away, if that were possible.*

*Atticus peeked open his eyes and stared up at the
stained-glass Jesus on the cross. "I've come here to
pray, because my prayers are answered here."*

*"But Atticus, why are you here?" The voice
sounded younger, more vigorous, but kinder, too.*

*"This is where I lost everything and gained
everything." Atticus lifted his head from the altar. His
church, his tiny chapel, this was where he felt closest to
God. Surely the Angel of the Lord understood that.*

"This is a place of beginnings for you."

"Yes." Atticus scrubbed his tear stained face.

"Atticus, why are you here? You are no longer at the beginning of your journey."

"I didn't think you'd hear me in the new church," Atticus replied lamely.

"What have you to say that I need to hear?"

"I," Atticus shrugged childishly. "I haven't said it yet."

Silence trembled along the beams and rattled the glass windows of Grace, Joy, Hope, Love, Matthew, Mark, Luke and John.

A sob caught in his chest, "I'm sorry. I'm so sorry. I love her. I need her. I took her before we were married. I'm sorry."

"Atticus," the voice was gentle and came from just above his head. "You are forgiven."

Atticus slumped back over the altar railing, exhausted.

"But Atticus," the voice dwindled farther away. "Why are you here?"

"What?"

"Why are you here?" A different voice came from just behind his shoulder. "I need you, Daddicus, Daddy. Why are you here?"

Atticus turned, blinking in the dim light of the sanctuary. A grown woman stood on a pew. Her tunic was leather and a quiver of arrows nestled behind her shoulder. The staff she held was thick and mahogany. Her red hair fell in a braid over and in front of her left shoulder and down to her waist. Her ears stuck out like jug handles on each side of her head.

"Who are you?" he stood.

She laughed. "I am no one. Not yet. Why are you here, daddy? I need you. I can't come through."

"Come through?" Atticus felt dizzy.

"Why are you here?" She faded away, leaving only one word behind, "Daddicus!"

Atticus sat up and tumbled down the altar steps. He was in the small chapel. The lights were off, the temperature freezing. He'd fallen asleep praying. He remembered his dreams. Suddenly, sure of it, he dashed down the aisle and ran toward his home: Gwen was in labor and there was something wrong.

Gwen's body lay crumpled at the bottom of the porch steps. One slippered foot was on the bottom step. Her fuzzy robe was bunched around her waist, exposing her bare legs to the chilly air.

"Gwen! Gwen!" Atticus shouted as he stumbled beside her. She moaned but didn't open her eyes. He felt her body contract as her moan deepened. She was in labor.

Without thought, Atticus picked her up and slid her onto the seat of his truck. Cold, the engine sputtered and finally caught. Gravel and clay splattered behind the truck as it fishtailed down the drive. Without thought, he turned right, toward the compound and the clinic instead of left toward the hospital. He glanced down as he shifted gears. A small circle of warm blood was on his thigh, where her head rested. The soldiers Morgan had arranged to guard the gate recognized the truck and waved him through. It bothered him, this trust in his truck. It might not have been him. His truck might have been commandeered by dark warriors. Atticus tsked at his thoughts. He should be concentrating on Gwen. He should be praying. Instead, he was worrying about military and security strategies.

He slammed against the cement stop before his brakes caught. The truck jumped up onto the barrier and bumped back down. Gwen groaned and shuddered convulsively. Atticus ran around, banged the clinic doors open and yelled, "Chi! Get Chi! Gwen's hurt!"

He snatched the truck door open and gently pulled out her body. Her head lolled sideways, the stream of blood was visible in the clinic's fluorescents.

Chi was beside him, jogging along as he shouted orders to a nurse. They ran to the triage room and Atticus laid Gwen on the examining table. She curled and cried out in pain.

"Contraction. How far apart?"

Atticus ignored Chi or didn't hear him.

Chi pulled up an eyelid and tenderly probed the bleeding wound on her forehead. The nurse came in with a cart. "Blankets," Chi ordered. "She is hypothermic."

He moved around the table and examined Gwen fully. "Dilation, five centimeters," he told the nurse. "How long has she been like this? Atticus! How long?"

"I don't know. I was in the church. I don't know." His ears roared, his head felt light – too light. His fingers and toes were ice.

Chi grabbed his arm and flung him into a chair. Grasping the back of his neck, Chi shoved his head onto his knees. Atticus fought, but Chi was stronger. Eventually, he let the preacher sit up.

"Now, tell me about Gwen." The doctor picked up a suture and began sewing her cleansed wound.

The elders sat or stood around the entry hall of the clinic. They'd come and gone throughout the evening, patting Atticus on the shoulder, hugging him, bringing him sandwiches and coffee which he left untouched beside him.

After three hours at Gwen's side, Chi had forced him away. He was useless there. He had no knowledge of medicine.

After six hours, Chi sat beside him, sending everyone else away. "She is still unconscious, but she is almost fully dilated. "We will need your help to deliver the baby. But I would feel better if she were in hospital."

Atticus refused to move her. "You designed this clinic for battle wounds. It's the best we could design. I don't want anyone else near Gwen."

Later, he heard Sara whisper to Rawan. "It's been nine hours." The sounds of exhausted wailing echoed down the hall. "But she's still unconscious."

The nurse poked her head into the entry way. "Preacher, it's time."

They draped him in a paper gown and mask. He sat behind her, supporting her back against his chest. Her head lolled against his shoulder.

"What do I do now?" Atticus' voice was hoarse with

unshed tears.

"You could pray," Chi smiled beneath his mask. "The rest will be up to Gwen."

Atticus felt the contraction ripple across her belly and around to her back. Her eyes flew open convulsively but she was still unconscious; she screamed. Atticus held her and prayed.

"The head is crowning," Chi commented calmly. "Now the shoulders. One more push, Gwen, and then you can rest."

Atticus saw his daughter's ears first. They were huge. She wailed immediately, and then mewed and fought her way out of her mother's womb. The nurse wrapped her in a white towel and whisked her to a nearby table. The baby gurgled and wailed again. The beeping from the heart monitor slowed.

"You have a daughter," Chi placed a squirming bundle into Atticus' arms. Her ears stuck out, her eyes were squinted shut and her mouth open. Tiny pink lips, soft pink tongue, bluish skin, wispy red hair. She was beautiful. Atticus sobbed and kissed his daughter's face repeatedly.

Gwen slumped against him still unconscious, no longer racked by contractions. The heart monitor's beeping slowed noticeably.

To Atticus, the nurse's voice seemed to come from far away. "We're losing her."

"Move," Chi commanded. "Atticus, move aside."

Rawan helped Atticus sit in the nearby chair. His baby gurgled joyfully in his embrace; his love lay in a coma across the room. Atticus aligned himself with

God through prayers of gratitude.

Time flowed past him.

"We have her stabilized. Go lay down on the bed.
I have had Rawan set up a cradle next to the bed. I
will wake you if I need to."

Atticus placed the beautiful baby into the basinet,
bent over and kissed her. Then he lay down and
immediately went to sleep.

"Daddicus?"

*He lay on a granite slab beside the water fall in the
Meshapa, staring up at the clouds. He turned his head
at the sound of the woman's voice.*

*She was there, staring down at him: jug-handle
ears, thick red braid, quiver of arrows. "Daddicus, why
are you here?"*

*Atticus sat up, "I thought she'd be here. She loves
this spot."*

The young warrior frowned. "She's not here."

*Atticus stared around the heather-scented valley.
"No, but I don't know where to find her."*

*"Of course you do." The red-haired woman
crossed her arms, so much like Gwen. "She needs you.
You have to go to her."*

"Where?"

"He's killing her."

Atticus leapt to his feet. "Where is she?"

"It is a different place than this. An evil place."

"Can you take me there?"

*The woman nodded and took his hand. He wove
his fingers between hers, and the landscape shifted.*

Bodies of dead and dying littered the sloping hillsides around him. Rivulets of blood and gore traced their way through the grass. Spikes with lumps of writhing flesh decorated one side of the hill above him. Smoke roiled in chunks at the top of the hill he was on.

"Shergoque." Atticus glanced up at the woman still holding his hand. "The Battle of Shergoque. This is where Sanchor was lost."

The woman nodded.

A man shouted in anger. Atticus and his daughter turned to look in that direction. Gwen, glorious in battle, stabbed at the man who stumbled backwards. He was tall, with jug-handled ears. A black cape flapped around him, leather leggings and metal guards were all dull gray.

Gwen was bleeding from gashes on her skull, shoulder and thigh. The dirt on the rest of her body was smeared with blood, looking like brownish gray patches of muck. Her feet were bare, her hair was blunt cut short. As her opponent stumbled backward, she lunged, Bear on the Mountain.

The man retreated further, unable to block all of her blows. He fell to one knee and jabbed out with his staff, hitting her above the knee – wasp sting.

Atticus heard the bone crack and watched in horror as she crumpled. He ran, still hand in hand with the red-headed warrior running at his side.

Black clouds boiled across the sky. Lightning crackled in streaks through the thunderheads. Atticus raised his left hand above his head and pulled the lightning from the sky. The man in the black cloak knelt beside Gwen, stabbing his cudgel into her stomach. Atticus flung the bolts at him. He had no other thought than to kill this darkness. To eradicate it from the universe. The shaft of light struck the man and splintered, blasting holes in the ground around him. The man's head jerked up in surprise. Slowly, as Atticus ran closer, the man stood.

Lightning crackled and struck around them as the two men faced each other.

"I know you're there," the Strategia Oscuro sounded surprised. "Show yourself."

The woman gripped his hand tighter and shook her head.

Gwen crawled on her back and sat up out of reach of Sanchor's staff.

Sanchor waved his hand above his head. "Be still," he commanded. The clouds rolled away, the wind died down. The air grew icy cold, but calm.

Gwen rolled onto her good knee and began to crawl away. Sanchor cackled madly. Running at her, he launched a kick into her side that cracked ribs. She screamed and jabbed backward with her staff, but missed him completely.

Atticus lunged forward, but was held back by the woman's iron grip. "You cannot save her here."

"A woman?" Sanchor laughed. "Why can't I see you, woman?"

She was silent.

"No matter," Sanchor turned back to look down at Gwen, wallowing in agony at his feet. "I don't want to save her. I want to turn her."

"Never," Gwen whimpered.

"How? How do I save her?" Atticus whispered.

"A man's voice now? How many of you are there?" Sanchor stepped away from Gwen, closer to them.

"The dreamer must awaken," the woman spoke clearly.

Sanchor cackled again. "Do you hear that, love? Wake up! Wake up and all this will be over." His staff jabbed into her broken knee. Her scream muted his taunts for her to awaken.

"He's dreaming. This is his dream," the woman stated.

Atticus looked up at her. "Can you take me to Doug and bring us both back here?"

She nodded.

The world shimmered.

The scent of pine filled his nostrils, and cinnamon and baked turkey. Children laughed and chased puppies around a huge Christmas tree loaded with presents and ornaments. Christmas carols rang through the air and snow pasted white icing against the windows. A fire crackled warmly in the huge stone hearth. A peace, a joy, a place of love; Atticus yearned to linger here. His cry startled the children and puppies to silence. "Doug!"

"Here. I'm here. I'm Doug," a young boy stood up.

"He's killing her. You have to fling him out of the dreaming."

The young boy held his hand out to the girl beside him. Taralyn shape-shifted into a warrior, tall, fierce, muscular. The puppies were suddenly mastiffs and Dobermans and Rottweilers with studded collars. Doug was dressed in desert fatigues and battle gear, a bazooka in his arms.

The woman who was also Gwen's infant reached out and touched Doug's arm.

The world shimmered again.

"Gwen! Hold on! We're here!" Atticus ran up the hill.

"Atticus," she turned. "My Atticus."

"What?" Sanchor toed her leg. She screamed in agony.

"You cannot turn me, Sanchor." She tried to prop up on her elbows and shook her head. "Atticus is here. He's going to take me home."

Sanchor peered blindly down the hill. "Why can't I see you? Where are you, 'My Atticus'?"

"You can't see him." Gwen swallowed painfully. "He's a part of my dream, not yours." She collapsed onto her back. "My Atticus. My dream."

"This is my dream. I command here." Sanchor looked around and pointed at the corpses. "Arise! Find this Atticus. Kill him."

Dark soldiers stood up from where they had lain dying or dead. They took up fallen swords and staffs. A whoosh preceded an explosion as Doug' bazooka blew a hole in Sanchor's walking dead.

The dogs attacked. Taralyn pulled a battle staff from behind her back and launched herself along with her pack.

"You'll never turn my Atticus. He serves the Light."

Sanchor reached down and pulled Gwen up by her hair. "Your Atticus? Don't you love me anymore, Gwen?"

She stopped struggling.

He shook her viciously. "Answer me. Do you still love me?

She looked at Atticus and then turned to Sanchor. "No," she said simply.

He bellowed with rage and flung her away from him. The sky darkened to plum and red streaked through it, like veins pulsing with blood. His clothes and skin darkened, and then blackened, and then was the absence of light itself. He was becoming a door.

"Wake the dreamer!" the woman with jug-handled ears cried. "Wake the dreamer!"

Doug stepped forward.

Atticus watched Doug closely. The young man cocked his head. That was it. He simply looked at Sanchor and cocked his head.

A light breeze lifted a ripped corner of Gwen's gown and fluttered it, where she lay alone and still on the hillside.

Atticus swooped like an owl in flight, and landed beside her body. He wrapped her in his arms, trying to warm her. "Gwen," he whispered. "What are you doing here?"

Gwen couldn't answer.

Doug, Taralyn, and the woman knelt beside them.

"Gwen, it's time to come home. Your daughter needs you." Atticus kissed warmth into her forehead.

"Mom, I need you." The woman touched Gwen's

shoulder. "Mom, why are you here? I need you to come home."

Doug and Taralyn held hands and began to pray.

"What are you doing?" Atticus whispered.

"We're forming a portal to take us home," Taralyn answered.

The circle shimmered above their heads and slowly sank down on them as a silver dome.

The world shifted.

The ringing phone shattered Tyler's dreamless sleep. "Hello?" he asked as he looked at his bedside clock.

"Tell Taralyn I'll be there in seven minutes."

"What?"

"Tyler, tell Taralyn –"

"I'm here!" She had picked up the extension in her room.

"Seven minutes," Doug stated.

"I'll be ready."

"It's four fifteen in the morning!" Tyler shouted as the phones disconnected. "Have you lost your mind?"

"Yes," Taralyn answered from across the hall. "Certifiably psycho-babe, right here. After what I've just seen." She poked her head into his room while pulling on a sparkly hoody. "Come on! Get dressed!"

Tyler opened his mouth but found he had nothing to say. He stood and reached for the jeans he'd slung over the chair last night, only six hours ago.

Doug and Taralyn danced down the clinic hallway, hand in hand. Tyler followed blearily behind.

"Atticus!" Doug shouted.

The preacher stuck his head out of a side room and then came out to fling his arms around the young man. Taralyn squeezed into their embrace and kissed both men. Atticus grinned and hugged Tyler.

"In here," he pulled them inside.

Gwen was sitting in bed, smiling down at her baby. She looked up and held out one arm, enfolding first Taralyn, then Doug in an embrace.

"This is her?" Taralyn touched the baby's cheek. "This is your daughter, the warrior?"

Gwen nodded.

Tyler observed from the doorway. "Any time you'd like to fill me in, that would be nice."

"Dad," Taralyn threw herself at him and hugged him ferociously.

"They saved me," Gwen's voice was hoarse. "Your daughter, Doug, and Atticus. They saved me."

"And our daughter. Don't forget her." Atticus kissed Gwen's head and cupped the infant in his hand.

"Oh," Tyler grunted. "Thanks. Clear as molasses."

Taralyn giggled and went back to Doug' side.

"Before the baby was born," Atticus moved aside as Chi readjusted a machine at Gwen's side. "Gwen was pulled into a dream by a Strategia Oscuro named Sanchor."

"In this side of reality," Chi added, "she lapsed into a coma."

Gwen nodded at both men.

"My beautiful daughter came and took me to her, where she was being tortured." Atticus again touched

317

the infant, who was suckling from Gwen's breast.

"In your dream?" Tyler asked.

The four people nodded.

"She told me I had to awaken Sanchor because it was his dream. So we went and got Doug and Taralyn."

"And my puppies," Taralyn grinned.

"Puppies?" Gwen squawked. "They were the most ferocious canines I've ever seen!"

"They all came back with us and Doug knocked Sanchor out. End of dream."

Doug continued. "But Gwen was dying, so we thought of a way to bring her back."

Taralyn grinned, "We formed a portal of Light within the dream."

"And we all woke up," Atticus concluded.

"You were tortured in this dream, like Atticus was stabbed by the sword in a dream?" Chi pushed Atticus aside again and began to examine the new mother.

"In the dream, I had broken ribs, a shattered knee cap, contusions, abrasions, and several gaping wounds."

Chi sighed, "Cracked ribs, probably. A fractured tibia, and bruises all over. Plus the six stitches I put in your forehead last night."

"They'll heal," Gwen assured him.

"You mean," Tyler glared at Doug and his daughter. "What happens in these dreams can have an impact on reality?"

Atticus nodded.

Chi held up one hand. "What is damaged in the

dreams is reflected in real life? We have witnessed this twice now, yes?"

The three dream-walkers nodded.

Chi's eyes flew open as his face broke into an expression of joy. "If injury reflects injury, why not healing?"

Tyler finally stepped all the way into the room. "Why could not I heal people in my dream? Feed the starving? Cure the dying? Why could not I do this?" He looked at Atticus, who shrugged.

"Atticus, teach me this dream-walking," Chi demanded.

Atticus hesitated.

Taralyn immediately replied, "I will."

Chapter 51
The Misunderstandings

They were snuggling on the porch swing. Taralyn had set the temperature for autumn with just enough nip in the air to make snuggling close acceptable. She traced Doug' shirt buttons from his neck downward. When she reached the top of his jeans, she wiggled her finger between the shirt pieces and tickled the patch of skin just below his navel.

Doug grabbed her hand swiftly and pulled it to his lips slowly. He kissed her palm and then, still holding her hand, sat up a little straighter.

"Doug, can I ask you something?"

"Anything." He stared off into the dreamscape, marveling at the late season lightning bugs and the scent of pine trees.

"Are you a virgin?"

He glanced down at her, but answered evenly, "No."

"I am."

Doug tried not to smile.

"Some girls at school were talking."

Doug waited.

"Do you know," Taralyn wiggled straighter on the swing. "Have you ever heard – or experienced – 'bolt the barn door, Betty' sex?"

Doug gulped and choked on a laugh. "What?"

"Both the barn door Betty sex," Taralyn repeated, Doug governed his expression. "Why?"

"It's not like I'm clueless, you know. I just wondered if you've ever had that kind of sex."

Doug sat up and faced her. "Taralyn, the kind of sex I've had before is none of your business."

She squinted at him, a sure prelude to her anger.

He stood up and leaned against the porch railing, facing her. "The only two things you need to know is that I love you and that you will remain a virgin until your wedding night if I have anything to do with it." He pushed away from the railing, standing tall. "And that's the end of this conversation."

She stood slowly and slid her arms around his neck, pressing against him. "You love me?"

"Yes, Taralyn, I love you." He held her arms and kissed her lightly.

"Don't you wonder what it'll feel like?" She pressed kisses along his collar bone. He moaned. "I think about it all the time. I think about how your hands feel, and your lips, and your tongue. And I wonder about other parts of you."

Doug's fingers clawed into her shoulders as she pressed against him. The railing refused his retreat.

She was breathing hard; he was gasping.

"Don't you want me, Doug?" She kissed him as she had never done before.

For an instant, there was nothing in the world he wanted more than Taralyn. He grabbed her shoulders and shook her. "Don't tempt me, Beth!"

The look of shock on her face made him realize what he'd said.

"You called me Beth," she whispered, drawing her hands up to her lips like a child afraid of the dark.

"Taralyn." No other words came.

"Beth was my mother's name."

Doug released her and kept his hands up as if surrendering.

"Doug?" Tears spilled over Taralyn's cheeks as he disappeared out of the dream.

Matt glanced up from the desk and smiled in greeting. "Hi, Taralyn. How did your exams go?"

"Aced them, no worries." She plunked into the chair opposite him.

"What brings you to the compound?" Matt folded his hands politely instead of pouring over the blueprints for the new barracks which he so longed to do.

"I seem to have a talent for dream-walking. Atticus wants to know if you'd be willing to learn how."

"Sure. I already told Doug," he hesitated as her face screwed up in disgust. "He says he is basically just a participant, but to expect him or you any night soon."

Taralyn stood up. "It'll just be me. Tonight."

Matt stood as well and blocked the door before she could exit. "Taralyn, has Doug done something I need to kill him for?"

Taralyn froze, thinking and battling the tears which

sprang into her eyes.

"It was a rhetorical questions, sweetie."

Taralyn glowered.

"Unless Doug really did do something terrible." Matt wrapped his arm around her shoulders and directed her back to his desk. She cried and leaned against him, shaking. She hiccupped an embarrassed laugh and asked him for a tissue.

"Tissues are for wimps. Have a scratchy paper towel."

She wiped her eyes and blew her nose. Tossing the wad of brown paper into the little gray metal can beside his desk, Taralyn mumbled. "Thanks. I can't talk about it to anyone."

"Sure you can. Me." He perched on his desk.

"Doug doesn't love me. He just used me because he can't have the woman he does love."

"He used you?" Matt towered to his full six foot eight inch height, his beard bristled.

"No! Not 'used' as in boinked." Taralyn crossed her arms. "What is it with men and virginity? There is more to love than that."

"Of course there is." Matt settled back down. "It's just that men have this competitive strength, they want to be the first at everything. Trace it back far enough and I'll bet you your class president was the first kid on his block to draw a happy face on the wall with piss."

Taralyn gulped a giggle.

"And there are other firsts women know nothing of: first to grow pubic hair, first to have wet dreams, the first to get some cheerleader into the back seat and as you so elegantly stated, boink her."

"Scientifically, you're talking about the need to perpetuate DNA."

Matt blinked. "Keep talking like that – you'll stay a virgin."

"Hey!"

"Sorry," he held up a hand. "We're animals. We have basic needs – food, shelter, procreation. 'Be the first to meet these needs'; that's the true golden rule of man."

Taralyn sucked her bottom-lip thoughtfully. Matt mentally shook his head at how cute Taralyn was without her realizing it. "But there's more to us than animal instincts. We have a soul. The soul gives us other needs – belonging, companionship, kindness, all leading up to perpetuation of the soul. Sex perpetuates the body, love perpetuates the soul."

Matt held his arms out as if to embrace her. "You have everything necessary to perpetuate the species. Legs, boobs, face of an angel, rear end so tight you could –"

"Matt!" she blushed.

"Believe me, if I were any other man, Doug would never have had a chance. I would have been there first, underage or not."

Her face clouded.

Matt chuckled, "Even Atticus thought I was in love with you." He stood up and cocked his head. "I'm not. So relax. I'm very much in love with someone else."

Taralyn didn't relax; she peered at him. "Who?"

"Doesn't matter. Well, it does matter, just not in this

conversation. The point I'm laboring toward is that sex has everything to do with procreation; love does not. You can love someone and never touch them sexually. You can love someone without the slightest thought of having children together. Or, you can say you love someone but all your emotions are on the physical plane. It's a deep emotion, devastating and thrilling. A relationship built on sex can be solid and last a lifetime. But it falls apart in the face of true love." Matt crossed his arms, still leaning on his desk. "I've seen both kinds of relationships. I've experienced both kinds. You haven't. Doug is your first love, right?"

She nodded.

"But you are not his."

Her face wrinkled in anger.

"You think he's still in love with someone else."

"He called me by her name." Taralyn's lips pursed.

Matt shuddered and thought for a moment, trying to get his words right. He went for levity. "At least it was a woman's name, not a man's."

She gave him a look of confusion. "I knew you wouldn't understand."

"I do, Taralyn. I do understand. His brain wasn't active when his body was. You elicited feelings that physically reminded him of another place and time. It doesn't mean he still loves her, or ever did."

"He called me by my mother's name."

Matt's bottom slipped and he barely caught himself from crashing to the floor. His face darkened. Matt walked around his desk and grabbed up his battle staff. "You'll have to excuse me now, Taralyn.

I've got to go kill Doug."

Atticus was in the process of knocking on Matt's office door when Taralyn's cry of "Stop Matt, Don't!" was all it took to enrage him. He crashed through the door and tackled the bear of a man.

"Atticus?" Taralyn grabbed at his shoulder as he gripped Matt's shirt, trying to throw him off balance. The giant just looked down at his preacher with confusion, his battle staff dangling from his fist.

"Help!" Taralyn stuck her head out the door and yelled. "Atticus, stop it! Don't hurt Matt!"

"Yeah, Atticus," Matt spoke softly down into the smaller man's crimson face. "Don't hurt me."

As Doug, Tyler and Juan flew into the office, Atticus stopped shoving against Matt's immovable chest. He took a deep breath and his face lightened. He took another gulp and growled, "Keep your hands off her. I've told you before."

"Off who?" Taralyn asked. "Oh my God, Matt, you're in love with Gwen?"

"What?" Atticus snapped, piercing her with a look.

"Gwen?" Tyler repeated dumbly.

Juan put his hand on his hip, snapped his head and snarled, "Excuse me?"

Only Matt saw the humor. He looked around, fighting a grin. "There seems to be a misunderstanding – several misunderstandings here."

"I know what I heard – Taralyn begging you to leave her alone."

Taralyn held up a hand, "I was begging him not to kill Doug."

Tyler asked, "Why does Doug need killing?"

Atticus answered, "Because Matt's in love with Taralyn."

Juan puffed further, "Este que?"

"No." Matt spoke softly. "Taralyn's a sweetie. If I could have children, I'd want them to be like her. I love you, Taralyn, but I'm not in love with you. Is that OK with you?"

"Fine by me," she replied.

Doug asked, "Are you in love with Gwen?"

"I'm in love with Juan." Matt stepped away from Atticus. "Not that my love life is anyone's business."

Every eye turned to Juan. He grinned and bowed his head.

"So, why were you going to kill Doug?" Tyler asked.

Matt looked squarely at Taralyn. "Misunderstandings happen. As we all witnessed in the last five minutes. Could it be you misunderstood, not what was said, but the context in which it was said?"

Taralyn glanced sideways at Doug and nodded. "Then, everyone out of my office, except for Juan. I have work to do."

Chapter 52
The Dream World

The belly-whopper splashes were accompanied by squeals of children's laughter. Atticus walked slowly, wandering through the woods toward the sounds. Over the bushes, between the trees, he glimpsed an old tire swing pendulating; brown legs stuck through the hole. The bushes rattled as two boys sprinted past in an energetic game of tag. "Hey Pastor!" one of them yelled.

The sun was warm and a light, sweetly scented breeze ruffled his hair. Another splash and Atticus was splattered with ice cold droplets.

"Visolela!" a squeaky voice shouted.

"Over here," he heard a young girl reply.

Atticus took another step and stopped in a sandy clearing around a spring. A dozen children swam, ran, or lazed around the pool.

"Hey Pastor!" A boy of about seven ran up and took his hand. "Look at this cool swimming hole Taralyn made us!"

"Brother Rutger?" Atticus allowed himself to be pulled forward.

"Jah, that's me!" the boy grinned.

Atticus peered at each child. Visolela, with her curly hair cut short and her skin a warm chocolate, as a six year old. She bobbed in the water next to Sara. About five, the blond, blue-eyed Sara had her hair braided in two pigtails. Tyler was hanging upside down from a looping oak tree, his belly was sun burnt and his eight year old face red from being upside down for too long. Mitchell was practicing staffs with Doug; both boys looked to be about ten.

The brown legs slipped out of the tire swing and plummeted into the clear water below.

"Hi, again, pastor!" The two tag-players returned, arms around each other's shoulders: Juan at seven and Matt at nine.

"Who's that?" Atticus pointed at the spongy mass of black curls making its way across the pool.

Juan and Matt giggled and ran away.

A whisper of white skin and red hair reached down and helped the child out of the pool. She hugged him and wrapped a thick blue towel around both of them. Atticus could hear their teeth chattering. The girl glanced across the pool and grinned. Her ears stuck out like flags, but her eyes danced with love, "Daddicus!"

Atticus took a deep breath and swelled with pride. "Hi, baby girl."

His daughter, six years older in this dream than in real life, ran into his embrace. The boy, abandoned in half of the towel, took a step back and looked frightened. Atticus knelt, eye-level with the child.

"Who's your friend, Natalie?"

"He won't tell me his name. But he's one of us."

"You're not the doctor; he's still on duty tonight."

The boy shook his head.

Atticus studied his sweet face. "Whom do you serve?"

The boy shrugged and pointed at Natalie.

"He doesn't talk yet," she explained. She left her father's arms and got under the towel with the stranger. The boy smiled into her face with such adoration, Atticus caught his breath.

"Look what we found!" A scrawny red-head with blotchy freckles and skinned knees raced into the clearing beside another tomboy: his wife and Taralyn. They bore a towel between them filled with blueberries, strawberries and calamondas.

The children squealed and gathered around, eager for the sweet and sour treats. Atticus recognized Beatrice in the face of a tanned eight year old girl with long brown hair. Samir was there, a young six year old without the whip scars Atticus knew laced across the adult's back.

It didn't matter how old they were in the real world, in this dreamscape, they were all children.

Atticus observed the child sharing a calamonda with his daughter. Who was he?

"Do you like the swimming hole, Pastor?" Taralyn peered up at him.

"It's wonderful," he nodded.

"No! No camels, Samir!" Sarah shouted

The children rolled with laughter as a camel appeared and disappeared just beyond the clearing.

Atticus awoke feeling happy. His wife snuggled next to him. His infant gurgled in the next room. Sunlight peeked through the sides of the green cotton curtain. His elders had learned dream-walking so quickly. Within one month, Taralyn had taught them all how to shape shift and control the settings to a much finer degree than he could.

The first barracks held eight hundred fifty seven children from six different worlds. Work on the other two barracks was progressing slowly, due to the fierce early winter they were having.

Gwen sighed and curled closer to him, "That was fun."

"Taralyn has a great imagination. I could never dream-weave like she does."

"You have other talents," his wife assured him.

"Yes, I do," he grinned and pulled her closer.

Chapter 53
The Silent Child

They moved the morning practices into the new fellowship hall due to the weather. Basinets were set up to hold Kayien, Natalie, Rasom's new baby, and a few toddlers who had been carried through the portals of light recently.

Atticus kissed Natalie and laid her beside Kayien. He turned and caught Visolela staring at the infants, her eyebrows furrowed and lips thinned.

"What's wrong?" he asked immediately.

The Nigerian frowned and shook her head. "It is nothing."

"Visolela?"

"I am sure it is nothing."

"Is Kayien alright?"

She looked away in silence.

Atticus took her elbow and lowered his voice, "Visolela."

"He does not," Visolela began. "Chi says it is just temporary. Because he was premature and because I am so old."

"You're my age – thirty-seven. You're not old."

"He cannot hear. Kayien cannot hear."

Atticus wrapped her in his arms and sighed in relief. "Thank you for telling me, sister. I'll pray about it. There's a reason for everything. We learn from times of adversity."

He glanced over at Kayien. The little baby was holding hands with Natalie. It hit him suddenly: Kayien was the unnamed new boy in the dream.

"The problems, as I see it," Tyler looked around the elders and took a deep breath. "Finding a way to key into one exact world, rather than just opening a portal anywhere on any world."

They stared at him in worried silence.

"You know," Beatrice inclined her head. "If you'd said that a year ago, I would have thought you were crazy."

The elders laughed.

"You did it," Taralyn pointed at Gwen. "You came back to this world. Can you remember how?"

Gwen shifted uncomfortably; it was time to feed Natalie. "I prayed that God's will be done. But honestly, I just wanted to come home."

"There's no place like home," Sara chirped in a Dorothy-mimic.

"Maybe it is that simple," Matt mused. "We open doors on many worlds because we have no idea what the other worlds are like. But if we could focus."

"Isn't that what we do to begin with?" Rawan asked. "Like dream-weaving and prayer? We focus our energies."

"We feed the demon," Mitchell agreed.

"What, Maxwell's Demon? I thought you said it just opened and closed the doors." Taralyn put her hand on his arm.

"Well, maybe we can do more than that. It's worth a try."

"I agree." Chi nodded. "Gwen, you're the only one here who has been on another world. Is there a place you remember strongly?"

Gwen blushed. Atticus grinned and replied for her, "The Pool of Meshapa."

"Let's do it!" Rutger stood up.

"Wait a minute," Tyler frowned. "We're not ready to go. We have no provisions or weapons. If we get stuck on the other side, we'll need a way to survive."

"I didn't mean we were going to walk through," Rutger put his hands on Rawan's shoulders to steady himself. He glanced around: Tyler, Doug, and Beatrice didn't meet his gaze. "Are we?"

"Not right now." Gwen's words didn't assure him.

"We could just peek through, like some of the soldiers do when we open a portal," Mitchell suggested excitedly.

"We can't do it right now." Gwen crossed her arms over her swollen breasts.

"No, not now," Visolela agreed.

"Let's eat and discuss all the repercussions," Atticus stood and raised his hands. "Sweet Lord, you told us to go to all nations, and I don't think you'll mind what planet those nations are on. We just need your wisdom, Lord. Guide us and guard us along the path of righteousness. Amen."

Gwen and Visolela headed into the nursery and had to separate their children. Natalie wailed, Kayien just squirmed, reaching out for Natalie. The mothers rocked as they breastfed their infants.

"Who do you think he'll send?"

Visolela looked surprised. "He is your husband, what do you think?"

"Doug."

Visolela nodded. "Or Tyler."

"I don't think he'd send Tyler until the complex is completely secured and Taralyn turns eighteen."

"Maybe Rawan," Visolela posed.

Gwen agreed. "I think a healer would be better accepted than a doctor."

"Rutger cannot go right now. His wife's health is failing."

Gwen blinked, "He's ninety-five years old! Atticus wouldn't send him."

"Would he send you?"

"I wouldn't go," Gwen stroked Natalie's cheek.

"What about the Jols? Does he mean to send them back?"

Gwen nodded, "The adults. And the Sysroms, the Grallons, the Faleavers. All of the adults will go back to their worlds and spread the news of our refuge for children."

"Who does he think will take care of the children?" Visolela scowled. Kayien blinked up at her and smiled, milk spilling around his lips.

"He hasn't discussed it with me."

The women exchanged glances. "I think Beatrice wants to move into the barracks, like a den mother." Visolela rocked and spoke softly. "I would like to do that, also." She glanced at Gwen fearfully.

Gwen smiled reassuringly. "I think that would be perfect for you."

Visolela grinned and sighed with relief. "If we had one parent for one hundred children, that would mean we would need thirty adults eventually."

"You've thought this through." Gwen commented.

"Yes, I have." Visolela's eyes shone. "And we already have the thirty adults. The elders' families could each take one hundred children. That is Doug, and Tyler and Taralyn – or Tyler and then Doug and Taralyn when they marry, Rutger and Kaela Perkins, their three daughters could each take a group; Beatrice; Matt and Juan; Mitchell's family; Rawan, Chi and I; Eduviges. Twelve – enough to begin with the first barracks. And then there are Patsy, Samir, and other members of the church in good standing who could become elders. I think Ormed and Gilga are old enough, since they are married. If they are going to stay."

"Visolela, this is brilliant." Gwen leaned forward and took her hand. "Matt's redesigning the barracks. He can put a suite next to each section, two on each floor, five floors." She lowered her voice. "And I think we would all be safer living within the compound."

"I think we should divide the children into groups according to their gifts."

"How do you mean?"

"We are too divided. The Jols, the Shallons, the Faleavers, I think we should all be of Atticus. So we will need to make a concerted effort to divide and regroup the children."

"I'm listening," Gwen said cautiously.

"The children with musical talent should go to Eduviges' and Patsy's pods. Those strong in prayer should go to Mitchell. Physically strong – laborers – should go to Matt. Those who can learn our technology should go to Tyler. When Taralyn and Doug have their own group, they should have those who can dream-weave. Healers could go to Rawan."

"What about you? Who do you want in your group?"

Visolela looked down into her son's beautiful face. "The special ones," she whispered. "My husband and I will take the special ones, wounded and maimed, silenced by war and grief."

Gwen fought sudden tears.

"You will tell Atticus? You will speak to him for me?"

Gwen nodded immediately.

Chapter 54
The Bowl

Atticus listened to the introit. Children, adults, and instruments led the congregation into expectancy. Beatrice gave the invocation and led the service through to the prayer of confession. He led them through the Lord's Prayer. He had dispensed with the children's sermons, since they made up more than half of the congregation. He seated them after a beautiful rendition of Gloria Patre. Then he launched into his sermon.

He had given his sermon a great thought and prayerfully revised it several times this week. He was a little terrified by the swiftness of the unfolding events around him, but he felt that calm center he knew was the hand of God on his heart. He took a deep breath and, trusting God, began.

"Once upon a time, there was a father who had two sons, and he gave each of his sons a gift. To one son, the father gave a bowl. It was fine earthenware, intricately patterned and painted with a glossy finish. The son, pleased with this beautiful gift, put it on a shelf in his house and displayed it proudly to anyone who came to see him. His wife dusted it every day and his children were allowed to look at it – without touching it – and promised that one of them would inherit it eventually."

Atticus began to pace. The voice mic Le'Vander had rigged up for him was pinned to his collar. "The second son was also given a bowl exactly like his brother's: fine earthenware, intricately patterned and brightly colored and glazed. But this second son had no house in which to display it. He had no wife to dust it nor children to promise it to. So the second son thanked his father and tucked the bowl inside his pack and set off down the road.

"Soon, he came to a group of people. They were gathered around the muddy shore of a shallow but wide pond.

"What's going on? He asked the people. A child spoke up. 'We are dying of thirst, but there are too many of us, and the water is too muddy to drink because we've stomped all along the shore.'

"The second son took out his bowl and walked into the middle of the pond. He scooped up clean water and returned to the child. She drank deeply and didn't die of thirst. So the second son spent his whole day using his bowl to give clean water to the thirsty crowd." Atticus shrugged, "Or words to that effect."

He returned to the pulpit. "The Bible is full of stories about gifts. Noah was given the gift of boat-building. Joshua was given the gift of military strategy. Jacob was given the gift of dream analysis. Esther was given the gift of consultation. In the New Testament, Jesus tells parables about gifts and how they are used or ignored." Atticus swallowed his fear and continued. "What does the Bible tell us about gifts?"

No one called out an answer as they would have done in the small church across the cemetery from his parsonage. He sighed. "Does God tell us to hide them?"

"No," Rutger called.

Atticus smiled gratefully at the old man. "Does God tell us to bury them in the back yard?"

"No!" Patsy grinned up at him.

"Does he admonish us to keep them only to ourselves?'

The Jols replied as one, "No!"

"What does God expect us to do with his gifts?"

"Use them," came several voices.

Atticus nodded. Slowly now, "I want you to think – I want you to imagine – what would have happened if Noah had not used his boat-building gift? Think about the consequences, not only to his family, but to the generations to come. Now think about how stupid he looked, building a huge ark in the middle of the desert. And think about how painful it must have been for him, watching the flood waters rise. Hearing the screams of his drowning neighbors and friends. He only had room for the animals that God had told him to take."

Atticus paced, glanced at his wife, and stopped. "It wasn't fair. You know it wasn't fair, to force a man to choose between the world and God."

Atticus rubbed his face and returned to the pulpit. "Noah wasn't forced to choose. He was given the right to choose. He had freedom of will. He chose to build the ark because he had placed his life in the hands of God, and it was his faith, his love of God, that saw him through the ordeal to the glory beyond.

"Joshua was hiding with the women when his people went to war. But when he heard the voice of his God, he chose to become God's warrior. The Bible passages about Joshua teach great military strategies. Strategies we might never have learned if Joshua had chosen not to fight the Battle of Jericho.

"Time and again, the Bible tells us to use the gifts God gives us. It doesn't promise us that our lives will be better for it. As a matter of fact, people who are given gifts from God usually have horrible lives filled with loss, betrayal, pain, and ridicule.

"But I would remind you of two things. The first is the benefits of the gift God gives you pass down through the generations. And two – we are not bodies with a soul. We are souls who at this time exist in a body. "Who here has not suffered loss? Not one of you. Who here has not been betrayed? Not one of you. Who here, while suffering on a world, knows that the gifts of God eventually lead us to heaven? We all do. That's why we're here.

"We have all been given gifts and – today – right now – we can choose to have a nice, safe, pain free life where we keep the gifts unused, or we can have a life of strife, torment, constant adventure, and use God's gifts for the glory of his kingdom and the benefit of generations to come."

Atticus nodded. The fluttering of fear had gone,

displaced by the warm pressure of power. "Use your gifts."

He glanced at Gwen holding Natalie and sat down.

Patsy stood and raised her hands. The choir rose as the musicians readied their instruments. "Jerusalem, Judea, Samaria, and the ends of the earth!"

Atticus bowed his head. He hadn't discussed the sermon or the anthem with Patsy, but she'd obviously been talking with God. It was a perfect anthem for the mission God had set before them.

Over one-hundred adults from six different worlds stayed after the morning service at Atticus' request. They stared up at him expectantly. He stood before them, in front of the altar steps.

"This is a place of sanctuary, of refuge. A haven for children. We will have room for almost three thousand children. We need you to go and get them and bring them here."

Taralyn and Doug exchanged glances from their pew behind the refugees. They knew Atticus was going to present the idea today; they were surprised at how straight-forward he'd said it.

"An elder will travel with each group and when you have gathered enough children, the elder will open a portal back here. Gather no more than two dozen at a time; do not draw the attention of the Darkness to this refuge. I will send my elders out once every season."

Doug put his hand over Taralyn's. They'd argued about it, and she was still angry, but they both knew he had to be one of the elders to go.

"We will raise your children in the Light. It will take years to build the army, but from the stock of three thousand children, we can begin to send back trained warriors each Winter's Night. We will train them, and when they are ready, we will return them to fight at your side, to hold back the Darkness."

Atticus took a calming breath and said firmly. "You will leave tomorrow."

The crowd erupted; Atticus counted to ten silently and then raised his hand.

"You represent six worlds. We have room for three thousand children. I require you to find four hundred children from each world to send to us for refuge. Four hundred children. They must be old enough to take care of themselves but not old enough to shave or menstruate."

There was another outcry that subsided when Atticus again raised his hand.

"We promise to feed them well, keep them healthy, raise them in the Light, and love them as our own."

A tall pock-faced woman stood and shook her fist. "I'll not leave my children!"

"I know exactly how you feel, Sister of Sisrown. I would not leave my children either. I'm not telling you to leave your children here. I'm telling you that you will leave here tomorrow and return to your world and help gather children who are in need of refuge. You are being sent to find children who will benefit from the training we can offer them.

"You were given a gift. The knowledge that this is a

place of refuge for children is a gift from God. God requires that you pass on this gift. But the choice is yours. It always has been yours. It always will be yours. "My choices are more limited than yours. It is my responsibility to tell you that for every adult who does not want to leave here, you are stealing the place of a child. And I won't allow that. The barracks were built for children. These children will be trained to hold back the Dark to the best of our ability. They will each be taught how to pray, how to open portals, how to dream-walk and dream-weave, and how to fight.

"You have choices – go home and bring back children to be trained here. Or go home. Or leave the compound and find your way in this world. You leave tomorrow after morning exercises and breakfast. Each of you will be given a week's supply of food. You may take your belongings and anything you were given while here. And if you want to take your children with you – no matter where you go – knowing what it is you are taking them from – then take them.

"We hold no one against their will. But we will keep no one over the age of reason – boys who can shave, girls who can menstruate. This is the will of God as revealed to me by the Angel of the Lord."

Chapter 55
The Army

The portals opened one at a time, with a band of ex-patriots focusing on one specific location for each planet.

Atticus raised his hands; his voice carried across the parade ground and echoed in the crisp winter air. "When they question who you are, tell them you come to serve the Light. But tell them that you are more than this. Tell them, *Comes the Warrior, to Build an Army, to Hold Back the Dark!*"

The Yseluta went first. Seventeen men led by Larry stepped bravely through the shining door in the air and disappeared.

Juan led the Leinads home.

Rawan glanced fearfully behind her as six Sisrowns stepped with her through the portal into a fiery desert. No children accompanied them.

Doug embraced Tyler and then turned to Taralyn. "I'm going to miss your birthday. So here's your present." He knelt and handed her a little black box.

She bit her lip and wordlessly slipped the diamond ring on her left hand.

Doug stood up and kissed her. "I'll see you on the porch tonight."

The Jols began going through. Olmed hugged Gilga goodbye; she was pregnant and had chosen to remain with Mitchell's family.

Suddenly, Ricean threw her arms around Tyler's neck and kissed him passionately. He blinked and fumbled to return her kiss. Then Ricean released him and dashed through the portal.

Samir embraced his cousin who had come to Georgia to run his shop in his absence. He looked longingly at Sara, but she didn't see him. "The Faleavers say they have camels," he told Atticus as he followed them to their world.

Eduviges looked terrified and began to shake as the portal to Eurnied shimmered open before her. Patsy's clear voiced filled the air, "Abide with me, Fast falls the evening tide."

Eduviges blew her a kiss through teary eyes and walked into the jungles of Eurnied.

ABOUT THE AUTHOR

Evelyn Rainey has had five novels published by traditional small press publishers in the last four years: **Minna Pegeen** (Comfort Publishing), **Bedina's War** (Comfort Publishing), **Perky's Books & Gifts** (Bedlam Press), **The Island Remains** (Whiskey Creek Press) and **Laughing Humans** (Portals Publishing). She edited and has a short story in **Stories for All Seasons**.

A frequent guest author and panelist for Science Fiction/Fantasy conventions and writer conferences, she also writes the Science Fiction/Fantasy Books column for **BellaOnline** – the second largest women's emagazine in the world. Previously, she wrote the Veterans column for **BellaOnline** for three years. She has been published in *Zero Signal, Lakeland Ledger, Polk County Democrat, World Treasury of Golden Poems, Youth Alive, Wesleyan Magazine* and the *Polk County Poetry Anthology.* As the summer of 2015 blossomed, she ranked in the 14,000 range for Fantasy Author and the 5,000 range for Historical Romance Author on **Amazon.**

Her online presence includes her website http://Evelyn-Rainey.com , Amazon Author page (amazon.com/author/evelynrainey), Goodreads (goodreads.com/Evelyn_Rainey), Facebook (EvelynRaineyAuthor) and Twitter (EvelynRainey). She enjoys corresponding with people who have read her books and/or who want to discuss the Art and Business of writing.

For ten years, she facilitated **Writers for All Seasons** and now facilitates **Writers at Unity**. She has been an educator for thirty-some-odd years. With degrees and certificates in Early Childhood, Elementary, Middle School Integrated Curriculum, Gifted, ESOL, and Journalism, she currently teaches Robotics to gifted Middle School students at Jewett School of the Arts. Prior to that, she provided consultation for Gifted students and their teachers in traditional classrooms as well as alternative facilities including jails. Outside of the school system, she is an herbalist, a master of crochet, a singer and she loves to do book-signings.

Following her bliss, Rainey now owns and operates two traditional small presses: **Bliss Books Online** (Building Life-long Inspirational & Successful Strategies) and **Portals Publishing** (The Best Books are Portals to a New World). Both are imprints of her **Denouement Literary Agency, LLC.**

Discussion Guide

1. Value: What spiritual lessons were presented throughout the story?
2. Attitude: How closely did the attitude of the story itself match with your attitude about life?
3. Authenticity: The idea of a halo actually being a wormhole is not original to this story. What are your thoughts about the possibility that prayer or despair could open passages to other worlds?
4. Point of View: Who told this story? Why?
5. Cause & Effect: In your opinion, what were the initial events which caused the biggest motivation for the characters and the plot to develop?
6. What if… Find an event which, if it had not occurred, the major events would not have unfolded. How would the story have changed? How might it have stayed the same?
7. Conflicts in characters: With whom does Gwen have the most conflict? With whom does Atticus have the most conflict? Within the main characters, what are their inner conflicts? How are these resolved/Are they resolved?
8. Conflicts in setting: How does the setting – location, time, socio-ecological circumstances – create conflicts? How are these resolved/Are they resolved?
9. Conflicts along plot line: Which conflict was the most disturbing to you? Was it resolved by the denouement?)
10. Compare/contrast: Choose two characters or two major conflicts and compare how the author developed them. How are they alike? How do they differ? How would the story have been different if these two things were not developed in this fashion?
11. Main Idea established by title and book cover: When you first saw the cover and read the title, what were your thoughts about the main idea? Were those thoughts supported or changed over the course of reading the book? How so?
12. Main Idea established by values/morals: Do the values "Children, righteousness, truth, the love of God, friendship, etc.) and the morals "darkness must be conquered at all cost, a killing blow is the best way to

dispatch someone lost to the darkness" expressed in this book support the main idea "Good triumphs over Evil"? Conversely, does the main idea of this novel support the values and morals expressed?

13. Main Idea established by supporting details: Think of this book as a building. Which supporting details would be considered weight-baring so that if they were removed, the whole infrastructure would collapse?

14. Genre: What parts of the story are pure Fantasy? What parts determine the subgenre Christian Fantasy? How significantly would the story change if it were not this particular genre?)

15. Plot – Premise: What part of the premise drew you in and made you want to keep reading?

16. Plot – Rising action: Consider and discuss the pace of the rising action and developing conflicts.

17. Plot – Climax: Was the climax what you expected? Were you satisfied by it or did you wish something else had happened?

18. Plot – Falling Action: Consider and discuss the pace of the falling action and resolutions of the conflicts.

19. Plot – Denouement: This is the first book in a series of seven. In what ways did the story's characters and conflicts end up? What was left unanswered? What had you wished happened differently?

20. Validity and accuracy of information: What things were inaccurate or invalid?

21. Flow and fluency of language: Quote three of your favorite parts of the story. Discuss the flow and fluency of the language used.

22. You: Who were your favorite characters? Why?

23. You: Are you a stranger to despair? Are you a stranger to joy? Which do you choose?

CHALLENGE: After reading Comes the Warrior, you probably know how to do Morning Meadow by heart. For one month, every day, do the Morning Meadow. Discuss what physical and emotional changes occur over that month.

ABOUT Bliss Books Online

"Building Life-Long Inspirational & Successful Strategies"

What We Offer

✓ We publish in three versions: trade paperback, e-book and audio
✓ We distribute worldwide in English.
✓ We offer standard royalties for each of the versions based on net.
✓ We provide the book cover by a professional designer.
✓ We provide the author 10 copies as the advance.
✓ We post the author's discussion guide on the nation's largest book club database.
✓ We promote the book to the media (the author's local newspapers and radio stations) and the representative editor of the book's genre at BellaOnline (second largest women's e-magazine in the world)
✓ The author is responsible to do the research, but we will announce the book to as many groups for which the author can give us email addresses and/or meet-up contacts in the United States, Great Britain, Australia and New Zealand.

- ✓ We can help set up book signings and speaking/lecture tours.
- ✓ We will nominate the book for at least one, but possibly several literary awards throughout the contract's duration.
- ✓ We can help set up as much of the author's platform as the author wants – the author does the hard work; we'll assist and advise.
- ✓ We continuously assist the author with promotion strategies throughout the contract's duration.

You may also be interested in **Portals Publishing**
"The Best Books are Portals to a New World."

PortalsPublishing.com

Both BLISS Books Online & Portals Publishing are imprints of **Denouement Literary Agency, LLC**
DenouementLit.com